"WHAT HAVE THEY DONE WITH NEW YORK?"

"This ought to be a park—this field we're on. And there ought to be skyscrapers all around us: enormous structures—a hundred stories tall, some of them."

Belinda was getting uneasy. Something else was about to go wrong.

The ship's loudspeaker hummed, then said, "This is the Central Park Spaceport, a fully automated mechanical entity capable of independent thought and action. Built in the twenty-third century amid the ruins of legendary New York City, I am a product of the last and finest stage of human technology...

"Through me, oh humans, your dead relations greet you. For two hundred years I have waited for someone to come back home..."

To The Resurrection Station

ELEANOR ARNASON

AVON
PUBLISHERS OF BARD, CAMELOT, DISCUS AND FLARE BOOKS

TO THE RESURRECTION STATION is an original publication of Avon Books. This work has never before appeared in book form.

AVON BOOKS
A division of
The Hearst Corporation
1790 Broadway
New York, New York 10019

First Avon Printing: October 1986

AVON TRADEMARK REG. U.S. PAT. OFF. AND IN OTHER COUNTRIES,
MARCA REGISTRADA, HECHO EN U.S.A.

Printed in the U.S.A.

K-R 10 9 8 7 6 5 4 3 2 1

For Patrick Arden Wood

I am but mad north-north-west;
when the wind is southerly I know
a hawk from a hernshaw.

     —*Hamlet*, Act 2, scene 2

The Ghost of Gorwing Keep

Rain ran down the carriage's windows. They were all closed. Nonetheless, Belinda could hear the grunts and moans of the thornbucks that pulled the monstrous conveyance down a muddy country road. Jolting and splashing, on the carriage went. Toward what end? Belinda wondered. She looked at her guardian, sitting across from her and toying with his music ring. Back and forth he twisted the ring's crystal. From it came the faint sound of a bone harp and sometimes a few bars from one of the Brandenburg Concertos. She stared at his pale thin face, remembering his sudden appearance at her school. She had returned to her room after a lecture on astrophysics and found him there, pacing back and forth, rain dripping from his overcoat, spotting the worn old wireroot carpet, which her roommate had bought at a native fair.

"Pack!" he'd said.

"Why?"

He stopped in front of her, took hold of her

shoulders and shook her. "You are a year short of your majority, my sweet. For the time being, you'll do what you're told and ask no questions."

What choice did she have? She had packed and gone with him, weeping a little when she kissed her roommate good bye. Dear Marianne! Where would she find another friend like her? Certainly nowhere in this desolate landscape. She looked out at the bare-branched dripping wood and shivered.

Just then the carriage bumped around a turn in the road. Ahead of her she saw a huge old house. It had been built in the settlement days. She was sure of that, after one look at the low concrete walls, the shallow domes and the narrow plastic windows. By this time, two centuries after settlement, the pale concrete was streaked dull red and brown. Most of the metal domes had collapsed. The plastic windows had gotten cloudy. Ick, Belinda thought.

Her guardian leaned forward. He looked excited and happy. "That is Gorwing Keep."

Her guardian's home. Was it to be hers, too? She sighed, remembering her room at school—small, neat and bright, full of her plants and the native artifacts Marianne collected.

The carriage went through the Keep's front gate, past the gate house and up to the front door.

"The house was built by Godfrey Hernshaw, the captain of the settlement ship," her guardian said. "He named the planet. Did you know that?" He looked at her.

Belinda shook her head.

"New Hope was the name of the ship. It was his idea to give it to the planet. Here humanity would

begin again, and do better than it had on Earth."
Her guardian paused. "—What a man he was! In
his time, this was at the center of the largest estate
on the planet. He had seven sons. Three of them
were presidents of the world council. There has
been a Hernshaw living in this house ever since
Godfrey. I am the last." The thought seemed to
upset him. He frowned, leaned back and said nothing more till the carriage stopped at the Keep's
door. They got out. The door slid open, and her
guardian said, "Welcome to Gorwing Keep, my
dear."

Belinda shuddered and thought—be resolute.
What else was there to do? She went into the dark
front hall. An ancient humanoid robot stood there.
It bowed, making a grinding noise, then said,
"Please follow me, miss. Your room is ready."

After a moment's hesitation, she followed the
venerable machine. Clanking and grinding, it led
her through a series of corridors, going further and
further back into the house. The air was cold and
damp and had the musty smell of long-shut closets.
Belinda shivered. Oh, to be back in Port Discovery!
At last the robot stopped in front of a door that
slid halfway open, then ground to a halt.

"Nothing works the way it should anymore,"
her guide said. "And what does the master do
about it? Nothing, except play with that old music
ring. The captain's first wife brought it from Earth.
If only the captain were still alive!" It pushed the
door the rest of the way open. "After you, miss."

She went in. The room was large, paneled with
rustwood and lit by a fire in the fireplace. An
old-fashioned bed, its posts carved by native
craftsmen, stood in the room's center. On it lay a

native gown made of barkcloth and decorated with the tiny bright red shells of river clams.

"The bathroom's that door there, miss," the robot said, pointing. "The master would like you to put on the gown on the bed."

"Why?"

"Who can say, miss? The Hernshaws have never explained anything. They get that quality from the captain. It's the only quality of his that they still have. You should have seen the captain, miss—so tall, so full of energy, with such a bright quick eye. He had only one eye, when I knew him. The other was injured on the trip out and had to be removed. I'll wait outside and guide you to the dining room when you're ready."

She waited till the robot was gone, then went into the bathroom and turned on the shower. The shower nozzle hissed, then rattled. Finally it produced the spray she wanted. She undressed and showered. Ah! How good the water felt, after a full day spent in that awful carriage. She scrubbed herself all over, then stood, her eyes shut, feeling the spray beat against her back, and the hot water run down her body. At last, reluctantly, she got out and dried herself. The towel around her, she went into the bedroom and looked at the dress on the bed. It was pretty, all right. But she didn't want to put it on. She didn't like the planet's natives. Even their artifacts made her a little uneasy. The one thing about Marianne she didn't like was her mania for native art. She shivered, remembering the red shell eyes of Marianne's idols. Well, as much as she feared the gown, she feared her guardian more. She picked up the gown and took it into the bathroom to put it on.

When she was ready, the robot led her through more corridors to the main dining room. Her guardian was there, sitting at the great table, drinking wine. He looked at her and smiled slightly. "Sit down, my dear." He filled a glass for her. She sat down and tasted it. It was some wonderful old vintage—mellow and sweet, far different from the cheap wines she'd drunk in student bars in Port Discovery. She sipped it slowly and looked around. The room was lit by dim lights and paneled with the dark wood of the indigo tree. Starmaps hung on the walls. She'd seen a few of them before at the Port Discovery observatory. From the side, they looked to be two or three centimeters thick—as, in fact, they were. But from the front, they were windows into space. They seemed to go back forever. Even after two centuries, points of light still burned in their black depths.

"Wonderful, aren't they?" her guardian said.

She nodded. "I've never seen so many."

"They're heirlooms, part of the Hernshaw treasure—as is my music ring and the robot. They were great collectors, Godfrey and his sons." He stared at the fire in the fireplace and absently ran a finger around the rim of his glass. At last, he sighed and looked at her. "I suppose I'd better tell you why I brought you here."

"I'd certainly like to know."

"How to begin?" He drank the rest of his wine, then refilled the glass. "In the first place, my dear, your name isn't Belinda Smith. It's Belinda Hernshaw."

"What! I'm related to you, then?"

He smiled slightly. "Does that bother you?"

"It's good stock," the robot said. "Or it used to be, anyway."

Her guardian frowned. "You may go, Number 39."

The robot clanked away. Her guardian waited till it was out of the room, then went on. "You are my niece, Belinda, the daughter of my brother—a young fool, if ever there was one!" His right hand was resting on the table. He clenched it, then noticed it was clenched and opened the fingers. "Ah well. He's been dead a long time. He fell in love with one of the gray folk, my sweet, and he married her."

The gray folk. That, she knew, was a backcountry name for the natives. She waited anxiously for her guardian to continue. Where was this story leading? She wasn't sure she wanted to know.

He drank more wine. "After a year or so, the woman had a child. She claimed it was my brother's."

"That's impossible. Humans and natives cannot interbreed."

"I told Gilbert that. But he believed the woman—the more so, because she died soon after the babe was born. He had nothing except his daughter then."

She began to suspect what the story's end would be.

"I'll be brief," her guardian said. "My brother died when the child was a year old—killed by a ghostbear we were tracking through the snow. It turned and attacked him." Her guardian shut his eyes and shuddered. "I still dream about that." He opened his eyes. "I killed the beast, but too late. Gilbert lived just long enough to make me promise to care for the child." He stopped and sipped his wine. "I kept that promise, Belinda, though I never believed the child was really a Hernshaw. Still, my brother had acknowledged it. I found a respectable family that was willing to care for the child and sent it—sent her—to all the best schools. You are that child, Belinda my sweet."

She could feel the quick beat of her heart, feel the tightness in her throat. "No. It's impossible. I don't look like a native."

"You never did, even in infancy. But there's no question about it. A native woman bore you."

"There are physiological differences between humans and natives. Different blood types, different heartbeats. Surely my doctor would have noticed them."

Her guardian nodded. "He did. But I paid Dr. Boucher to keep quiet, and to make sure no other doctors saw you."

He was right, she realized. She'd always been treated by Dr. Boucher. She had a rare cardiovascular condition, the doctor had told her, and it required a specialist's care. She could still hear her heartbeat. She listened. Was there an alien pattern there? No. Of course not. The whole story was ridiculous. She looked around at the dark walls, the dark old furniture, intricately carved by native craftsmen. A place like this was certain to produce morbid fantasies. Her guardian had gone crazy.

But she could hardly tell him that. "This is all very interesting," she said finally.

"Is that all you have to say?"

"It's very confusing, guard— I mean, uncle. I need time to think."

He gulped down the rest of his wine, then picked up the silver bell that rested on the table and rang it.

Clank, whirr, clank, whirr. In the robot came.

"We'll have dinner now, Number 39."

Belinda stood up. "I don't feel well, g— uncle. I'm not hungry."

Her guardian nodded. "Show Miss Belinda to her room, and bring me another bottle when you return."

She said good night, then followed the robot through dark hallways.

"So you're a Hernshaw, miss," it said. "I suspected as much. You look like the captain's first wife. Ah, there was a lady! A little dainty thing, but a crack shot, with a black belt in karate. She was the armaments specialist on the settlement ship. All the captain's best sons were by her."

"You heard what my guardian said?"

"It wasn't hard, miss. —Mind the stairs here. They're starting to crumble. —My hearing is excellent. The captain used to say that I could hear the wool growing on a sheep's back. I can't, of course, since there are no sheep on this planet. I've often wished there were, so I could find out if the captain was right."

"It's all impossible," Belinda said. "I can't be half Hernshaw and half native. Humans and natives can't interbreed."

"This far out in the backwoods, anything is possible, miss. Just remember that. This is your room."

They stopped, and the robot forced the bedroom door open. Belinda went in. "There's a flask of brandy in the bedside table, miss. Good night."

The door ground shut. She heard the robot clank off down the corridor. All at once, she was weeping—almost silently but with great sobs that shuddered through her body. She pulled the native gown off her and dropped it on the floor, then sat down beside the fire to weep.

By the time she stopped, the fire was almost out. She was cold, dressed only in her underwear. Her eyes and her throat hurt. She got up, groaning because she was stiff, and went into the bathroom to wash her face. When she was done, she looked at herself in the bathroom mirror. Was that the face of a half-breed, of a semi-alien? She refused to believe it. True, her hair was a native color: soft, dull brown with silvery highlights. Her face was pale, and her eyes were light gray. Those were native colors too. But her features were human— delicate, not sharp and bony like native features. "No," she said out loud.

She turned out the bathroom light and went back into the bedroom, over to the bedside table. The flask was there: small and made of silver, with "To Iris from Godfrey" engraved on it. Iris. Was she the captain's first wife, the armaments specialist? No matter. Belinda opened the flask and gulped down half the brandy in it. She shuddered and recapped the flask. Her gut felt warm. Already things around her were beginning to get fuzzy. She looked at the gown, which lay crumpled at her feet, then slowly bent and picked it up. It had been woven, she knew, from threads twisted from the fibrous bark of the clothbark tree. The fabric was coarse and lumpy and felt harsh against her skin. Still, it was pretty. She laid it gently over the back of a chair. Time to go to bed, she thought.

Things would seem better in the morning. She pulled the covers back and climbed in.

She woke the next day to the sound of the robot pushing her bedroom door open. She sat up. Her eyes felt dry and scratchy, her head ached, and things seemed no better than they had the night before.

"Good morning, miss. I see you've been crying." The robot set a teatray on the bedside table, then clanked to the closet. "Have some tea. You'll feel much better. The master wants you to wear this today." It pulled out another native gown, this one dyed red and decorated with lots of fringe. At the end of each piece of fringe was a tiny, pearly spiral shell. "Those shells are from a snail-like creature that the natives consider sacred. The captain used to eat them stewed in a kind of bouillabaisse. The snails, I mean. Not the natives."

She sighed. "All right. I'll wear it."

The robot nodded. She poured herself a cup of tea and sipped it. The room was cold, she noticed. Gray light came in through the cloudy plastic window. She could dimly see the trails raindrops made as they ran down the outside of it.

She didn't believe she was a native. But she felt disoriented. Everything safe and comfortable seemed to be moving away from her. Already she had trouble visualizing Port Discovery—the streets of painted houses and the rows of flowering iris trees. The house she'd grown up in had been pink. She was sure of that. But what about the tree that shaded it? Had its blossoms been lavender and yellow or violet and pink? She was no longer certain. Belinda sighed and finished her tea, then got up and got dressed.

As usual, the bedroom door opened only half-way. She squeezed through and saw the robot waiting in the corridor.

"Now I see your mother in you," the robot said. "That was her dress, the one she wore when she married Mr. Gilbert."

"Oh no." She stopped and looked down at the fringe and the tiny shells.

"Yes indeed. This way, miss." The robot clanked off down the corridor. She followed. "Quite a spectacle it was. Be careful," it said as they turned into a new hall. "The ceiling's falling, and there are bits of it all over the floor. A native shaman performed the ceremony—right here, in the main living room. I thought the master—the present master, I mean—was going to be sick at the sight of all those gray folk, doing their marriage dance on the captain's fine old carpet."

"This is all too confusing for me," Belinda said. "I can't make sense out of it."

"Who ever said that life had to make sense?"

They turned another corner, went up a flight of stairs and ended in a little room. The walls were windows, all of them cloudy with age. There were plants in pots on the low window ledges: firefern, groundstar and tiny dwarf iris trees. A table was at the room's center with breakfast waiting on it and a young man sitting at it, who stood as they entered.

"Miss Hernshaw, this is Claud Alone-in-the-forest," the robot said. "You two are cousins."

"Oh," Belinda said.

The young man nodded and mumbled something she couldn't understand. Though he wore human clothes, he was clearly a native—tall and slight, with a pale skin and light brown hair. His face was all sharp angles: prominent cheekbones, deep-set slanted eyes, a jutting nose and a pointed chin. In her opinion, he was ugly—except for his eyes, which were a pale greenish brown and fringed with long thick colorless lashes. His eyes were lovely, she decided, though pretty strange looking.

"The master will be here shortly," the robot said and left them.

As soon as it was gone, Claud said, "This is terrible." His English was good, but his voice was the voice of a native. It was high-pitched. It lacked resonance; and it lilted oddly.

"What is terrible?" Belinda asked.

He pulled out a chair. "Please sit down, and excuse me if I pace."

She sat down and poured herself a cup of coffee. Claud paced to the end of the room, then turned and paced back.

"What's wrong?" she asked.

"Do you know yet why that fellow brought you here?"

"To tell me I was a Hernshaw." She added cream to her coffee. Her hand was trembling a little, she noticed. Claud's nervousness was making her nervous.

"No." He shook his head.

She added sugar to her coffee. "Then why?"

"Your maternal relations demanded you back. A marriage was arranged for you when you were born, Belinda, and now it's time for the ceremony to be performed."

"What!" She dropped the sugar spoon into her coffee cup.

"You're supposed to marry me," Claud said,

sounding anguished. "Why was I ever born?" He kept on pacing.

She ought to be horrified, she realized. But so much had happened in the past two days that she was no longer capable of responding properly to anything. She pulled the sugar spoon out of her cup, then used it to stir her coffee. "You speak very good English for a native."

Claud nodded. "I went to the native school in Port Discovery and then to New Harvard. It was while I was there that I met my true love at one of the native fairs. I went to buy some pickled nashri. There she was, buying a wireroot carpet. What a sight she was! Her hair was dark red like a firefern, and her face was ruddy and freckled, like the blossom of the spotted iris." His voice had grown soft. He stopped and stared at one of the cloudy windows.

"Red hair? She was human?"

"Was and is. We have to meet furtively, of course. What would her friends and relatives say? And now I'm supposed to marry someone else."

She looked down at her coffee cup. Oh Marianne, Marianne, she thought. Why didn't you tell me? For her roommate's hair was red, and her face was covered with freckles. Who else could it be? She imagined Marianne in the arms of a gray man and shuddered. Why didn't these people shut up? She didn't want to know their secrets. She drank some of the coffee, then looked at Claud. "Can't you refuse to marry me?"

He shook his head. "No."

"Why not?"

He looked at her. A fleeting glance. She had a

sense that he was surprised. "I am not human, Belinda, though I have lived among humans for years."

"What does that mean?"

"Humans love to confront one another—and us, when we let them. They are always taking a stand on one thing or another. They think it is a virtue to be inflexible—like a miredrake that has lived too long. The skin grows hard. The animal cannot move. It lies under the house, locked in position, hissing angrily at anything that comes near. Someone has to crawl in with a knife and put the poor animal out of its misery."

He paused for a moment. Belinda drank more coffee. He went on. "To us, there is nothing to admire in this kind of rigidity. We think reality is complex and not always certain. It is hard to know the right and wrong of a situation. Listen to other people! Especially to the other people in your tribe. And always be ready to compromise."

"Oh," said Belinda. This fit with what she knew about the natives. They were timid. They hated any kind of quarrel. Though it was possible to push them too far. Then they exploded into a brief violent fury. The anger did not last long, but while it lasted, the natives could be dangerous—as the early settlers had discovered. Nowadays, humans let the natives alone as much as possible.

"You are willing to let these people ruin your life?" she asked. "And my life too?"

He nodded. "Yes. I have no desire to imitate human behavior. I have seen where it leads." A shudder went through him. "I think that's why I'm so nervous. I have lived for years with people who *like* to argue. It has not been easy." He bit a fingernail. "Another person might have learned to argue, if only in self-defense. I did not. I have become more and more timid."

Belinda said nothing.

Claud went back to pacing. After a moment or two, he spoke again. He seemed to be thinking out loud, arguing with himself. No. He could not be arguing. He had just told her that he hated to argue. He was having a discussion.

"I will not stand up to the elders of the tribe. They'd be furious, if I told them that I would not marry you. I was raised to marry you. That's why I was sent away to school—so I'd know how humans thought, since you were raised a human." He paused and scratched his nose and frowned. "I have to be fair. The elders had no choice. I am the only male in the tribe who's the right age and the right degree of kinship. I have to marry you. If I don't, who will?"

"I might possibly be able to find someone."

"But not in the tribe. As you may or may not know, among our people alternate generations are endogamous. Since your mother married outside the kinship group, you may have to marry within it. The elders told Gilbert Hernshaw that all his wife's children would have to marry back into the tribe. He said that was fine with him."

"Now, what right did he have to decide my life for me?"

Claud stopped at the table. He fiddled with a butter knife. "He was in love, Belinda. He was willing to agree to anything in order to get your mother."

"That was Gilbert," her guardian said behind

her. "Always inconsiderate. I begged him not to marry that woman."

Belinda looked around. Her guardian was standing in the doorway, dressed in an old-fashioned tight-fitting suit.

"I was his brother, his twin," her guardian said. He came into the room. "Who could be closer to him? But do you think he paid any attention to my opinions? No. Never. Only one person ever mattered to him. Gilbert Hernshaw." Her guardian sat down. "Coffee, please."

She poured him a cup of coffee. Claud went back to pacing.

"Claud doesn't want to marry me, g—uncle, and I don't want to marry him."

"You have no choice in this matter, my dear. Nor does— Will you please sit down? You're making me nervous."

Claud sighed, then took a seat and helped himself to a roll.

"That's better." Her guardian sipped his coffee, then uncovered a warming dish and spooned stewed ebony pears onto his plate. "You may not realize it, Belinda, living in Port Discovery, but most of this planet still belongs to the natives. Out here in the backwoods, we do our best to get along with them. The elders of the Stone Tree tribe want you to marry Claud. I'm certainly not going to argue with them about it. I advise you not to, either." He sprinkled sugar on his pears. "I don't see what the problem is. The elders don't care where you live or how you live. They're only interested in bloodlines. You and Claud can live like humans, if you want to—even live in Port Discovery.

You won't be forced into one of those wretched hovels."

"Just a minute," Claud said. "I spent my childhood in a native house. They're not all that bad."

"I defer to your experience. More coffee, please, Belinda."

She refilled his cup, then set the pot down and shook her head. "It wouldn't work, uncle. Claud loves someone else. So do I." I most certainly do, she added to herself, thinking of Marianne's red hair shining in the sunlight and her wonderful green eyes—Slavic eyes, almond-shaped and slanted. Things were getting so complicated, she thought. If only the past two days could be undone. If only she could be back at college. But college seemed so far away. Even if she got back to Port Discovery, things wouldn't be the same. She knew about Marianne and Claud now. What a betrayal that was! How could Marianne have done it? She sighed and buttered a breakfast roll.

Her guardian finished his pears, uncovered the scrambled eggs and helped himself to them. "To be brutal, my dear, you have no choice. We are fifty kilometers from the next human estate, and there is no way out of here except by carriage. My coachman, as you may or may not have noticed, is a native, a member of the Stone Tree tribe. How far do you think he will drive you? My radio is not working at present. And finally, you are a native, my sweet. According to treaty, you are subject to native—not human—law. If you got to a human settlement, you'd only be returned here." He took a roll and bit into it. "Reconcile yourself to the situation," he said as he chewed.

She looked at Claud's pale, sharp-angled face

and thought of Marianne. Never. Somehow she would get away. But she said nothing to her guardian except, "We'll see."

She finished her breakfast, then excused herself. Claud stood too. "Can I go with you?"

"Yes," her guardian said. "Get to know each other better. Go visit the terrarium. Number 39 will show you the way."

Belinda nodded, and the two of them left together. The robot led them through dark hallways to a huge, domed room. The dome was transparent. Below it grew plants brought from Earth two centuries before. Their foliage was an extraordinary, intense, almost luminous green. The air itself seemed to have a greenish tint, which paled into gray in the room's upper reaches, close to the dome. Belinda stopped and stared. "How wonderful!"

The air was warm and moist, full of strange odors. Pale green flowers bloomed right above her, hanging down out of pots.

"Our house is full of wonders," the robot said. "Those things above you are orchids. The captain's second wife liked them. I never did like her. I'll be outside if you want me, Miss Hernshaw."

It left. Belinda and Claud looked at one another. "What are we going to do?" she asked.

He frowned and bit his lip. How human he looked, she thought. But he wasn't. His almost human appearance was an accident of evolution. In spite of it, he was utterly alien, utterly inhuman, utterly different from her. Then she remembered that she was supposed to be a native.

Claud looked up at the leaves above them—enormous, frilly and bright green. "How can I think here? This place makes me nervous."

She was nervous, too, though she hated to admit it. The plants' green was too vivid. The warm, moist, rich air made her dizzy. "There has to be a way out!"

"What?" Claud began to pace again. "Hernshaw was telling the truth. We can't get away. The woods are full of Stone Tree warriors. They even have a couple of mind-watchers watching us. Can't you feel them?"

"No." She felt a prickling sensation spread across her back. Like all humans on the planet, she knew that the natives had psi powers. Like most humans, she preferred to forget the fact. It was too horrible, imagining those woodland skulkers looking into human minds or making ashtrays move in human houses.

Claud stopped pacing and stared at her. "That's odd. One of the watchers is old Starbird. You can always tell when he's watching you. His presence is like a rock in the middle of your head."

"I can't feel anything."

"I don't understand that. Your mother was very gifted. She could mind-watch from a hundred kilometers away, or so my mother told me. She could bring birds down out of the sky and fish up to the water's surface. She could even mind-move small objects, and that's a rare talent. My father said it was a great pity Ania Groundstar was born into the exogamous generation. She would've been a wonderful wife. What man could fail as a hunter or a warrior, if he had her help?"

"I suppose so."

"Are you sure you can't sense Starbird? He's got a hard cold slick feel to him like a polished stone."

She shut her eyes and tried to figure out what

was inside her head. The usual memories were there—Port Discovery in the summer sunlight, her foster mother fixing fish stew, and the expected anxieties—would she get out of this mess and back to school before finals began? She noticed as well a lot of facts about natives, stars, stones and birds, also a slight tension headache. But she couldn't find the hard, cold, alien presence Claud said was there. She opened her eyes and shook her head.

"You must be a psychic idiot, Belinda. It's nothing to be ashamed of."

"I'm not ashamed."

"You can still lead a useful life, though there are things you'll never be able to do."

"All I want to be able to do is get out of here."

Claud shook his head. "It can't be done."

She felt herself growing furious. What was wrong with this oaf? He had gone back to pacing. Up and down the concrete aisle he went. "He's lying about living in Port Discovery. The elders aren't going to let us out of their sight, at least until we procreate. We'll be stuck in a hut in some native village with rain dripping through the thatch and miredrakes grunting underneath the floorboards—and the elders listening at the door to make sure we're making love." He stopped, twisted a leaf off one of the plants and shredded it.

"I don't see why it's so important that we marry."

"Part of it is religion. If certain things aren't done in certain ways, then the ocean monsters will rise to the ocean's surfaces, causing terrific tidal waves. Didn't you learn that stuff in Introductory Comp. Soc.?"

"I haven't taken it yet."

"Oh." He tossed away the plant shreds. "The

rest has to do with your mother's psi powers. Such powers are hereditary. The elders don't want the tribe to lose whatever powers you have or are carrying."

"This is all too silly for words."

"It may be silly, but it's going to ruin our lives." He pulled another leaf from one of the plants and tore it up.

"No." She shook her head. "I refuse to let it." She looked around her at the strange wonderful plants from Earth. "Maybe there's something in this house that will help us. It's full of ancient marvels."

"What?"

"Robot?" she called.

A moment later, she heard a clanking and whirring behind her. She turned.

"You called, miss?"

"Yes. Did you hear our conversation?"

"I couldn't help it, miss. You were talking loudly, and the terrarium door isn't very thick."

"It doesn't matter. Do you think the captain would approve of what my guardian—my uncle—is doing?"

The robot stood still, humming loudly. In this light, she could see it clearly. Its steel surface was crisscrossed with scratches. One of its eyes had gone dead and was dull gray instead of luminous blue. Why hadn't she noticed that before? Had it just gone dead? At last the robot swiveled its head from side to side. Its neck joint made a grinding noise. "No. He would not approve. He took care of his own. He would never have surrendered one of his family to a bunch of barbarians."

"Watch it," Claud said. "Those are my people out there."

"Can they tell what we're doing?" Belinda asked.

Claud shook his head. "All a mind-watcher can do is tell where a person is and what kind of mood they're in. The really good ones can pick up fragmentary images, but old Starbird is just barely adequate. I don't know who else is with him, but it's no one first rate. The Stone Tree tribe doesn't have a first rate mind-watcher. We are very hard up for psychics."

"Good," Belinda said. She looked back at the robot. "Is this the right way for the Hernshaw family to come to an end? With this kind of betrayal?"

After a moment the robot said:

"Broeth munu berjast ok at bonum verthast.
Munu systrungar sifjum spilla."

"What?" Claud asked.

"It's a stanza from the captain's favorite poem. It's about the end of the world, and it means—

"Brothers will fight and kill one another.
The children of sisters will break their kinship."

The poor old machine, Belinda thought. Its world really was ending. It had been programmed to serve the Hernshaws, to see this one family as everything. Now the last two Hernshaws were turning on one another. With a start she realized she was starting to think of herself as a Hernshaw. Well, as bad as that was, it was better than being a native. She looked at Claud. He was biting his

lip and one of his eyelids was twitching. How ugly
he was! Even his wonderful hazel eyes didn't help
all that much.

"I'll help you, miss," the robot said. "The captain would have wanted me to." After it said that,
it stood for a while, staring straight ahead. Belinda
bit her fingernails. Claud shifted from foot to foot,
as if anxious to get back to pacing. At last the robot
said, "Most likely the master will drink himself
into insensibility after dinner. He does that most
nights. After I've put him to bed, I'll take you into
the storage wing. Maybe we can find some means
of escape there."

Claud shrugged. "It's better than doing nothing,
I suppose. I'm going to take a walk. Maybe I'll
meet some of my kinfolk and find out what the
elders are planning."

"What shall I do?"

"Be patient, miss. If you want, I'll show you to
the library. The captain's collection of Earth music is famous. Or was famous, anyway. You humans forget so quickly."

"All right."

So they went to the library, a large room with
lots of windows. For some reason, the windows'
plastic hadn't gotten cloudy. Belinda looked out
and saw a brown lawn. Beyond it was the forest.
The rain had stopped, but the sky was still low
and gray.

"Make yourself at home, miss. I'll bring you
some coffee."

The robot left. She looked around at the room.
There was little in it: a pair of easy chairs covered with thornbuck hide, a rug made from the
pelt of a ghostbear and a huge desk. Behind the

desk was a chair, its high back carved with native monsters. There were two wooden gorwings atop the chair, their wings spread wide, their long necks stretched forward, their beaks open to show rows of tiny white shell teeth. Yech. Belinda shuddered, then started looking at the crystal cases along the walls. She found "Highlights of The Flying Dutchman" and put it in the ancient crystal-player. Strangely enough, the machine still worked. But the crystal was mislabeled. She had heard parts of "The Flying Dutchman" performed by the Port Discovery Symphony Orchestra. This wasn't it. Instead of Wagner's wonderful music, she heard a lot of whining string instruments and a man's voice singing:

"If we can make it through December,
Everything's going to be all right, I know.
It's the coldest part of winter,
And I shiver when I see the falling snow."

What was this stuff? The recording sounded incredibly old, full of crackles and hums. The singing went on:

"If we make it through December,
Got plans to be in a warmer town come summertime,
Maybe even California.
If we make it through December, we'll be fine."

The robot returned, bringing a cup and a pot of coffee or—to be more accurate—pseudo-coffee. The colonists had brought real coffee with them from

Earth in their store of frozen genetic material. But the plant did not thrive here. A local bug, the coffee weevil, ate every bean. The colonists made do with a drink brewed from the fruit of the yellowpod tree. It didn't look like coffee, but it stimulated, and it had a wonderful aroma. Not like the aroma of coffee, the old records said, but almost as good.

The robot set the cup down and filled it with yellow coffee. The singer in the crystal sang:

> "Got laid off down at the factory,
>   And their timing's not the greatest in the world.
>   Heaven knows I've been working hard,
>   Wanted Christmas to be right for Daddy's girl."

She switched off the player and took the crystal out. On one of the facets in tiny silver letters was "The Golden Hits of Merle Haggard." Who was Merle Haggard? Why had Captain Hernshaw brought his music with him from Earth?

"Do you like that song, miss? It's appropriate enough. From the looks of the sky, we're going to have snow." The robot went to the desk and got out a bottle half full of brandy. "Do you want some in your coffee?"

Belinda nodded. "Who was Merle Haggard, anyway?"

"I don't really know, except that the captain liked his songs."

"Well, I don't." She put the crystal back into its case. She took down "The Jupiter Symphony" next and looked at the writing on the crystal. It said,

"Thus Spake Zarathustra" by Richard Strauss. She put the crystal back.

The robot poured brandy into her cup, and the coffee darkened a little. "That's the captain's desk."

"I suspected as much." She glanced at the sharp-toothed gorwings and the writhing interwoven monsters that were carved in the wood.

"He used to sit there and listen to the reports his sons radioed in from all over the estate. You should've seen him, miss. In his last days, he had a long gray beard, and he'd twist it and tug at it while he listened. If you're a Hernshaw, you're his heir. You know that, don't you?"

"What?"

"Gilbert Hernshaw was older than the present master. By some ten minutes, as I remember. My memory isn't what it used to be. Faulty circuits, I suppose."

"Are you sure of this?"

"More or less. Things come and go, miss. Sometimes the world seems so clear and certain. Then I forget the crucial connections, and everything falls apart."

How could that metal voice sound pained? But it seemed to her it did. The robot bowed, making a grinding noise, and left. She kept looking through the recordings till she found one she thought she'd like—"Folksongs of the Asteroids." The crystal was inside a case labeled "Great Moments of Chinese Opera." She put it in the player. While the music played, she curled up in a chair and drank the coffee. She must have slept badly the night before, for she was soon drowsy. She finished the coffee, leaned back and shut her eyes. For a short while the music kept her awake with shrill whistling and plinking sounds and the sad tale of a space-wreck. Then she went to sleep.

When she woke, several hours later, it was snowing outside—large fluffy flakes that came straight down, melting as soon as they touched the ground. The crystal player had shut itself off. She felt groggy and headachey. For a moment, she didn't know where she was. Then she remembered, sighed and stretched.

"You may well sigh," Claud said.

She looked around and saw him sitting in the captain's chair, smoking a native cigar. He waved at the windows. "They're all out there, every male in the tribe who's old enough to hold a spear. They plan to hold the marriage ceremony tomorrow night. The moons will be in the 'ru' configuration, which is considered lucky for marriages, night-fishing, and the making of narrow-necked pots."

"Oh no."

"Oh yes." Claud puffed on his cigar. The tip remained ash-gray. He sighed, picked up a lighter and flicked it on. "The old women are coming here tomorrow morning to purify you. I have to go off in the woods and take a ritual bath in running water. In this weather, mind you. I'll probably catch a terrible cold."

She stood up. "We'd better tell the robot."

"I already have."

"Oh." She sat down.

Claud lit the cigar, then snapped down the lighter's top. "The only good news I got was that old Starbird is uttering dire prophecies. He says he can sense Godfrey Hernshaw's ghost. The ghost is somewhere close by, he says, and it's very angry. According to him, no good will come of this."

"Of what?"

"Forcing the two of us to marry. Unfortunately, no one believes Starbird. They say he's not good enough to sense a ghost."

Could the mind-watchers really sense disembodied spirits? Was this the proof of an afterlife that humanity had always wanted? She decided to worry about those questions later. She had too much on her mind as it was.

"The robot said it would bring our lunch here. Your guardian rarely eats lunch. He drinks it instead."

"Oh." So her guardian was a problem drinker. How little she had known about him up till now. Not that she had particularly cared. She had always been interested in the here and now. Marianne said she was narrow-minded. True, perhaps. But she'd been happy enough, concentrating on her schoolwork and her plants and Marianne. She got up and went to one of the windows. It was still snowing. Now the snow was staying on the ground. Already there was a thin cover of white over the lawn. She felt cold and depressed. Her life seemed as desolate as the landscape in front of her. She turned suddenly and looked at Claud. "Marianne Duval was my roommate at college."

"What?" Claud dropped his cigar, then picked it up before it could burn the desk.

"Did she tell you anything about me?"

"Only that you are terribly prejudiced against natives. Are you?"

She nodded.

"But you are a native."

"I didn't know that till yesterday. Besides, I thought I was supposed to be only half native."

Claud shook his head. "That's impossible, Belinda. Humans can't interbreed with us. Gilbert Hernshaw couldn't possibly be your father."

"Then who was?"

He shrugged. "Some passing stranger, a member of another tribe."

"I'm getting more and more confused." She went over to the player and turned it on. "The Song of the Bare Rock Miners" began.

Claud frowned. "Turn that off, will you? I've never been able to tolerate Earth music."

She turned the player off.

"Thank you. It sounded awful." He relit his cigar.

"Well then." She took the crystal out and found another one. The case was labeled "Whalesongs and Other Sounds of the Deep." The crystal itself contained bone harp music, as she'd discovered earlier. She put it in the player. They listened to that till the robot brought them lunch.

After lunch, Claud suggested that they go look at the stables. Belinda glanced outside. Everything was white now, and the snow was falling more thickly than ever. It did look inviting. Snow rarely fell in Port Discovery. When it did, it usually melted as soon as it hit the streets and the bright-tiled rooftops.

"All right. I'll have to change though."

Claud nodded. "I'll meet you in the front hall."

She went back to her room and changed into pants and the warmest shirt she had. There was a heavy jacket in the closet, also a pair of boots that were only a little too big. She put these on and went to meet Claud. Together they went out into the snow, across the white lawn, their heads bent and their hands in their pockets. A wind had started to blow. It whirled snow into their eyes and whipped their hair back and forth. Around the house they went, through a little side garden, between leafless bushes. It felt good to get outside, Belinda thought. She'd been suffocating in the house. She looked at Claud. His hair was white. There were snowflakes caught in his eyebrows and on his thick lashes. For some reason the snow made him look less alien. They crossed the back drive and entered the stable courtyard.

"What do you want?" someone asked. Her guardian's native coachman came out of one of the boxes. He was leading one of the thornbucks, a huge beast with long legs and powerful-looking shoulders and haunches. Its gray coat was winter-shaggy. Atop its head were two long curving horns with sharp spikes all along their upper edges. The coachman stopped. The thornbuck looked at them with pale yellow eyes, then snorted.

"Don't think you can steal any of my bucks," the coachman said. "They're none of them broken for riding. Besides, I'll have my eyes on you."

"You certainly are suspicious," Claud said. "All we wanted to do is take a look around. It's stifling inside that house."

"Well, be careful what you do in my stable."

Claud nodded. The coachman led the buck across the courtyard and into another box. Claud stamped his feet to get the snow off his boots. "So much for that idea. It wouldn't have worked, anyway. We couldn't have gotten past the Stone Tree sentries."

"You were thinking of stealing a thornbuck?"

"Yes. The important word is thinking. I doubt if I'd steal a buck, even if I could. As I said before,

I'm terribly timid. Would you like to walk in the woods?"

She nodded. They left the courtyard and crossed a little river on a bridge. There was ice along the banks, but the river's center was still unfrozen. The water was clear with a slight greenish tinge. She could see right through it, down to the pebbles on the river's bottom. She stopped and watched the water slide below her. How lovely it all was—the white banks, the falling flakes of snow, the fast-moving water. She shivered from a combination of coldness and delight. After a moment, they went on into the woods. The wind decreased, and the snowflakes came straight down. Overhead, something screeched. Snow fell on them. She looked up and saw a tiny furry silver-gray manikin, that shook the branch it clung to.

"That's a timish," Claud said. "The humans around here call it a snow monkey. It's supposed to be a relative of ours."

The creature screeched again, then leaped into another tree and started climbing. They watched it until it disappeared around the tree's trunk, then went on. The path turned a corner. They saw a native warrior ahead of them, standing in the path's center, leaning on his spear. He was taller than Claud and even uglier, his face very long and narrow with a pointed nose and chin. His hair hung down in little braids with shells dangling from their ends. Even his moustache was in braids: two long ones that ended in silver bells. His leggings were buckskin, decorated with fringe, and his jacket was brown fur. "What want?" he asked in English.

Claud answered in one of the native dialects.

The warrior frowned and tugged at his lower lip. "No," he said at last. "Go back."

"What did you say?"

"I told him we were taking a walk. He doesn't like the idea. I don't know if you are interested, but his name is Rissa Needleburr, and he's a cousin of yours."

"Yes," the native said.

It was impossible. How could she have anything in common with this savage? The savage smiled, showing broken teeth. "Good meet—" He stopped, then looked at Claud. "Na?"

"Kin," Claud said. "It's good to meet kin is what he's trying to say."

Oh yeah? she thought.

Claud scratched his nose. "I guess we'd better turn back. He won't let us go any further."

She shrugged, and back they went. The snow fell more and more lightly. Belinda looked up at the gray sky and saw a pair of birds circling way way up.

"Gorwings," Claud told her. "They're pretty unusual around here this time of year. Those two probably belong to old Starbird. He keeps all kinds of nasty pets."

She shuddered. "I feel so trapped."

"You ought to. You are."

They recrossed the bridge and went back around the house to the front door. There was a native there, drawing something in the snow that lay across the doorstep. He straightened up and turned to face them. How ancient he was, how bent and wrinkled! His bare legs were bone thin: his sandaled feet were covered with cordlike veins; his barkcloth shirt was open to show a sagging belly and shriveled privates. "Woe! Woe!" he cried in English. He waved his hands in the air, then hobbled away.

"That's Starbird." Claud looked at the design in the snow. "I think that's to ward off ghosts. He must really think the captain is around."

"In that case—" She kicked the snow till she'd obliterated all the lines the shaman had drawn.

"I hope you know what you're doing." He rang the doorbell.

"I don't believe in ghosts, but right now I'll take anyone's help," Belinda said.

The snow had stopped. The air was still and seemed colder than before. Half way across the lawn, Starbird was dancing or having a seizure, she wasn't sure which. The door opened.

"Come in. Come in," the robot said. "The master has passed out early today. We can go and look at the storage wing right this minute."

"Give us time to thaw out."

"Certainly, miss. This way, if you please."

It led them to a room with a fireplace and lit the fire, then brought them coffee and brandy. They took off their coats. Claud stood in front of the fire, his hands stretched out toward it. The ruddy light gave color to his face and made his hair a human shade of brown, or so it seemed to Belinda. She settled herself into an easy chair. The robot poured the coffee.

Claud sighed. "I can't take this weather anymore. I've spent too much time in Port Discovery."

"Why did you come back?"

"Don't you remember what your guardian said? We're subject to tribal law, to tribal authority. The elders sent for me. I knew if I didn't return, they'd have me brought back in manacles." The robot gave him a brandy snifter. He emptied it with one gulp. "Do you think I liked leaving? Do you think I liked the look on Marianne's face when I told her?"

"Did you tell her you were going to get married?"

He shook his head. The robot refilled his glass. "How could I? I couldn't bear to hurt her that much."

She would've been hurt all right, Belinda thought, knowing that her two loves were going to marry one another and leave her alone. Or did Marianne have more loves, who would comfort her? Belinda felt tired. She sipped her brandy and watched the fire.

"About the storage wing, miss," the robot said.

She shook her head. "Not now. I have to have time to rest."

Claud finished his brandy. "I'll go."

"You're sure you won't, miss?"

"Yes." She set down her snifter and shut her eyes. After a moment, she heard them go. She kept her eyes shut a while longer, then opened them. The flames flickered. The wood snapped and crackled. Belinda felt depressed.

"39!" It was her guardian, shouting in the corridor. "Where are you, machine?"

She went to the door and opened it. There he was, his hair all tousled, his clothing wrinkled, his face pale and sick looking.

"G—uncle?"

He stared at her, bleary-eyed. "Where is the robot? I want something to drink."

"There's brandy in here, uncle."

He pushed past her, stumbled to the table and

poured himself a snifter of brandy. With one gulp, he drank half of it, then shuddered and sat down. "I had the dream again, my sweet. Gilbert and the ghostbear. Pray God you never have such dreams." He drank some more brandy, then refilled the snifter. "It's always the same, Belinda. The ghost-bear coming out of the thicket. Then Gilbert rais-ing his gun and pulling the trigger. Then there's the click, when the hammer hits the empty cham-ber." He stopped and drank more brandy.

"Empty?"

He looked up at her. His face was flushed and his eyes unfocused. "Yes. Of course. The bullets were in my pocket." He drank the rest of the brandy, then refilled the glass a third time.

Oh no, she thought. Not more confessions.

He nodded, staring at the fire. "You would've had the house, the Hernshaw inheritance, every-thing. A native bastard in the captain's high-seat. That couldn't be, Belinda. I had to stop that." He shivered, then laughed shakily. "And I did. I did. Tomorrow, you will be where you belong."

"But why did you take care of me, if you felt that way? Why didn't you simply give me to the natives when I was a baby?"

"I couldn't do that. I promised Gilbert. I couldn't break my promise. Not a promise made to a dying man."

He was crazy, she decided. They were all crazy—her guardian, Claud, the robot, the entire Stone Tree tribe. Maybe there was something bad in the air around here.

All at once, her guardian clutched his forehead, then slumped back in his chair. The brandy snifter fell from his hand, its dark contents spilling across the pale brown carpet. Was he dead? she wondered. She went closer. As she did so, he started to snore. No. Merely dead drunk. She picked up the snifter and set it on the table, then got her own glass and sipped from it.

She sat down in the chair opposite her guardian. He snorted and groaned, then went back to snoring. Belinda drank a little coffee. Well, she wondered, who was she? The heir to Gorwing Keep or a native bastard? Or neither. She liked the last idea best.

The fire snapped loudly. She jumped and spilled a few drops of liquor on the chair's barkcloth upholstery. She rubbed at the spots, but they didn't go away. Maybe it didn't matter. Maybe the house was hers. Not that she'd ever get it, the way things were going. Instead, she'd get a hut in a native village and Claud for a husband.

The room's door whined open. Claud came in, followed by the robot.

"Did you find anything?"

Claud shook his head, then helped himself to some brandy. "There's nothing there except a lot of dusty old machinery that doesn't work."

"We can't be sure of that, sir. We didn't get a chance to try all the machines. I thought I heard the master calling me," the robot said to Belinda. "So we came back."

Belinda pointed at her guardian. "He came in here looking for you and had a drink. Then he said he'd murdered his brother."

"What?" Claud said.

"Do you think he did, Number 39?"

"It's hard to say, miss. He says a lot of strange things when he's drunk. Some of them are true and some aren't. If you'll excuse me . . ." It gathered her guardian up in its metal arms and carried him out of the room.

Claud sat down. "What now?"

"I don't know. But I'm not going to give up—I don't think I am. I wish I had some idea of how to get out of here!"

Claud nodded in agreement. He sipped his brandy, staring at the fire. It was burning low. The dim light softened the angles of his face. She felt a sudden frightening rush of affection for him. Good old Claud. He wasn't all that bad, really, for a native.

After a moment, she recovered herself. It must be the brandy, she thought and set her snifter down. "I'd better go to bed. I'm feeling funny." She stood up.

Claud nodded a second time. "Good night."

She went back to her room. There was a light on, and a fire burned in the fireplace. One of her nightgowns lay on the bed. The ubiquitous Number 39, she thought. She picked the gown up. The soft feel of its fabric reassured her, as did the delicate floral print. How could harm come to anyone wearing a flannel nightgown? She carried it into the bathroom, hung it on a hook and turned the shower on.

She was a long time showering. She refused to think about her present problems. Instead, she worried about what courses to take next semester. She never studied well in the spring. What she needed, she thought, as the water hit her shoulders and back, was something easy like art history. But she'd already taken as much art history as she needed. Music history then? Or Introductory Earth

Lit.? She got out of the shower, still undecided, dried herself and put on the nightgown. She climbed into bed and lay a while, looking at the firelight on the ceiling. Then she went to sleep.

She slept badly, waking often. A couple of times, she woke shaking and turned on the light, looking around for something that shouldn't have been there—a monster or a native. But there was only the bedroom furniture. She lay with the light on till she felt more or less calm. Then she went back to sleep.

The last time she woke, it was morning. Gray light came in the clouded window. The robot came in the bedroom door, carrying a teatray. "Good morning, miss. How did you sleep?"

"Terribly."

The robot made a clicking sound and set the tray down, then poured her a cup of tea. "I thought about the master's confession last night."

Belinda sat up and took the teacup. "Yes?"

"It took me a long time to think it through. I don't think as well as I used to. Did I tell you that?"

She nodded, sipping the tea. It was a pale transparent red color and very bitter. She liked it, though a lot of people didn't, including Marianne.

"In the end, I decided to go to Gilbert Hernshaw's room. The present master told me to close it up, after Mr. Gilbert died. No one's been in it for almost eighteen years. I found this."

There was a silver warming dish on the tray. The robot lifted the cover. Underneath was a crystal cube. Belinda picked it up and turned it in her hands. It was maybe ten centimeters along each side. Within it, silver wires crisscrossed. They were so thin that she couldn't see them except when the light hit them at just the right angle.

"Do you know what that is?" the robot asked.

"A memory cube." She felt around it till she found the slight depression on one side. She pressed in there. All at once, the cube was full of light, and there was a human head in it, tiny and perfectly three-dimensional. She was looking at its back. She turned the cube till she saw the face. It was a man's face, very like her guardian's, but younger, with a far healthier appearance. The strong features seemed full of energy. There was a look of intelligence in the large light-colored eyes. Surely the curl of the full lips indicated good humor.

The man said, "This is for you, Belinda." She almost dropped the cube. "If you've been properly educated, you'll know Tennyson's lines in *In Memoriam*:

"Be near me when my light is low,
    When the blood creeps, and the nerves prick
    And tingle; and the heart is sick,
    And all the wheels of being slow.

"That's how I feel tonight, Belinda. You're in the next room, asleep in your crib. My brother Godfrey is in the dining room, drunk as usual. There's no one else in the house except Number 39, the old family robot. I'm sitting here, missing your mother and feeling sorry for myself. So I've decided to record a message to you, to explain what happened, how you came about." The man in the cube stopped talking. She saw him lift a glass to his lips and take a drink. He lowered the glass, then said, "I wish you could have seen your mother. She was beautiful, though not the way humans are. She wasn't soft and delicate. She had the harsh hard beauty the natives have. I loved her the first time I saw her. As Shakespeare says, 'Whoever loved, that loved not at first sight?' "

"That's balderdash," the robot said. "I remember—" It paused. "I forget what I remember."

"In any case, I married her. She had more than beauty, Belinda. She had intelligence too, an extraordinary force of character and psi powers." The man in the cube sighed. "I'll never find another woman like her. I know that." He drank some more of whatever he was drinking. "I wanted to have a child by her. I wanted the next heir of Gorwing Keep to have her qualities instead of the damn sickly Hernshaw qualities that Geoffrey and I have."

"The young whelp," the robot said. "What did he know about being a Hernshaw? He spent his life reading books and thinking in poetry."

She looked at the old machine. How its one blue eye glittered! Was it breaking down? Its conversation was getting increasingly strange.

"I know interbreeding is supposed to be impossible. Supposedly, humans and natives are two entirely separate species—similar only because they both evolved to fit similar ecological niches. I never believed this. Myself, I believe in Dr. Sigbert Schwartz's 'Diffusion Theory.' According to Dr. Schwartz, both species evolved from the same original stock. I studied with him at New Harvard, Belinda. I can still remember him stomping back and forth in front of the class, saying, 'Look at the natives, ladies and gentlemen. What do they look like, except to the blind eye of a bigot? They look like *us*.' He'd stop for a moment and glare at his students. And then he'd go on. 'Appearances do not always deceive. They tell us much that is true —Go to Settlement, to the museum! Look at the displays that show us life on Earth. Compare a lion and a house cat. They look alike. They *are* alike. They are related, as everyone knows who has read a book on evolution.

" 'We have not had the time—nor the resources— to compile a history of the evolution of New Hope. Still and all, we know the goldwattle and the gorwing share a common ancestry—As any fool can see! The relationship is visible.

" 'So is the relationship between us and the natives. But for the natives we make an exception. We deny the importance of appearance. We babble on about convergent evolution; and we look for anything—any minor difference—that will make them seem stranger and more alien.

" 'Why do we do this, ladies and gentlemen? Because of prejudice. Racism. Blind folly. False pride. And every kind of unscientific stupidity.'

"At this point, Belinda, he would turn bright red and have to stop and drink a glass of water and take a pill.

"In any case, he argued that both Earth and our planet had been colonized by a people that he called 'The Master Race.' The colonization was comparatively recent; and the two groups of colonists have not yet evolved into separate species. He believed that it was possible—in theory—for humans and natives to interbreed. We are genetically compatible, according to him; but—over the millennia of separation—we have become immune to one another. When a crossbreed is conceived, the mother's immunological system perceives it as alien and attacks it and aborts it. 'In isolation, in a test tube,' the doctor said, 'human and native cells show no aversion to one another. Ova and spermatazoa match easily and naturally. If I had the scientific resources of our ancestors, I could produce a crossbred test tube baby. Alas, I do not.''

Suddenly, she couldn't bear to listen. She turned the cube off and watched its picture disappear. Then she drank some tea. The room was cold. She shivered.

"Aren't you going to listen to the rest, miss?"

"Later. Rebuild the fire, will you, please?"

The robot nodded, then set to work.

Belinda finished the tea and poured herself another cup. She had reached the point where she had too much new information. She couldn't assimilate any more. She'd felt this way before, while studying for tests. She looked at the fireplace and saw the first small flames leap up out of the kindling. At least she would be warm. She sipped the tea. "Could I have breakfast here, robot?"

"Certainly, miss."

The robot brought her breakfast, and she ate it beside the fire: fresh ebony pears from her uncle's greenhouse, an omelette, toast, jam, and coffee.

While she ate, the robot got out a new dress, this one so covered with shells that she couldn't tell the fabric's color. The shells were white, pale pink, and slate blue. They were tiny and sewn into a floral pattern—a blue vine with white flowers that went up and down the dress, over a shimmering pink background.

"That's your wedding gown, miss. Lovely, isn't it? It took the tribal seamstresses half a year to make it. But you can't wear it till you've been purified. Right now, you have this to wear." It brought out another gown, sleeveless, made of dark brown barkcloth.

"I'll freeze in that."

"Be that as it may, you have to wear it. Think of your poor cousin out in the woods in a loincloth."

"Claud?"

The robot nodded. "They took him off for his cleansing a little after dawn."

Belinda shuddered and set down her coffee cup, then picked up the memory cube. She pressed the depression. The man's head reappeared. The bright light of the room he sat in shone out of the cube's sides and through her hands, making her fingers glow red. She set the cube down.

The man said, "As I mentioned, your mother had remarkable psi powers. She was telepathic, which is pretty common among the natives, and she was telekinetic. That's a rare talent, Belinda. She could only move small objects and those not far. But it was an amazing sight—ashtrays floating in midair, dice tumbling across the table, apparently of their own volition, my slippers sliding across the floor toward me. And while there was an upper limit to the size of the things she moved, there was no lower limit. I firmly believe that she could have moved subatomic particles, if I'd been able to explain what they were to her. But I couldn't. I confess, I have trouble myself understanding what goes on inside an atom. Microbes, however, she could understand. I taught her how to use a microscope. Once she saw the microbes, she had no trouble moving them. In time, Ania discovered she could sense microbes without seeing them, the same way she could sense birds and fishes and river clams. After that, she moved the cells around without using a microscope to look at them." The man sighed, then sipped from his glass. "Those were happy days. We were both terribly excited, both full of tremendous energy. Nothing seemed impossible. As Wordsworth says, 'Bliss was it in that dawn to be alive, But to be young was very heaven.' In the end, we devised a plan. Ania would use her telekinetic powers to protect our baby against her own immunological system. She would keep her lymphocytes—those are the cells that attack alien organisms—away from the foetus."

"That is ridiculous," Belinda said loudly.

". . . Of course, the baby would be vulnerable to disease until it developed its own lymphocytes. But we had to take that risk."

The man in the cube stopped. There was a frown on his tiny face. "I never really knew how Ania did it—how she was able to maintain a psychic filter day and night, waking and sleeping for eight months. Obviously, her psi powers were subject to subconscious control as well as to conscious control. She told me all she had to do was say to herself 'do such-and-such' before she went to sleep, or when she wanted to think about something else. But there had to be more to it than that. She was terrible at explaining things." The man sighed. "In any case, for eight months any lymphocyte that came close to you was transported to another part of Ania's system. The effort exhausted her. How much I did not realize until the end. After you were born, she was unable to regain her strength. She lingered for a while—then died." He stopped and looked down, then looked up again. "That's how you were bred, Belinda. That's how you came to be." The cube went dark. The recording had ended.

Belinda shivered. "Can that be true, robot?"

"What am I to say, miss? But Gilbert Hernshaw was a very honest man."

So she was a half-breed! A native and a Hernshaw at the same time. Surely this changed her present situation. If she was half human, she could hardly be subject to native law. She stood up. "I have to take the cube to my uncle."

The robot swiveled its head from side to side. "He won't care, miss. He wants Gorwing Keep. He wants you out of the way."

"Are you sure?"

"Yes. If you show him the cube, he'll destroy the recording."

She sat down. "What'll I do?"

"Get dressed and go to meet the old women. There's still a whole day before the wedding. I'll think of something."

"What if I refuse?" asked Belinda. "What if I say, 'I won't put on the dress. I'll stay in this room. I won't have anything to do with the ceremony of purification.'"

The robot looked at her for a moment. Then it spoke. "I cannot force you to do anything, miss. But the natives can—and will. If need be, they will drag you screaming through the ceremony. Think of your dignity! Remember that you are a Hernshaw!"

"Oh," said Belinda. She thought for a while. "All right. I'll take part in the ceremony. But not in the wedding!"

"Of course not," said the robot. "I promise you, Belinda, I will think of something."

"I hope so."

She put on the brown dress. The robot led her to the front hall. The old women waited there. There were a dozen of them, all dressed in their finest clothes: shell-covered dresses and tall cone-shaped hats with clusters of feathers at their tops. They carried ceramic whistles, wooden rattles, and smoldering firepots.

"Welcome, Belinda," someone said in English. Out from among the old women a young woman came. She was thin and pale with light blue eyes and flaxen hair. Her dress was dyed blue and decorated with white shells. "I am your cousin Lusa Windingvine. I'm here to interpret for you, so you'll understand the ceremony."

"Oh," Belinda said.

The old women set down their firepots. The room was filling with fragrant smoke. Belinda felt a little dizzy. Was there something in the smoke? Two ancient ladies hobbled forward and took her hands.

"Go with them," Lusa said.

They led her to the center of the room and tugged at her arms till she sat down. Then they hobbled off. Lusa sat down next to her. "The first part of the ceremony is the singing, Belinda. I'll translate the songs for you."

"Where did you go to school?"

Lusa smiled. "I didn't. I am Geoffrey Hernshaw's mistress. He taught me English."

"But I thought he hated natives."

Lusa shrugged. "Who else can he sleep with, this far into the backwoods?"

The old women seated themselves in a circle around Belinda and began to shake their rattles.

"As for me," Lusa said, "I belong to the exogamous generation. I can't marry the man I love, since he's a member of the tribe. I don't much care who I sleep with."

"What a lot of silly customs you people have."

"Are human customs any better?"

"I'm not sure."

The old women began to sway back and forth. They shook their rattles and blew on their whistles.

"They are going to tell the story of the creation of the world."

An ancient, shriveled, bent-over lady began to sing. Her voice was shrill and uncertain.

"She is telling how the Great-Fish-That-Is-The-Origin-Of-Everything shaped a nashri bean from the phlegm in its throat, then spat the bean out."

Another woman took up the song, a huge fat lady wearing a cone-hat covered with red shells. Her voice was deep and hoarse.

"The bean floated on the water's surface for days," Lusa said. "Then, all at once, its hard shell broke open and two people climbed out. They were the Divine Twins, Istai and Nu. They sat on the floating bean for days, not knowing what to do, till a passing monster decided to eat them. Then Nu took a sharp piece of the bean shell and stabbed the monster to death."

The fat lady stopped singing and gasped for breath. A third old woman began to sing.

"After that, Nu made a loom from the monster's bones, and Istai tooks the monster's sinews and wove all the land in the world."

Belinda was getting stiff, sitting in one position,

but she was afraid to move. The smoke from the firepots made her eyes water. She felt dazed. Where was Claud? Where was the robot and their means of escape? The song went on.

"Tiny bits of sinews fell into the water and became fishes," Lusa said. "Other bits flew up into the air and became birds. Still other bits fell on the new-made land and became animals. In this way, the world was created. As for Istai and Nu, they paddled their bean to land and built a house from the bean shell. They lived there together and had many children."

The song ended. Several woman began to blow softly into their whistles. How sad, how eerie that sound was! Belinda felt suddenly cold.

"This song is about the children of Istai and Nu."

The fat woman started singing.

"When the children were old enough to marry, they decided they didn't want to marry one another. They sent for Ashai Isaru, the great magician, the wisest of them all, and said, 'Brother, make more people, so we can marry outside the tribe.'

"Ashai said, 'I can't make more people, nor can anyone, except for the Great-Fish-That-Is-The-Origin-Of-Everything. But if you want, I'll go ask him.'

"His brothers and sisters said, 'Yes.' Ashai tied stones on his feet and jumped into the ocean, sinking all the way to the bottom, where the Great Fish was."

Now all the women sang together, shaking their rattles loudly.

"They're describing the Great Fish," Lusa said. "Its eyes were like two moons. Its nostrils were

like two caves. It was so long that Ashai couldn't
see the end of it. As for its scales, they were like
the shields warriors bear into battle. Its fins were
like the sails of fishing boats. When it opened its
mouth, its teeth were like spearheads or the peaks
of mountains."

The women stopped singing, all except the ancient bent-over woman. She kept on in her quaver-
ing voice.

"Ashai said to the Great Fish, 'Grandfather, please
make more people, so we won't have to marry one
another.'

" 'No,' the Great Fish answered. 'I won't do that.
There are too many of you already. You make too
much noise and disturb my sleep.'

"So Ashai untied the stones that were tied to his
feet and swam up to the ocean's surface. After
that, he went home and sat in his house and
thought. He thought for many days. Then he went
to see his sister Ania and asked her to weave him a
dreamcoat."

The women started singing again, shaking their
rattles and swaying from side to side.

"They're describing the coat. It was woven from
bright feathers and decorated with shells. There
was nothing in the world that was lovelier."

The women stopped. One woman sang alone.
She was very thin and had a wart at the end of her
nose. Her eyes were light brown, close to yellow.

"When the coat was done, Ashai put it on and
entered the Great Fish's dreams. With his magic,
he created an illusion: a land full of villages. In
every village there was a shrine dedicated to the
Great Fish. People came to the shrines, bringing
gifts and singing the Great Fish's praises. The smoke

from the sacred firepots rose on every side. 'All this will happen,' Ashai said, 'if the people on the land above you continue to breed. But if they find no mates, they will have no children. There will be no one left to worship you, Great Fish. I am a true dream, and I do not lie. If you listen to me, all will be well.'

"After that, Ashai left the Great Fish's dreams and went home. As for the Great Fish, as soon as it woke, it made more people."

With that, the singing ended. The women put down their instruments and stood. Lusa helped Belinda to her feet. "Now, the ritual bath. It's supposed to take place in a bath hut, but Geoffrey hasn't built one. We're going to have to use one of the bathrooms here."

They led Belinda to the master bathroom, singing and blowing their whistles. They bathed her and smeared her body with aromatic lotions. The oldest woman painted a design on her belly with red paint. It blurred at once, intermixing with the lotions.

"That is to promote fertility," Lusa said.

The woman painted two more designs, one on each thigh, using black paint this time. "Those are to ward off malevolent beings, such as midnight clutchers."

"What?"

"They are invisible beings that try to attack women at night. If they manage to impregnate the women, they bear monsters."

Ick, Belinda thought. Her head ached. The women had brought their firepots with them, so the bathroom was full of steam and smoke. She felt more and more dizzy. Somehow, the women had gotten

hold of the wedding gown the robot had shown
her. They put it on her, put shell necklaces around
her neck and bracelets on her arms.

It couldn't be evening, Belinda thought hazily.
What was the hurry? She was pretty sure now that
the smoke was drugged. The old women were all
grinning foolishly.

"Come," Lusa said and took her hand. Back they
went through the dark cold corridors, all the women
singing. Something was wrong, Belinda realized.
It seemed as if the marriage was going to take
place at any moment. She tried to worry, but the
smoke had done its work. All she managed was a
kind of numb grief

They reached the front door. Her uncle was there,
in a shimmery dark purple formal suit. She saw
the robot standing in a corner. In through the
front door came dozens of natives, dressed in their
best clothes, playing whistles and bone harps and
beating on xylophones that they'd bought from
human traders. Claud was among them. She stopped
and stared at him. He was wearing a shell-covered
loincloth, a shell necklace and tall boots made
of snow monkey fur. His hair was braided. On
his arms were bracelets made from bone and
wood. He looked tired, unhappy, and very ugly.

No, Belinda thought. This couldn't really be
happening.

A silver-haired old man led Claud forward, singing all the while in a shrill flat voice. When they
got close, she saw how dark Claud's eyes were. The
pupils were enormous. He too had been drugged.
The old man took her hand and placed it within
Claud's, then shook a rattle, looking up at the
ceiling. The natives formed a ring and began

dancing. The room was full of sweet-smelling smoke, full of the shrill voices of the natives and the sound of their rattles, all shaking in unison. Her head throbbed. She felt as if she were about to pass out.

"The shaman is invoking the Great Fish," Lusa said. "Also the spirit of Ashai Isaru and the spirits of your ancestors. He's saying, 'Be present, oh ancients. Protect your children.'"

One of the young men stepped out of the ring of dancers and blew his whistle. How sweet the piping was! The shaman raised his arms and shouted something.

"He's crying, 'Great Fish, bless us. Great Fish, bless us,'" Lusa said.

Another youth came toward them, carrying a bowl made of polished indigo wood.

"That contains water from the sacred fish pond at the shrine of the Great Fish. When the shaman pours that over you and Claud, you will be married."

She clutched Claud's hand and looked around desperately. Off to one side her uncle stood, smiling faintly, tapping his cane in time to the music. The robot stepped out of its corner. What was it going to do?

She didn't find out, for at that moment the front door slid open. A gust of wind blew in. In staggered old Starbird, a gorwing on his shoulder. The creature flapped its wings and shrieked.

The dancers stopped. Starbird raised one hand. He held a staff in it, elaborately carved and inset with bits of shell. The gorwing folded its wings and hunched down. Its steel gray feathers looked shiny and hard like scales. Its eyes were red. It opened its beak and made a clacking sound. Belinda saw its tiny sharp teeth. She shuddered.

"Nesh ini ashu," Starbird cried. "Otai otana!"

"He's saying the house is haunted," Lusa explained. "There's a ghost here, that has to be driven out."

"Retin," the old man beside them said.

"The shaman has answered, 'The excrement of thornbucks.'"

"Oon, oon," Starbird screamed and pointed at the robot. The gorwing stretched out its neck and hissed.

"He said, 'There, there.' The robot is haunted."

The robot moved forward. In the sudden silence, Belinda could hear the grinding and whining of its internal machinery. Its blue eye blazed. The natives near it moved away. When it reached the room's center, it stopped. After a moment, it said, "A mind transfer. We tried a mind transfer."

"What!" her uncle cried. "What's wrong with you, 39?"

The robot turned its head and looked at him. "I'm regaining my memory, Geoffrey."

"How dare you call me that?"

The robot made a crackling noise. It was laughter, Belinda realized.

"It was after my third heart attack," the robot went on. "My body was failing fast. I was going to die, unless I got out of it. But where could I go? Fortunately, one of my sons was a neurologist. My second wife taught him. She'd been the chief neurologist on board the ship. It was possible, I knew, to record the electro-chemical patterns that make up a human mind and transfer them into an artificial brain. It had been done on Earth. My son said he thought he could do it, here on this planet. It was risky, but I had no choice."

The old machine paused. Everyone was staring at it. Her uncle looked sick, and Claud seemed to be waking up finally. He looked surprised.

"Something went wrong. Or did it?" The robot paused again. "No, by God! Those young whelps of mine tricked me. Now I remember the sidelong looks, the whispers, the snickering. I was so sick I didn't understand what was going on. Guy must have put a standard servant program into the robot, after he transferred my mind. A fine joke that was, to make their old father think he was a robot servant."

"Godfrey Hernshaw!" old Starbird shouted and pointed his staff at the robot. The gorwing shrieked. The crowd of natives moved uneasily.

"Retin," the shaman said.

"It's a lie," her uncle shouted.

The robot turned. "Did you know about this, Geoffrey? Damn you." It started toward him. Her uncle screamed and ran out of the room. On his way, he kicked over a firepot. Burning resin spilled out onto the wireroot carpet.

Now the natives were fleeing through the front door, yelling and flinging aside whistles, rattles, and harps. Belinda stayed where she was, hand in hand with Claud, watching everyone else run.

"Well, that was certainly odd," Claud said after the last native was gone.

Several firepots has been turned over, and the carpet was burning in several places. But she still couldn't manage to get worried about anything. She watched the spreading flames with mild interest. "What do we do now, Claud?"

He scratched his head. "Damned if I know. I'd like to get out of these clothes."

"Later," the robot said as it came back into the room.

"Did you get him?" Belinda asked.

"No. I decided it was more important to get you out of here. You're my last living descendant, except for that cur. And I suddenly remembered something about the storage wing. Come on."

"What about the fire?"

"Let it burn. Worse things are going to happen to Gorwing Keep."

They left the room. The robot led them back through the dark damp hallways. How strange, Belinda thought. A few days before, she'd had no relatives. Now she had dozens of cousins, a wicked uncle and a five-times-great-grandfather, who was still alive inside a robot. Did she want this much family? If not, what was she going to do about it? They came to a door that didn't open till the robot pushed a button in its center. Slowly then it swung forward. They went through into a hallway that was metal, not concrete. The door swung shut. The robot turned a wheel on the door's back. "No one can follow us now. Hurry. I want to get out before the natives come back. I don't want to hurt them."

They followed it down the hall, through a series of doors that opened, then closed behind them. There was a different smell in this part of the house, a smell of metal and machine oil. The hall wasn't lit by daylight coming in through cloudy windows, as was the rest of the house. Instead, it was lit by a dimly glowing rod that ran along the ceiling. The floor was thick with dust. The air was still. When she breathed it, she tasted metal.

Clank. Clank. The robot's footsteps echoed between the metal walls. Where were they? Belinda
wondered.

"This is the storage wing?" Claud said. "The
doors along the hall lead into rooms full of broken
machinery."

"We didn't go far enough forward," the robot
said. "The passenger quarters are further on."

"The what?"

"This is a spacecraft, Belinda. It's one of the
settlement ship's lifeboats. I built my house around
it. I figured some day I might need a quick getaway."

"But doesn't Geoffrey Hernshaw know about
this?" Claud asked.

"I don't think so. My first wife knew, but she
knew how to keep a secret. I never told my second
wife or any of my sons."

"Why not?" Belinda asked.

"I like knowing more than other people." They
went through another door. The robot said, "We're
in the passengers' quarters now. It's only a little
further to the bridge."

The light-rod glowed more brightly here, and
the dust was thicker. They kicked it up, as they
hurried onward. Claud started coughing. The robot stopped and pulled open a tiny door halfway
up the wall. Inside were rows of buttons. The ancient machine pushed one. After a moment, Belinda
heard a low whine. Her ankles felt suddenly cold.
She looked down. The dust was moving, being
sucked into vents in the wall and floor.

"It doesn't sound too bad," the robot said. "I
just hope the engines sound as good. Come on."

They continued forward, through section after
section, till they came to a door that didn't open.

"The bridge is just beyond. The door's set to open when the right message is spoken. Now what was it? My memory isn't what it used to be. Have I mentioned that to you?"

"Yes."

"You see. I'd forgotten. Two centuries wasted, and now this body is breaking down, the way my old body did. Let me tell you one thing, Belinda. If there's an afterlife, those sons of mine are going to suffer."

She had a sudden vision of the captain hunting his sons through hell: an old man, stark naked, his gray beard flapping in the fire winds.

The robot stood still for a while, evidently thinking. Claud shifted from foot to foot and scratched his nose. At last the machine chanted:

> *"Geyr Garmr mjok fyr Gnipahelli.*
> *Festr mun slitna, en freki renna."*

Claud frowned. "What's that?"

"A line from my favorite poem. It means—

> *"Garmr bays before Gnipahellir.*
> *The bonds break and the wolf runs."*

"What does that have to do with anything?" Belinda asked.

"I thought, if I ever used this boat, it'd be because things had gotten very bad. And I was right, Belinda. This is the end of the House of Hernshaw. When this boat takes off, it'll blow Gorwing Keep apart."

"What about my uncle?"

"He'll die. Do you mind?"

She thought a moment. "Not very much."

Just then, the door began to open, whining and grinding all the way. Beyond it was a dark room, where lights suddenly appeared, flickering across screens and shining in rows. All over the domed ceiling, panels began to glow. There was enough light now so Belinda could see the acceleration couches and the instrument clusters atop poles beside the couches. Scenes began to appear on the ceiling panels: gray clouds, bare woods, a wide white lawn.

"Get on the couches and make sure you have all the straps fastened," the robot said.

They did what they were told. When they were done, Belinda turned her head and saw the robot fasten itself in. After that, it pulled the instrument cluster into position above it. "Two centuries," it said. "I wonder if either one of us can still fly, old lady." It reached up, twisted a rod, then pulled it downward. More lights came on. Overhead, a speaker crackled.

A woman's voice—deep, soft, and very pleasant—said, "Welcome aboard Lifeboat Number 11. I am fully automated and programmed to take you to a place of safety. Have no fear. Now—everyone please look at his or her instrument pole. If all the lights are green, then you are safely strapped in. If any of the lights are red, please check all your buckles. If there is anything you do not understand, ask your cabin monitor for help. I am now going to blast off. Get ready, everyone."

The engines roared, the rockets fired, and the boat took off. A sudden terrible weight pushed Belinda into her couch. Just before she passed out, she wondered, Where to next?

Further Revelations

By the time she came to the rockets had stopped, though she could still hear the engines. She felt very light and a little bit queasy. She looked up. The ceiling panels showed black sky and stars.

Space! She was in space! For a moment she thought she was going to lose her breakfast. Then the sick feeling was gone. It wasn't her head that was spinning, she realized. It was the sky. Stars drifted across the ceiling. Slowly her home planet came into sight.

"Oh no," Claud whispered. "Great Fish, preserve me."

Belinda stared up at white cloud belts and green oceans, shining in the sunlight. There were ochre patches too. Were they deserts or were they the forest of the temperate zone, autumn yellow? She didn't know. The planet filled all the panels. The whole ceiling from side to side was white, green, and ochre. It was a wonderful sight, but it made her uneasy. That enormous mass shouldn't be above her. She closed her eyes.

A bell rang. "Attention, everyone," the autopilot said. "I have found an apparent place of safety. It is the planet below us. Please make sure you are safely strapped in. I am about to start my descent."

The rockets fired. A great roar filled Belinda's ears. A great weight pressed her down, and she began to feel a shuddering motion. She kept her eyes closed. The lifeboat seemed to tilt. The shuddering motion got worse. She opened her eyes and saw green water above her. Sunlight glittered on it, and there were long streaks of foam. They were going to crash into the sea! She closed her eyes again. Now the lifeboat seemed to be turning over. Was it starting to tumble?

The turning stopped. The sound of the rockets got louder. She was pretty sure the pressure was going to squash her flat. There was a thud. The rockets stopped. One by one, the engines were cut off. In the quiet she could hear Claud chanting a prayer—not in a native language but in English. He must belong to the Reformed Native Church, she thought. Their liturgy was in English.

"Great Fish, protect me.
 Keep me from harm.
 Protect both my legs.
 Protect both my arms.

"Protect both my eyes
 And my ears and my nose.
 O wonderful fish
 From which everything flows."

How silly the natives were, worshipping all those gods and magicians. It was much more civilized to worship a single god with no physical presence and hardly any personality traits.

"Well, what are you waiting for?" the robot said. "Get up."

She opened her eyes. The ceiling panels showed a cloudy sky and a wide field of cracked concrete. They had landed. They were safe! She started undoing her straps.

"Just a moment," the lifeboat said. "I haven't finished my tests. I don't know yet if this is a place of safety."

"You ignorant machine," the robot said. "Look around. This is a human spaceport."

"I don't have to take that. Not from you. You're a machine too."

The robot was silent. After all, what could it say?

"Everyone stay on their couches till I've finished my tests."

Something new appeared on the ceiling panels. After a moment, Belinda recognized it: a jeep. It bounced toward them over the broken concrete. Behind it came half a dozen thornbucks, carrying uniformed riders.

"You see?" the robot said. "Those are humans."

"Patience, patience," the autopilot said.

The jeep was close enough now, for Belinda could see its red-and-white stripes. It was the police.

"They certainly look human," the autopilot said. "But appearances are often deceiving."

The robot got off its couch. "Open up, will you?"

"Not yet, and please sit down."

The jeep stopped. The thornbuck riders reined

their steeds. They all wore red uniforms with white trim, and one of the riders carried a flag that flapped in the wind. On it were the words, "Law and Humanity." On the side of the jeep was written "Settlement Police." So they had landed in Settlement. Well, that made sense, Belinda thought. The planet's only spaceport was there. It had been abandoned, of course, since no starships had ever come to the planet—except for the first one, the settlement ship. But the port beacon still functioned. The lifeboat must have followed it in.

"All right," the autopilot said. "I have just discovered a human cold virus in one of my air samples. I consider that adequate proof that this is a human settlement. You may go."

The bridge door whined open. Belinda undid the rest of her straps and got up. "Claud?"

Claud fumbled with his buckles, undid them and stood. He was extremely pale, and he looked ridiculous in his native finery. He was trembling, she noticed. She held out her hand. He took it. Together they followed the robot through the lifeboat. When they reached the airlock, the autopilot said, "Be careful. If there's any trouble, I'll be here, ready to take you to another place of safety."

The robot opened the airlock. A gust of wind blew in, warm and wet. Belinda smelled smoke and tasselgrass. Through the open lock, she saw the sky, full of huge gray clouds. She sighed. She was almost home.

Something started shrieking. She jumped.

"It's the emergency slide," the robot said. "I activated it. Come on, you two."

The shrieking stopped. The robot sat down on the edge of the airlock, gave itself a push and went through the airlock, out of sight. Belinda ran forward, dragging Claud after her. She was in time to see the robot go down a long metal slide to the ground.

"Come on," she said. She let go of Claud's hand and followed the robot onto the slide. What an exhilarating experience! Her dress was pulled up till it was barely decent. The shells on it came snapping off and flew into the air around her. Her hair flapped. She started laughing. When she reached the slide's end, the robot caught her, swung her around and set her down. A moment later, Claud reached the slide's bottom, the shells from his loincloth flying up and pattering down behind him. The robot caught him too.

"My God, they're natives," one of the mounted policemen said.

"This one is," the robot said as it set Claud down. "But the girl is Belinda Hernshaw, the heir to the Hernshaw inheritance."

"Then why is she dressed like a native?"

The other policemen nodded. The one in the jeep said, "Native lover."

The robot turned and looked the policeman over. "It's a long story, and I don't see any reason to tell it to you. Please take us to your leaders." It walked over to the jeep and climbed in. "Come on, Belinda. Claud, hop to it."

Belinda followed the robot into the jeep, and Claud followed her. The jeep driver turned and stared at them, then shrugged and started his machine.

Off they went, bouncing across the field, while the mounted police galloped after them. Over the broken slabs of concrete they went, past clumps of yellow tasselgrass. Here and there she saw patches of red: firefern or scarlet groundstar, she wasn't sure which. The jeep's jolts threw her first against the robot, then against Claud, then back against the hard wooden seat. This was worse than the lifeboat. She looked back and saw a metal sphere resting on half a dozen legs. That must be the boat. There were rocket tubes sticking out of the bottom. They were fire-black, as was the sphere and the ground around it.

The jeep passed tumbledown buildings. By this time, the thornbucks were way behind them. Ahead of them were fields of tasselgrass and groves of trees. The jeep went onto a dirt road. It must have rained lately. The road was full of puddles, and the jeep's wheels spun up muddy water. Some of it hit her, spotting her dress. She looked at Claud. His face was speckled with brown. There was mud all over the robot too.

But the jeep didn't slow down. It bounced along the road. After a minute or two, Belinda saw a villa. It was long and low and pink, with overhanging eaves and a garden full of autumn flowers. They passed the house. She saw another villa beyond it. This one was yellow and blue. The jeep began—at last—to slow. Ahead Belinda saw the buildings of Settlement: close-clustered, tall and narrow with steep roofs. She hadn't been here since high school, when Miss Dieudonne had taken the whole class to see the Settlement Museum. The jeep passed a sign that said, "Settlement City Limits. Speed 40 kilometers. Watch Out For Goldwattles."

The road changed from dirt to asphalt. They went between rows of houses. Belinda looked around. She was beginning to recover from the space flight. She no longer felt anxious. Now she was curious. The houses were made of concrete, all cracked and stained. The roofs were tile. The doors and windowframes were corroded metal. In the little front gardens grew firefern, groundstar, goldenlace and touch-me-not. How glad she was to be home—or almost home, anyway. The jeep crossed a little square and stopped in front of an official-looking building.

"This is it," the driver said. "The police station."

"Thank you," the robot said and climbed out. She and Claud followed. Once out of the jeep, she stopped and looked around at the drab old buildings, the first ever built on the planet—unless one counted the miserable huts that the natives made. Across the square from her, a goldwattle wandered aimlessly to and fro. It was close to a meter tall, a flightless bird with bronze feathers and an enormous bright yellow wattle hanging below its beak. In Settlement, as in every human town, goldwattles were protected. They were terrific ratters, and they helped control the rats humanity had brought with it from Earth. She felt a sudden pride, remembering the achievements of her ancestors—the long trip through space and the long struggle with the wilderness. Surely it was a wonderful thing to be human. Then she remembered she was half native.

"Don't dawdle," the robot said. They all went into the police station.

Clank, whirr. Clank, whirr. The sound of the robot echoed between concrete walls. The jeep's driver led the way past door after door, each one labeled: "Department of Permits and Licenses,"

"Traffic Department," "Animal Control Department," "Department of Noise and Litter." At the hall's end was one final door, labeled "Department of Investigations."

The jeep driver knocked. Someone said, "Come in," and they entered. What a strange room, Belinda thought as she looked around. The walls were concrete and covered with weapons: native knives and spears and clubs, ancient laser-rifles made on Earth, and modern gunpowder rifles. There was a wireroot carpet on the floor and a wonderful old lamp hanging from the ceiling, made of wrought iron, all spikes and curlicues. In the room's center was a desk with a man sitting behind it. He looked them over, then picked up a pipe and began packing tobacco into it.

"They got off the spaceship, captain," the driver said.

"Did they?" He clamped the pipe between tobacco brown teeth, then lit it. He was as strange looking as the room, Belinda thought—bony and knobby and most likely very tall, though she couldn't be sure of that, while he was seated. His skin was brown, and his hair and eyes were black. A huge triangular nose jutted out from his narrow face. "An ancient human robot, a native—dressed for some important ceremony, I perceive, and—" He stared at Belinda. She felt herself blushing. "—A human dressed up as a native. Curious."

"She's human, captain?"

The brown man sighed. "Look at her, Hodgkins. Forget the clothes. Those are extraneous. Look at her face."

"She still looks native to me."

"You will never be a detective."

"Hell, captain. You know I want to be an animal control officer."

The brown man nodded. "So you do. Do you want to go now?"

"I don't mind. There's supposed to be a goldwattle biting children down on Boston Street. That's the kind of problem I can handle."

The driver left. The man behind the desk stood up. He was very tall indeed. "Permit me to introduce myself. I am Charles-Auguste Laframboise, Captain of the Settlement Police. If I may ask, who are you?"

"This is Belinda Hernshaw," the robot said, pointing at her.

"Ah?" The tall man stared. "Hernshaw, do you say?"

"Yes," said the robot.

The tall man looked thoughtful. After a moment, he said, "Please go on."

"The young man is Claud Alone-in-the-forest. And as for me, I am not certain how to answer you. Until today, I thought I was a simple robot, a servant of the House of Hernshaw."

"You aren't?" Captain Laframboise sat down. His pipe had gone out. He relit it.

"Today, I began to remember. Have you ever heard of mind transference, captain?"

"Certainly. Our ancestors on Earth used it. They could record the impulses that made up a mind and transfer them into an artificial brain. You aren't claiming—?"

The robot nodded its head, making a squeaking noise. "I am Godfrey Percival Hernshaw, captain. A hundred and sixty years ago, when I was close to death, my mind was transferred out of my body into this."

"Godfrey Hernshaw? *The* Godfrey Hernshaw?"

"Yes."

"I am amazed." The police captain got up and went over to the window. Outside there was a little park, full of iris trees. Their blossoms were long gone, and their leaves had turned autumn-silver. He stood some time, staring at the park and puffing on his pipe.

Claud started fidgeting, scratching his nose and shifting from foot to foot. Belinda felt a little restless too. Where was all this leading? She looked at the robot. Its head was turned, so its one bright eye could watch the policeman. What was it trying to do? She'd been perfectly happy as Belinda Smith. She didn't want to be a Hernshaw. She wanted to go home to her room at college, to her plants, and to Marianne.

"I can't believe you," Laframboise said at last. He turned. "The story is too strange. I simply cannot imagine Godfrey Hernshaw—that giant of a man—reduced to some kind of walking talking tin can."

The robot was silent for a while. Finally it said, "If you want to think I'm a robot, do so. I don't much care. What matters to me is Belinda's claim."

"Which is?"

"She is the daughter of Gilbert Hernshaw and the heir to the Hernshaw inheritance."

Why didn't the robot care about proving it was Godfrey Hernshaw? Belinda wondered. Maybe it realized that it had no real proof, nothing that would stand up in court.

"But what about Geoffrey Hernshaw?" Laframboise asked. "The present master of Gorwing Keep? Is he not the heir to the estate?"

The robot swiveled its head from side to side. "Geoffrey Hernshaw is dead. He kidnapped Belinda, who is his niece, and tried to force her to marry a native—Claud here. The three of us escaped from the house in an old lifeboat I knew about. When we took off, the house blew up, and Geoffrey was killed."

"Ah." Laframboise took out a pipe tool and used it to clean his pipe. "As it happens, I know a great deal about the Hernshaws. I'm fascinated by the history of the settlement and of the founding families. As I recall, Gilbert Hernshaw died without issue."

"Here." The robot reached up and twisted one of the rivets on its metal chest. A tiny panel slid open. The robot reached in and pulled out a crystal cube. "This is a memory cube, captain. Play it. It will explain Belinda's claim to the Hernshaw estate."

"You brought it!" Belinda cried.

The robot nodded. "I thought we might need it."

The policeman took the cube and pressed the depression on its side. Suddenly, the cube was full of light. Gilbert Hernshaw looked out and said, "This is for you, Belinda."

Laframboise set the cube down. "Please be seated."

They sat down, all three of them, and listened while Gilbert Hernshaw explained how Belinda had come to be born. She had heard it all before, of course. So had the robot. But Claud listened with an intent look on his face. From time to time, he bit a fingernail or scratched his nose. Captain

Laframboise leaned back in his chair and puffed on his pipe. His face looked tranquil and a little sleepy, his eyes half shut, his thin lips smiling very slightly. When the recording was over, he leaned forward and picked the cube up. "Extraordinary. These are remarkable things, these cubes. How precisely are they operated?"

"You press that depression to turn on the recording—as you did," the robot said. "If you press three times in succession, the recording is erased. Then, if you press once, you can re-record."

"I see." The captain fumbled with the cube, obviously feeling for the depression. When he found it, he pressed it with his thumb—three times, hard.

"What!" The robot stood.

"What'd you do that for?" Claud asked.

Laframboise smiled, showing large even brown teeth. "If you are Captain Hernshaw, robot, then perhaps you remember Jeannette Laframboise? But perhaps not. She was nobody important—a little pretty light-hearted lab tech, happy with her work and her fiancé, the stolid engineer Andrew Huggins. Happy, at least, until you noticed her. Do you remember?"

"Yes," the robot said.

"That is something, I suppose. You seduced her, and she had your child. Do you remember that too?"

"Yes. I gave her some money. What else could I do? I couldn't acknowledge the child. My wife was a black belt in karate and terribly jealous." There was a strange note in the robot's voice. Was it pleading?

"Do you know the rest? Huggins refused to marry her. She was no longer light-hearted, poor child.

She worked in her laboratory—sadly now, without hope or joy. At night, she went home to her tiny apartment and tended the baby. It was a little boy, the first Charles-Auguste Laframboise. It was my great-great-great-grandfather." The policeman refilled his pipe, then relit it. They all waited silently, watching him. Outside, the clouds were breaking apart. The pale gray leaves of the iris trees shone in the sunlight.

"When the boy grew older, robot, he learned whose son he was. He learned who had repudiated him, and he learned of the wealth he would never get even a part of." He smiled a brief twisted smile. "For close to two centuries, we have lived in the shadow of the Hernshaws. We've watched their rise and fall, knowing it was our money they enjoyed and our money they wasted. As for us, we remained unimportant people—like poor Jeannette. Our successes were nothing much. Our failures lacked grandeur. We were condemned to triviality. Do you know what that is like?" He laughed. "The girl will know. Now, at last, a Hernshaw will know how we Laframboises have felt all these years." He stopped, leaned back in his chair and sighed. "You may go. But stay in Settlement. I am going to send someone to Gorwing Keep to find out what happened there. It is possible that you will all be charged with murder."

"Oh no!" Belinda cried.

"I'm a native," Claud said. "You have no jurisdiction."

"We shall see. Now, please go." Laframboise shut his eyes.

What could they do? They left, going down the long hall and out the station door.

Once outside, the robot stopped. "Tricked again. I am getting old, Belinda."

"What do we do now?" Claud asked.

"We could go back to the lifeboat. But I think that would be premature. Instead—" The robot stared straight ahead. Its battered metal body glistened in the sunlight. Even its gray eye—the one that didn't work—gleamed dully. "Let's go find a hotel."

"We don't have any money," Claud said.

"Yes we do. I took the precaution of rifling Geoffrey's safe—this morning, Belinda, while you were being purified. Geoffrey was still passed out in his bedroom. I have all of Geoffrey's ready cash inside me, as well as the Hernshaw Tiara and a few other knickknacks. Come along." It clanked across the square and into Kuala Lumpur Street. They followed. A housewife working in her garden straightened up and stared at them, her mouth open. They must look terrible, Belinda thought. She knew her hair was windblown. Shells dangled off her dress at the ends of threads, and she was limping, since her sandals hurt her feet. She looked at Claud. He was a mess too. Oh well. She reached over and took Claud's hand, then dropped it when she remembered she was in a human town. It wouldn't do to be seen showing affection for a native here.

On they went, through narrow streets, past the ancient concrete houses. There was a brisk wind blowing, and clouds were moving quickly across the sky. Belinda felt cold. She was going to have to get some other clothes. This dress wasn't warm enough. Besides, the shells were falling off it. She was leaving a trail behind her—like the children in the old fairy tale. Would the birds eat her shells, the way they ate the children's bits of bread?

They came to a small park and crossed it. On the far side was Nice Street. What a peculiar name, Belinda thought. All the streets in Settlement were named after cities on Earth, just as all the streets in Port Discovery were named after old-time scientists and philosophers. There must be a city on Earth named Nice, though she had never heard of it.

"This looks all right," the robot said and stopped.

They were in front of a four-story building. There was a sign above the door. It said, "Nice Hotel." There were windowboxes at every window, each one full of flowers. How lovely, Belinda thought. She could see clusters of pale flowers—white groundstars, most likely—and tall spikes covered with purple spheres. Those were touch-me-nots. If the spheres were touched, they deflated, emitting whistles, shrieks, or hisses, depending on the variety.

The robot clanked inside.

"Come on," Claud said. He took her hand and tugged. She jerked away. "What?"

"You know how conservative Settlement is, Claud. It's worse than Port Discovery."

Claud's face turned red. "You don't want to be seen touching a native. Is that it? Well, Marianne told me you were a terrible bigot." He went on in.

Why did she feel suddenly sad? She didn't care what Claud thought of her. She looked up at the sky. It was almost clear except for some thin clouds, way up. She sniffed, then shrugged and followed Claud in. The lobby was dark. Worn old chairs were scattered here and there on a threadbare carpet. A huge fat lady sat behind the desk, knitting.

She looked up and said, "My God, a robot. What a shock. I almost dropped a stitch." She set down her knitting, then got a glass and a bottle out from under the desk. She filled the glass and took a big swallow from it. After that, she yelled, "Louise, come here."

"Mama?"

Belinda looked around and saw a tall girl standing in a doorway. She had a half-plucked bird in one hand.

"Look, Louise. A robot."

"Incredible," the girl said. "I didn't think there were any left. Does it want a room?"

"I haven't asked. Do you want a room, robot?"

"Two rooms," the robot said. "One for the girl. One for the boy and me."

The woman looked past the robot and saw Belinda and Claud. "No. No natives. I run a clean hotel. No rats. No cockroaches. No natives."

"Then we'll have to go elsewhere." The robot started to turn.

"Don't be silly, mama," the girl said. "We'll have the whole neighborhood in to see the robot, if we put it up."

"But natives, Louise."

"These are modern times. We have to give up our old prejudices, however much we may like them. Think of the money we'll make."

The woman sighed. "Very well. 3A and 3B." She took down the keys, while the robot signed the register. "Five dollars a night, breakfast included. That's five dollars a night for each room. Please pay in advance."

The robot opened the compartment in its chest

and took out a roll of bills. It peeled off a ten and laid it on the desk.

"My God," the woman said. "A millionaire robot. Louise, take them to their rooms."

The tall girl took the keys and led them upstairs. She moved gracefully, Belinda noticed. Her hair was light brown and worn in a coil. But it was too fine for the pins to hold it. The coil was loosening and unwinding. Up the stairs she went, then down a long dim hall. She still held the half-plucked bird. How long and slender her hands were, Belinda thought. Louise stopped and unlocked a door. "Here, miss. I think you'll like this one." She opened the door. Belinda went in. It was a lovely room, full of sunlight and the delicate scent of touch-me-nots. The bed had a clean white coverlet. A floral print hung on the wall. Through the window she could see the park. She sat down in the wicker-work chair, kicked off her sandals and sighed.

"The bathroom is at the end of the hall," Louise said. "I'll be back in a moment to get your water jug."

Belinda nodded. She heard the door shut, then heard the robot clank on down the hall. She closed her eyes, thinking how terribly tired she was. She was just drifting off to sleep, when Louise came back.

"Excuse me, miss."

She opened her eyes. The girl's hair had golden highlights. Her face was pale and delicate, and she had huge dark gray eyes.

"Would you like some tea? It would relax you."

"Yes, please. Thank you."

Louise picked up the water jug. "Are you really a native? You don't look like one."

"No."

Louise smiled. "I thought not. I'll get your tea."

She left. Belinda got up and went down the hall to the bathroom. She looked in the mirror and groaned. Her hair was all tangled, her face was spattered with mud, and her dress was a wreck. But what could she do? She had no other clothes. She didn't even have a comb. She washed her face and used the toilet, then went back to her room.

Louise brought the tea. She drank it. Then she went to sleep. When she woke, it was dark out. A cool wind blew in the open window. She sat up and turned on the light. There were half a dozen boxes on the wicker chair. "What?" she said out loud. She went over to the chair.

The boxes were labeled "Marabelle's Dresses." She opened them. There were two dresses, stockings, a pair of shoes and underclothes. There was a comb, too, and several hairclips. She laughed, then picked out underclothes and one of the dresses. First a bath, she thought. She hurried down the hallway to the bathroom. It was unoccupied. She went in and turned on the bathwater, then hung up the new dress. After that, she took off her native wedding gown. There were bare patches all over it where shells had come off. It was too bad, she thought. The dress had been pretty in a primitive way. She hung it up, then took off the native jewelry she had on. She looked at herself in the mirror. How tired she appeared, how wan and sad. It was hardly surprising, considering what she'd been through. She tested the bathwater, then climbed in. There was a pseudo-sponge on the tub's edge. She took it and started scrubbing off the magical signs that had been painted on her belly and thighs. Slowly, as she washed away the aromatic oils, she felt herself relax. When she was done washing, she sighed and sank down in the hot water. She lay there for as long as possible, half afloat in the warm soapy water and half asleep. At last, the water began to get cold. She got out of the tub and dried herself, then washed her hair in the wash basin, using the hotel soap.

When that was done, she dressed. How wonderful it felt to put on human clothes again. She wrapped a towel around her head and looked at herself in the mirror. The dress was soft russet-red, high necked and long-sleeved. It was close-fitting down to the waist, then flared out into a full short skirt. She put on the belt, which had a buckle made out of white shell. The buckle matched the little shell buttons down the front of the dress and on its cuffs. Very nice, she thought, though the towel around her head didn't match, being bright red. She smiled at her reflection and went back to her room.

Claud was there, sitting in the wicker chair. He was dressed in human clothes, and his long hair was no longer braided. He looked at her. "How are the clothes?"

"Who got them?"

"That girl, Louise. The robot gave her money."

"They're fine," Belinda said.

Claud looked down at his hands, which were clasped. He was rubbing his thumbs back and forth over one another. After a moment, he looked up. "I'm sorry about calling you a bigot, Belinda. You're right. Settlement is very conservative. It wouldn't do for the two of us to hold hands in public. But we can be friends in private, can't we?"

A strange tenderness filled her. He looked so forlorn. "Yes. Of course."

Claud smiled briefly. "The other thing I wanted to tell you is—I telephoned Marianne. I asked her to come to Settlement."

"Did you tell her I was here?"

He nodded, then frowned. "She said a strange thing. She said it was no more than she deserved."

Well, Marianne was right about that, Belinda thought. "Is she coming?"

"Yes. Tomorrow."

Belinda sat down on the bed. She wasn't really sure how she felt. Was she happy or anxious or both? She took the towel off her head and started combing her hair.

"She's coming in on the noon monorail."

"Oh." She got up and went over to the mirror to part her hair and put the hairclips in. "Well, we can deal with that tomorrow. I'm hungry."

Claud stood up. "There's a cafe downstairs in the hotel."

Belinda put on her new shoes, then looked at herself in the mirror. Very nice, she thought. She went downstairs with Claud.

The cafe was at the back of the hotel: a large room with lots of windows. There were small round tables and straight-backed chairs, hanging lamps and a metal-topped bar. The robot was standing at the bar, talking to a short woman who wore a priest's black jacket. "Belinda, come over here," it called.

She and Claud stepped into the room. Everyone there turned to look at them. Oh my God, she thought. Her hair was still wet and pretty stringy looking. She blushed. Claud was blushing too. They crossed the room, trying to ignore all the stares. Most of the customers were laborers, dressed in denim shirts and jeans. But there were two paint-spattered house painters; and a thin fellow, who looked like a bank clerk; and a pretty little shop girl, sitting all alone.

"Belinda, this is Mother Kowalski. She's a historian, a professor at Settlement College. Mother, this is Belinda Hernshaw."

"How do you do, dear," the priest said.

"And this is Claud Alone-in-the-forest."

"A pleasure." The priest shook Claud's hand. "I heard about the robot, and I had to come. My field of specialization is the early settlement period. I knew the robot had to date from then. Can I buy you two something to drink?"

"Wine," Belinda said.

Claud frowned. "Brandy and coke, I think."

"Louise, dear, get these nice people what they want."

Louise, who was behind the bar, nodded and fixed the drinks.

"The robot has been telling me that it was activated at the start of the settlement period, but that it was given a new personality when it was forty years old. As a result, it says, its early memories are confused. A pity. A terrible pity." The priest sipped at her drink. "Could I see the spacecraft? I went out to the spaceport, but there were police everywhere. They weren't letting anyone near the ship."

"It's not a ship," the robot said. "It's a boat."

"Well, be that as it may, I'd like to see it."

"We can't help you," Belinda said. "The police captain doesn't like us."

"Tck. I assume you mean Laframboise. His family has hated the Hernshaws for generations. Have you ever noticed how obsessed we all are with the past? We seem to live our lives in retrospect, here on this planet. Louise, dear, could you get me another drink?"

"Yes," Louise said.

"Why is that?" Claud asked.

The priest took the new drink from Louise and tasted it. "It's just right. Thank you. Why are we obsessed with the past?" She set down her drink and got out a clay pipe, then a tobacco pouch. "Most likely because we want to preserve our human heritage. We're a long way from home and surrounded by an alien people. If we didn't work hard at remembering who we used to be, we might become indistinguishable from the natives. That, of course, would be terrible." She packed tobacco into the pipe. "Louise, dear, do you have a match?"

"Here," Louise said and held out a matchbox.

"Thank you." The priest lit her pipe.

"Oh," Belinda said. "Could we get something to eat?"

"Certainly, dear. Just sit down, and Louise will get you a menu. The fish stew is very fine."

She and Claud sat down at a table by one of the windows. There were lamps outside, so she could see the little patio with potted iris trees.

"Mother Kowalski is right," Louise said when she came over. "Mama makes a really good fish stew."

"All right," Belinda said.

Claud nodded. "I'll have it too."

"Is the dress all right?" Louise asked.

Belinda smiled at her. "It's lovely. Thank you for getting it."

Louise blushed. "It was nothing."

They ate the stew and drank a local white wine, which was a little harsh but perfectly tolerable. Belinda started to get drowsy. She looked over at the bar. The robot and the priest were still talking. "Would you mind if I left, Claud? I can't keep my eyes open."

"No. Not at all." He stood up as she pushed back her chair. "Good night, Belinda."

She went upstairs, undressed and went to bed. She fell asleep almost at once. When she woke, it was mid-morning. Outside, there was sunlight, and she could hear birds shrieking and cackling. She lay a while, feeling sleepy and comfortable. Then suddenly she remembered—Marianne was coming to town. She sat up and remembered that Laframboise had threatened to arrest her and Claud for murder. "Oh no," she cried.

She started shaking, then said aloud, "Get a hold of yourself, Belinda." She got out of bed, got dressed, and went downstairs.

Claud was in the cafe, sitting at a table by a window and reading the *Settlement News*. Outside, she could see the patio and beyond it the Settlement River, shallow and slow moving, its clear water sliding over all kinds of stones. On the other side of the river was a row of barrel trees. Beyond them were houses.

Claud stood up when she came over. "Good morning. I got the *Port Discovery Communicator* for you. And try the omelette with herbs. It's terrific."

She sat down. Louise brought her coffee. Their hands touched accidentally when Louise set the cup down. Belinda felt a tingling sensation. She couldn't fall in love with someone new, she thought, looking up at Louise's pale delicate face. It would be disloyal to Marianne.

"Are you ready to order, miss?"

"The omelette with herbs."

Louise smiled. "That's a wise choice. Mama makes a wonderful omelette."

She left. Belinda watched her walk across the room. How graceful she was. She sighed, picked up the paper and glanced through it. There was only one interesting story in it, and that one covered most of the front page. It was about a professor at her own college. His field of study was ethical philosophy. Two years before, he had gone up into the continent's central highlands to study the ethical concepts of the mountain people there. Somewhere in the narrow valleys he disappeared. Searchers found his last camp and his abandoned jeep, but they never found him. Two days ago, he had walked into a human trading post. He'd had an accident high in the mountains, he explained. His head had been injured, and he'd lost his memory. A tribe of mountaineers found him and cared for him. He had stayed with them for close to two years. For close to two years, he traveled on foot through the cold mountain forests. He lived in huts made of leaves, and he learned to hunt with stone age weapons. He had forgotten he was human, and the people who found him had never heard of human beings. They thought he was a native from another tribe, one they'd never met. He had believed the same thing. Slowly, his memory came back. Bit by bit, he recovered his past. When he knew who he was, he left the tribe and came down out of the mountains to rejoin humanity.

What a fascinating story, Belinda thought. She'd certainly like to meet the professor. Maybe she would, if she ever got back to college.

Louise brought the omelette, and she put aside the paper. "Is there anything in your paper, Claud?" she asked.

He shrugged. "A brief article about our lifeboat. The police are refusing to talk about it, and no one else seems to know anything."

She ate breakfast. When she was done, Claud said, "We have an hour before the monorail comes in. Do you want to take a walk?"

"All right."

They wandered through Settlement, down the narrow streets, then along the river. The day was warm and sunny. Children played in the streets, and housewives worked in their gardens. Along the river, old men fished. An old lady fed crackers to birds in one of the squares. They stopped to watch the noisy flock. Most of the birds were rose-billed shriekers, but there were a few black-and-white birds that Belinda didn't recognize, and even one goldwattle.

At last, they headed toward the monorail station. They reached it just in time to see the train arrive. It chuffed into sight along the shining rail, black smoke spewing out of its twin smokestacks. Belinda felt a brief excitement. Then she began to worry. Who was Marianne going to choose—her or Claud? She bit her thumbnail, watching the train come closer and closer. There was gilt on the smokestacks. It glittered in the sunlight, then suddenly dimmed when the engine came into the station. The engine passed her. The station filled with clouds of smoke and with the noise of the train: the chuff-chuff of the engine and the clack-clack of the wheels on the overhead rail. The train slowed and stopped. Steam hissed out all along it. Forgetting that Claud was a native, she grabbed hold of his hand. "Where is she?"

"There," he cried and pointed.

She looked down the platform. It was Marianne all right—a short plump woman with dark red hair. The dress she wore was dark green, short and loose-fitting except where a belt pulled it in at Marianne's surprisingly narrow waist. It was sleeveless, revealing her round sun-reddened arms.

Belinda let go of Claud's hand and started running, shouting, "Marianne! Marianne!"

Marianne turned, cried, "Belinda!" and held out her hands. Belinda dodged past a native family and barely missed a little old lady with an enormous wicker suitcase. She reached Marianne, grabbed hold of her and hugged her. "I'm so glad. I'm so glad."

Marianne laughed. "Calm down, Belinda. Please, dearest, calm down. Hello, Claud. How are you?"

"Fine," Claud said.

"There's someone I'd like you—both of you—to meet. Please let go of me, Belinda."

Belinda stepped away from her. There was a man beside Marianne—a tall fellow with thick blond hair and a deeply lined, darkly tanned face. Who was he? He looked familiar.

"This is Nigel Bloodsworth," Marianne said.

Of course, Belinda thought. She'd seen his picture in the paper. He was the lost professor.

"He's my husband, Belinda."

Suddenly everything got blurry. She felt dizzy. "Oh," Belinda said. She fainted, falling back into Claud's arms.

When she came to, she was lying on a bench in the station's waiting room. Marianne sat beside her, fanning her with a newspaper. "Sweet, I'm sorry," she said when Belinda opened her eyes. "I didn't mean to shock you so much."

Belinda sat up. She still felt a little dizzy. She looked around. Claud and Nigel Bloodsworth were standing a short distance away, both looking worried. "Why, Marianne? Why?"

"I married him before I met you, dearest—the semester before you came to school. We kept it a secret, because my scholarship was from the Society for the Encouragement of Spinsterhood. I would have lost it if they found out I was married. Then Nigel went up into the mountains and disappeared. Everyone was sure he was dead. I went a little crazy from grief, Belinda. I did some things I shouldn't have done—such as getting mixed up with both you and Claud. My only excuse is that I haven't been entirely sane these past two years. I really am sorry, sweet."

Belinda frowned. "It's all over between us?"

Marianne nodded. "All over, darling. My place is with Nigel now. I intend to be true to him."

"But what about your scholarship?"

"I have only a year to go, and Nigel has two years back pay coming to him. He's going to put me through to my degree."

She started weeping while looking at Marianne's ruddy face. How she had loved those features: the wide brow, the eyes slanted above broad cheekbones, the little nose and the full-lipped mouth. She moaned and buried her face in her hands.

"Please, Belinda. Don't."

But how could she stop? Her loss was so great. She wept and wept.

At last, Claud said, "Let me handle this."

Marianne got up, and he sat down next to Belinda. "Stop it." He gripped her shoulders and shook her. "How do you think I feel? You were lied to by a roommate. I was lied to by a lover."

She lifted her head and stared at him, still weeping, her whole face wet with tears. "Claud," she said in a low voice. "Don't you understand? Marianne and I were lovers."

"What!" He let go of her and stood. "I won't believe that." He started pacing back and forth, biting his lip and tearing at his hair with one hand. Belinda watched him. Marianne and her husband were some distance away, standing hand in hand, looking embarrassed. "Marianne a pervert," Claud muttered. "It's horrible. It's impossible."

"Just a minute." Belinda got up and wiped her eyes. Her nose was running. "Do you have a handkerchief?"

"Yes." He pulled it out and gave it to her, then went back to pacing.

She blew her nose. "Don't you call anybody names, Claud. Remember all the perverted things the natives do."

"Such as?"

"You make love with your children."

"Only once, and that's for magical purposes. It's the only way children can become adults. Their parents give them their first spirit—their childhood spirit, and their parents have to give them their second spirit—their adult spirit." Claud stopped pacing. "I don't believe that, of course. But the more backward tribes still do."

"It's disgusting," Belinda said.

Claud's face turned red. "You've got no right to say that."

"And you don't have any right to call me a pervert," Belinda said. She handed back the handkerchief. "Thank you."

"You're welcome." He put the handkerchief away, then frowned and scratched his nose. "All right. No more name calling. But I have to think about this. Excuse me." He turned and walked away across the waiting room.

Belinda sighed. He too had abandoned her. How lonely she felt. She looked toward Marianne. Her husband came forward, holding out his hand. "Cry peace, Belinda?" he asked. His voice was deep and soft. He smiled, showing white even teeth. Both his upper canines were missing. That must've happened in the mountains, Belinda thought. Was it due to an accident or to a primitive rite? She shook his hand.

"Good," he said. "I don't like arguments. Now—let's go where we can get a drink. Marianne wants to know what happened to you, after your guardian took you away from school. She's been worried."

Belinda sniffed and nodded, and the three of them went out of the station. The sun was still shining, she noticed with surprise. Across the street there was a little bar, the New York. They went over and sat down in the cool shadows, under a painted wall that showed green hills, blue rivers and tall white towers. In the middle of one of the rivers was a woman holding up a torch. There were words in the blue sky above the towers. Belinda frowned and tried to make them out. They said:

> "It avails not, time nor place—distance avails not,
> I am with you, you men and women of a generation, or even many generations hence,
> Just as you feel when you look on the river and sky, so I felt."

The bartender came up and said, "That's from 'Crossing Brooklyn Ferry' by Walt Whitman. My father was a Whitman fiend. I myself consider his style overinflated. What can I get you to drink?"

"Red wine," Nigel Bloodsworth said.

Marianne nodded. "The same."

"I'd like white wine," Belinda said.

The bartender brought their drinks. They sipped the wine.

"Well, what happened?" Marianne asked.

Belinda frowned. "It's a long story."

"Tell it."

She told them everything that had happened at Gorwing Keep from the time she arrived to the moment when she and Claud and the robot blasted out in the lifeboat.

When she was done, Nigel said, "That's absolutely incredible."

"You don't believe me?"

"I didn't say that—or rather, I didn't mean that." He finished his wine, then lit a cigar. "So humans and natives are related. I'll believe that. After all, I've just spent two years being a fellow named

He-who-cannot-walk-quietly, who was a native."
He grinned. "Do you realize how many scientists
are going to look like fools because of you, Belinda?
It's too bad old Sigbert Schwartz isn't alive. He'd
love it. Are you planning to claim the Hernshaw
inheritance?"

"I don't think so. I don't have any proof, and I
don't want it. I don't want to be a Hernshaw."

Nigel frowned. "But you are one," he said slowly.
"When I first started to remember who I was, I
tried to forget again. I wanted to keep on being
He-who-cannot-walk-quietly. It seemed a lot safer.
But the memories kept coming. In the end, I went
to the shaman. Bartender, could we have another
round?"

"Certainly, sir."

The bartender refilled their glasses. Nigel went
on. "He was an old, old fellow. In a year or two,
he'd be too feeble to keep up with the tribe when it
traveled. Then he'd be left behind in the forest to
die. But he was still pretty clever. He listened to
me, and then he told me the story about the man
who lost himself." He drank a little wine. "I've
been trying to remember the stories I heard in the
mountains. I'm planning to write an essay. Anyway,
this story is about a shaman who had the power to
leave his body and travel around in the shape of a
bird. While he was gone, his body lay in his house,
as still as death. Well, one day when the shaman
was out of his body, the Snow Monkey Spirit came
by his house. He looked in and saw the shaman's
body. 'It's been a long time since I've been a man,'
the Spirit said. 'I think I'll try it again.' So the
Snow Monkey Spirit entered into the man's body
and became the man. He got up and went out of

the house. He cried, 'Hu! Hu! How fine this is!'
Then he took off through the forest, laughing and
singing.

"When the man came flying back, disguised as a
bird, he found his body gone. He shrieked with
fear, and he flew in each of the five directions. But
the Snow Monkey Spirit hid himself with spells,
and the shaman couldn't find him. Then the sun
set, and when the last light was gone, the man
forgot he had ever been anything except a bird.

"When the man didn't come home for supper,
his wife began to look for him. She was a famous
mind-watcher and far-caller. She sent out a mind-
call in all five directions, saying:

" 'Come home, my husband.
    Sit on your mat.
    Your supper is ready,
    Greasy and fat.'

"Now, the Snow Monkey Spirit didn't hear her,
for the message wasn't for him. But the bird heard
her and came, though it didn't know why. It flew
into the man's house and settled on his mat. Then
it stretched out its neck and took the meat above
the fire.

" 'Oh husband. Oh husband,' the woman said
and wept. Is this boring you, Belinda?"

"No. Not at all."

"Marianne?"

"No. Keep on."

"Well, the woman caught the bird and put it in
a cage, and she took it to a shaman."

" 'This is no ordinary bird,' the shaman said.
'This is a spirit bird.'

" 'It's my husband,' the woman said. 'And I want him back the way he was.'

"Then the shaman went to the man's house and searched it till he found some of the man's hairs, tangled in the fringe at the edge of his sleeping mat. In the ashes of the fire, he found a toenail that had not been burnt. He wove a collar from the hairs and hung the toenail clipping from it. Then he put the collar around the bird's neck. As soon as this was done, the man remembered who he was. 'Now, go and seek your body,' the shaman said. 'The toenail clipping will point the way for you. A bear cannot hide from its cubs, and a man's children will always find him out. In the same way, a body cannot hide from one of its parts.'

"After that, the bird flew off. The shaman followed as fast as he was able. Soon they came to where the Snow Monkey Spirit was, still in the man's body and terribly drunk, for he'd stolen a skin full of wine from someone-or-other. The shaman grabbed the body by its hair and jerked it upright. 'At last I have you, wicked fellow,' he cried. 'Now, I'm going to kill you.' He waved a knife in front of the body's face.

" 'Just my luck,' the Snow Monkey Spirit thought. 'I've got a body that belongs to someone involved in some terrible quarrel.' And he fled out of the body as fast as he could.

"Then the man's spirit re-entered his body. He stood up and embraced the shaman who had saved him. Together they went home."

"It's a nice story," Belinda said. "But what does it mean?"

Nigel frowned. "It made sense to me when I heard it. Let me see if I can think of a way to explain it." He sipped at his wine, then relit his cigar. At last, he said, "Even though the man forgot who he was, he was still the same person. He still carried his past within him. That was what his wife reached, when she called him."

"You may be right," Belinda said. "But that doesn't make me a Hernshaw. I've been Belinda Smith all my life. That's my past."

"Well, maybe your problem is different from mine," Nigel said.

"Yes, it is." She looked up at the bar clock. "I'd better go back to the hotel. It's lunch time."

"Can we go with you?" Nigel asked. "I'd like to meet your robot."

"All right."

They paid for their drinks and walked back to the hotel. The sun was almost directly overhead. The narrow streets were shadowless. The children were gone—most likely home to lunch. There was no one in the bright front gardens. Nigel shuddered. "I'm not used to all this yet. I haven't slept since I left the forest. The air's too still inside human houses. I feel as if I'm suffocating." He stopped and turned around, looking at the houses. "Look at all that concrete. Housewalls are supposed to move when the wind blows. You're supposed to hear the rustle of the leaves on the roof and feel all kinds of drafts. Only the dead live in motionless houses."

She felt a sudden liking for Nigel, even though he'd stolen Marianne from her. He too knew what it was like to lose the past. Would she ever regain even part of it? Would she ever get back to school?

They went on to the hotel. The fat lady was at

the desk, still knitting. "Good afternoon, miss. The robot is in the cafe with Mother Kowalski."

"Thank you," Belinda said. They went into the cafe.

It was packed. They pushed by the people waiting at the door and crossed the room to where the robot and Mother Kowalski stood beside the bar.

"Hello, dear," the priest said. She held out her hand to Nigel. "Professor Bloodsworth, this is a pleasure. How wonderful to have you back with us again."

"Hello, mother," Nigel said and shook her hand. "Let me introduce my wife, Marianne Duval."

"How glad you must be, dear," the priest said as they shook.

Marianne smiled and nodded.

"Captain Hernshaw, this is Professor Nigel Bloodsworth," the priest went on, looking at the robot. "Nigel, this is Captain Godfrey Hernshaw. You two have a lot in common. Captain Hernshaw just recovered his memory too."

Nigel laughed and shook the robot's metal hand.

"You told her about yourself?" Belinda said.

"Yes," the robot answered. "I saw no reason not to. We're going to need allies, if we're ever going to prove that you're Belinda Hernshaw."

"Though I don't know what I can do, my dear. Laframboise won't listen to me at all. No one respects the clergy anymore."

"We went out to the spaceport this morning," the robot said. "There were policemen everywhere. We couldn't get anywhere near the lifeboat. We went to see Laframboise, and he said he was making sure we didn't try to escape in the boat. The mother tried to convince him that he had no right to seize the boat. He said, 'I am the law.' "

"Unfortunately, he is right," the priest said. "The present chief of police devotes himself to the pleasures of the table. He is completely uninterested in anything he can't eat. Laframboise runs the police department."

"He said he'd asked the Air Police to check into the events at Gorwing Keep," the robot added.

The Air Police! Belinda remembered seeing their ghost-gray biplanes flying overhead at Settlement Day celebrations. She'd seen the flyers too on several occasions. They had sauntered through Port Discovery in their gray uniforms, their gray leather caps and their goggles. They had seemed to her to be like heroes out of old stories: handsome and arrogant.

"The Air Police told him there's nowhere to land in the area, but they'd try to drop a man and a radio at the nearest native village. Laframboise expects the man's report tomorrow."

Tomorrow she might be arrested and charged with murder. Belinda shuddered. "Can no one stop Laframboise?"

"Possibly," Mother Kowalski said. "Louise, dear, we'd like to get some drinks."

"Of course, mother." Louise smiled at Belinda, then went behind the bar. She refilled the priest's glass. Belinda, Nigel, and Marianne ordered wine. She served them.

"This situation is more complex than I thought," Nigel said. "What does this fellow Laframboise have to do with anything? You didn't tell us about him."

"He's threatening to charge me and Claud with murder," Belinda said.

"What?" Marianne cried.

"For the death of Geoffrey Hernshaw. He hates the Hernshaws, and he wants to cause me trouble because I'm a Hernshaw."

Marianne paled. Her freckles looked darker than usual against her suddenly white skin. "Can't anything be done?"

"Possibly, my dear, as I said before." Mother Kowalski drank a little of her drink. "There's a table free over in the corner. Could you seat us there, Louise?"

"Of course, mother."

They sat down, Louise cleared the table and brought new drinks. Mother Kowalski looked at the robot, who was sitting opposite her, between Belinda and Marianne. "Haven't you noticed, captain, how improbable the events of the last few days have been?"

The robot sat perfectly still, staring straight ahead. It's one working eye shone brightly. At last it said, "Yes. All those coincidences—ever since Belinda came to the Keep."

The priest nodded. "And Belinda herself is improbable—a hybrid that everyone thought was impossible, created by psi powers."

Belinda turned red. "What are you trying to say?"

"Be patient, my dear." The priest took out her pipe and lit it. "I started thinking about all those improbabilities, and I remembered something, a story from the early days. It's about you, captain. You were out in one of the survey planes, and you crashed more or less in the middle of the Great

Barren Waste. You were hundreds of kilometers from the nearest human camp in a waterless wilderness, and your radio had been wrecked in the crash. Do you remember?''

The robot nodded. "Yes. A band of natives found me, a miserable crew. They wore almost no clothes, and they had almost no tools. They lived on roots and berries and on whatever small game they could kill with their throwing spears. But they did save me. They took me with them and kept me alive till one of the planes looking for me came over."

"Do you remember Water Calling Woman? She was a member of the band. She could always find water, even in places where there simply wasn't any."

"I remember." The robot paused, then went on very slowly. "She was a slender girl, dark for a native, and naked—at that point—except for a little leather apron and lots of necklaces. They were made of disks carved out of eggshells. She was pretty. Very pretty. She had a delightful smile. My first wife had just died, so I took Water Calling Woman back to Gorwing Keep with me."

"What happened then?" the priest asked.

"We got tired of one another, and she married a local native." The robot paused again. Sunshine came in the window behind it, and its battered old body glistened. "She had two or three children. Then she killed herself."

"Whatever for?" Belinda asked.

"Her husband told me that she started seeing ghosts. They were her people. They said a great drought had come, and they couldn't find water, since she was no longer with them. They died, and their ghosts came to reproach her. She couldn't bear their reproaches. She killed herself. That's what her husband said. I didn't believe him, of course. I don't believe in ghosts."

"What interests me is the children." Mother Kowalski finished her drink, then signaled Louise for a refill. "Could Belinda be descended from any of them?"

"Yes," Claud said. He was right in back of Belinda. When had he come up? she wondered. "Hello, everyone." He sat down.

The priest turned and stared at him. "What did you say?"

"Water Calling Woman had two children. Nisu the Rainmaker and Sunia Bottlebush. Belinda's mother was descended from both of them—Nisu on her mother's side and Sunia on her father's side. Why do you want to know?"

"I think Belinda has inherited a very peculiar psi power. Her ancestress could find water where there wasn't any. Her mother could conceive and bear an impossible child. Around Belinda, I believe, the laws of probability don't work."

"Balderdash," the robot said.

Mother Kowalski smiled. "Let's wait and see. I believe that Laframboise will be foiled in some strange and improbable fashion."

Belinda frowned. "But if I'm making these things happen, why are so many of them awful? Why would I hurt myself?"

"I think, dear, that your power is far greater than your mother's or Water Calling Woman's. But it's also much less well controlled. They suspended the laws of probability for short periods only and only to get some specific thing they wanted very badly. You seem to have created a permanent null-p field. I assume you did it out of fright, when your guardian kidnapped you. You were trying to defend yourself, and you did pretty well, I must say. But you don't seem to be able to limit the field or turn it off."

"Oh dear." She felt suddenly uneasy.

"I repeat—balderdash," the robot said. "If Belinda has this mysterious power, why hasn't anyone noticed it before?"

"She was raised among humans," said the priest. "And humans know almost nothing about these kinds of power. To us, they are alien. They frighten us. Most of us would like to believe—these kinds of power do not exist."

"That is true," said Claud.

Mother Kowalski smiled at him and then went on. "Because we do not want to believe in such things, we do not see the evidence for their existence, unless it is so obvious that it cannot be ignored. And in the case of Belinda, I am inclined to think the power was latent, until the last few days. It existed more *in posse* than *in esse*, until Belinda was threatened. Then she hunted—unconsciously— for a weapon. She found the improbability field. She used it." The priest looked at Belinda. "And now you are stuck with it."

"Balderdash," the robot repeated.

Nigel leaned forward. "Then shouldn't we avoid Belinda?" His voice was very soft. "So long as we are within her field, strange things will happen to us too."

The priest nodded. "If you're afraid of the improbable, then you should keep away from her."

"No," Belinda cried.

"Don't worry, dear," Marianne said. "We're not afraid."

Belinda stood. "I'm getting a headache. I think I'll take a walk."

"Wait." Claud pushed back his chair.

"No. I want to be alone." She left the cafe, crossed the hotel lobby and went outside. There were three goldwattles in the street, wandering slowly past. She watched them for a moment, then crossed the street and went into the park. What if Mother Kowalski was right? A horrible prospect was before her: a life without rules, where anything could happen. She sat down underneath an iris tree. Above her, leaves rustled in the wind. She looked up. The leaves were silvery, edged with sunlight. How lovely. But was it real? Was it permanent? Maybe the leaves would turn into birds and fly away. She watched a while. The leaves remained leaves. Maybe the priest was wrong. She sniffed and rubbed her nose. But the theory had sounded so convincing. Everything had been taken from her now: her past, her dear love Marianne, and her sense of reality.

She sat for a long time, looking at the gravel at her feet. At last, she sighed and looked up. The sky had filled with large fluffy white clouds, and the sun was behind one of them. What now? she wondered. She had no idea. She sighed again and stood up. She might as well go back to the hotel. She had no better destination. She walked slowly down the gravel path among the iris trees. The wind seemed colder than before, and she had goose bumps all over her arms. She shivered as she crossed the street. Into the hotel lobby she went, then up the stairs. She opened the door of her

room. Claud was there, sitting in the wicker chair
and smoking a cigar.

He looked up. "Hello."

"What are you doing here?" She came in and
shut the door.

"I thought I'd better talk to you." He took a
flake of tobacco off his lip and put it in the ashtray.
"I know you're upset. Humans don't know anything about psi powers, Belinda. Don't listen to
what they say."

"Oh." She sat down on the bed. "But something
strange is going on."

Claud nodded. "I think the priest is right. You
do have a psi power, and it's not a common one.
But it's not what the priest thinks it is."

"Then what is it?"

Claud frowned and drew on his cigar, then blew
the smoke out. "When something important happens among our people, we hold a dance, and
everyone dances. Most people follow one pattern,
the traditional pattern. But some people dance
their own steps. If the people around them like
their steps, they'll do them too. Sometimes the
whole village will go from one pattern to another."

"What are you talking about?"

"Don't you see? Possibility is the pattern that
most people follow. But it isn't the only pattern
there is. There are people—we call them 'dance
makers'—who can hear other rhythms and do other
steps. Sometimes their pattern starts spreading,
because other people like it and decide to use it."

Belinda shook her head. "I don't understand."

Claud sighed. "You've set up a new pattern,
Belinda, just as Water Calling Woman did. In the
pattern her tribe danced, there was a desert around

them. But Water Calling Woman danced a pattern where the land was full of water. Because of that, she could always find a spring or pool." He scratched his nose. "The other tribe members didn't learn her pattern. I guess because they needed the desert. Most likely, they knew how to live in the desert and nowhere else. So they kept to their own pattern and died of it finally.

"Your mother danced a pattern where humans and natives could interbreed. Well, no one else learned the steps she did. Her pattern didn't spread. You're the only half-breed on the planet.

"But your pattern is spreading. I'm not sure exactly what it is yet. Things get confused when people start to learn new steps. Nobody is really sure what he or she is doing. But there must be something in your pattern that satisfies us, because we're trying to learn it."

Belinda frowned. "I still don't understand."

"In some ways, you're pretty stupid. I think it's the human in you."

"I won't listen to that. Get out."

Claud sighed and stood. "All right."

He left, and she lay down. She tried to think about what he'd said, but it made no sense to her. Oh well, she thought. Maybe the best thing to do was wait and see what happened next. She rolled over and closed her eyes.

She woke up a little after sunset, got up and combed her hair. The clouds were gone. Once again the sky was clear. It was a wonderful dark blue-green, with a band of golden light along the western horizon. In the park streetlights shone. Night-birds were making soft moaning sounds. She felt a lot calmer than she had before. She smoothed her skirt, trying to get the wrinkles out, then went downstairs.

The cafe hadn't opened for dinner, but Louise beckoned through the glass door. Belinda went in.

"You seemed upset at lunch," Louise said. "Are you all right now?"

"I think so." She frowned, looking out at the patio and the river.

"Why don't you sit down, miss? I have some tea in the kitchen. Tea always helps."

"Thank you." Belinda sat down at one of the tables. Louise went to get the tea. She came back in a minute or two, carrying a ceramic teapot. There were native designs cut in the clay, but the glaze was human. No native potter could have come up with that soft blue-gray. She had two cups in her other hand. They were the same color as the pot and had similar designs cut into them. Louise set everything down, then poured the tea.

"I've never seen a pot like that," Belinda said.

Louise smiled and nodded. "My papa made it. He was a potter and a student of culture." She sighed softly. "How much I miss him. Do you care for sugar in your tea?"

"No, thank you."

Louise sat down and picked up her teacup, smiling gently as she looked at it. "He believed in synthesis, miss. He said, if humanity was going to survive here on this planet, we had to learn from the natives—and teach them too. He practiced what he preached. He went into the backcountry and set up a pottery that used both human and native techniques. I grew up there, miss, in a big native-style house beside the pottery. I used to sit watching while he showed his native apprentices how to make glazes and how to operate a modern potter's wheel. He learned from them as well. Before he died, he could use their wheel and make their glazes. He knew every one of their designs and what it meant." She sighed again, then looked at Belinda. "Forgive me, miss. He's been dead five years. I should be used to it."

Belinda frowned. "But your mother doesn't like natives."

"No. As soon as papa died, we moved back to Settlement. Mama said she had suffered enough." Louise sipped her tea. "But I meant to talk about you, miss." She set the cup down. "Forgive me if I intrude, but it's obvious that something is bothering you. Your friends seem nice enough. Still, one is a robot and the other is a man. How much can they understand about a woman's mind and heart?"

Belinda looked at her pale delicate face. Her soft hair was loose and fell around her shoulders. In the dim light of evening it appeared very dark, almost black. Her full lips were gently smiling. What harm would it do to tell Louise her troubles? She sighed. "I lied to you before, when you asked if I were a native. I'm half native."

Louise frowned, then nodded. "I was beginning to suspect that—though I know it's impossible."

"What? How?"

"There is something very unusual about your psychic emanations. You lack the intensity that natives have. At first, I was sure you were human. No native could produce such faint and confused emanations, I thought. But there is something inhuman about your mind. I cannot explain what it is. But there's a certain strangeness there."

"You're telepathic?" Belinda asked.

Louise nodded. "You told me your secret. I will tell you mine. I am a native."

"What?"

Louise sipped more tea. "My parents—my foster parents, I mean—had one child, a daughter who died almost at once. Mama went into a terrible depression when the baby died. Papa feared for her sanity and her life. In desperation he turned to the local wise woman. 'Get her a child,' old Runa said. Fortunately, she had a grandchild she could spare—a baby girl, whose mother had died. The baby looked almost human, as had the mother. As you must know, some natives are indistinguishable from humans—at least until medical tests are done.

"Papa brought the baby home. Mama got the crazy idea that this was her baby, her little Louise. Papa tried to tell her the truth, but she wouldn't listen. She refused to understand." Louise looked up. "She raised me as her daughter, but papa told me who I really was."

"Wasn't it confusing?" Belinda asked.

"Yes. But it seems to me that life is usually confusing. People who think it's simple haven't done much thinking about it."

Belinda frowned. So Louise had the same problem she did. They were both of them caught between two cultures. Maybe she had sensed that somehow. Maybe that was why she'd been attracted to Louise. "Do you think of yourself as a human or as a native?"

"As both. Papa said I was an example of the synthesis he believed in."

Belinda frowned again. Louise reached over and took one of her hands. She felt a slight shock and a warm tingling sensation. Her face grew hot. She hoped the room was dark enough so Louise couldn't see her blushing.

"Believe me, Miss Hernshaw, you will go mad if you try to think of yourself as entirely human. Even I—living here as I do, in this town of narrow-minded people—even I remember my nativeness. I still remember the forests of the backcountry and the dark house of my grandmother, old Runa."

"But all my memories are human ones."

"That may be, but there is something in you that isn't human. Runa said I was the best mind-watcher she had ever met, and I can sense the nativeness in you."

"Well, I can't."

"You will in time."

Belinda pulled her hand away. She had a sudden terrible desire to kiss Louise. She shuddered and buried her face in her hands. Why was life so complicated?

"Don't cry," Louise said. She got up, came over and put her arms around Belinda. Belinda sobbed. "Poor dear. Don't cry." Louise's arms tightened around her. Belinda felt her whole body tingling. She was suddenly very aware of her breasts, her crotch, and her thighs. She shivered. Louise laughed suddenly. "So that's it." She bent her head and kissed Belinda on the lips.

"No." Belinda tried to push her back.

"You forget I'm a telepath, dear. I know very well what you're feeling."

Belinda thought about that for a moment, then nodded and pulled Louise down toward her. They kissed again, this time open-mouthed. She hugged

Louise. Her skin was extraordinarily soft. Her silky hair brushed against the side of Belinda's face.

After a minute or two, Louise pulled away and straightened up. "Let's go to my room. This place is too public."

They went upstairs, hand in hand. At last something was going right, Belinda thought. They entered a room on the fourth floor, and Louise turned on the light. There was a bed with a barkcloth bedspread, a wireroot carpet and a dresser, its top covered with native knickknacks. Louise pulled down the shade, then locked the door. She turned and looked at Belinda. Her full lips were smiling, and her gray eyes shone. "Come here."

Belinda came to her. They embraced gently and gently kissed. Belinda felt the touch of Louise's tongue on her lips and opened her mouth. It had been so long since she'd held anyone, she thought. She'd been so lonely. She pulled Louise closer. Their tongues touched. Louise moved her hands down Belinda's back till they rested on her hips. The kiss continued. At last, Belinda shivered and pulled away. She looked at Louise, her vision a little blurry, a great tenderness filling her. How lovely the girl was, her hair shining golden-brown in the lamplight. She reached up and touched Louise on the cheek. Louise laughed softly, took the hand and kissed the palm, then led Belinda to the bed. They sat down there, side by side, and kissed again. After that, things became confused for Belinda. A little later, she found herself lying down with Louise's hand up under her skirt and her hand inside Louise's blouse. Goodness, she thought. It had taken Marianne and her weeks to get this far. She kissed Louise again and felt Louise pull down her pants and reach between her legs. Everything was getting blurry, and she was no longer able to think. She pulled Louise's blouse open and kissed one of the pale brown nipples.

Somehow, soon after that, their clothes came off. Afterward, she wasn't sure how. She found herself kissing and caressing Louise's small breasts. Louise seemed most interested in her thighs. She rubbed along the inside of them and between them. Things became more and more unclear for Belinda. She grabbed Louise's head, pulled it toward her, and kissed Louise fiercely, biting her lower lip. Louise laughed and hugged her tightly.

She was always afraid of this moment, Belinda remembered with sudden clarity. This was when she stopped being a person and became an emotion. A moment later, the thought was gone. She concentrated on the feel of Louise's body, a little sweaty now and wrapped tightly around her. Soon that was gone too. All she had left was a feeling of warmth and motion and a sense of darkness, though her eyes were open and the light was still on.

Then—some time later—she was herself again. The darkness was gone, though she could still feel warmth and the motion of Louise's body. She kissed Louise, this time gently, and Louise hugged her a little, not much. They held onto one another a while longer, then let go and rolled apart. Belinda lay stretched across the bed, staring at the cream-colored ceiling. How comfortable she felt, how relaxed. She sighed softly. Louise sat up and pushed her hair back out of her eyes. "I have to get going. I haven't finished setting the tables in the cafe."

Belinda nodded. Reluctantly, she got up. They

made the bed together, then dressed and left the room. Outside, in the dark hall, they kissed. After that, they went downstairs. Louise went into the cafe, and Belinda went outside.

It was cool, and she didn't have a jacket. But she was starting to feel a little restless. She kept walking. On one side of her was the river, its dark surface shining in the light of the streetlamps. On the other side was a row of fat-trunked barrel trees. Their branches were short, knobby, and twisted, with clusters of leaves at their ends. Where the streetlamps were, the leaves glowed redly. She walked past the empty benches. Ahead of her, a footbridge crossed the river. The bridge had metal railings and lanterns of metal and glass. It was native work. The style was distinctive. Everything twisted and coiled, full of an animal energy.

Belinda stopped to watch a bug flutter around one of the lanterns, then went on. Something was bothering her, she knew—a vague melancholy, a barely perceptible discomfort. Was it Laframboise? No. This was something else. What? she wondered.

She looked up at the stars, picking out the constellations one by one: the Wheel, the Harp, the Miredrake. Sol was somewhere up there, inside the box of four bright stars that was the Miredrake's head. Over to the west were the Divine Twins, two blue-white giants blazing side by side. And east of her was the Fisherman. His net was overhead—a dim white glow that went all the way across the sky. That, she knew, was the Galaxy, seen edge on. On Earth it was called the Milky Way, not the Net, and it looked almost the same.

She was feeling trapped, she realized suddenly. Not by Laframboise, but by this town of narrow-minded people, as Louise had called it. Port Discovery was no different. How could she live there, she with her impossible heritage and her eerie psi power? She imagined herself back in school, going from class to class, worrying about finishing papers and finding a new roommate. Even if she hid who she was, the improbability field would still be there. Sooner or later, someone would realize that strange things happened when she was around. She'd probably be expelled.

"No," she said out loud. "I won't go back."

Then where would she go? She didn't know. She sighed and started back toward the hotel. At least, she thought, she had found a new lover. She smiled, remembering how Louise had looked, standing naked by the bed, her pale body shining in the room's yellow light.

When she got back, the cafe was open and once again full of people. She looked in and saw Mother Kowalski at the bar, talking to Louise. Claud and Marianne were sitting together at a table in the back. They both looked unhappy and uncomfortable. She felt someone touch her arm and looked around. It was Nigel Bloodsworth. "Hello. Let's go rescue those two from one another." He nodded toward Claud and Marianne, then led the way into the room. "Somehow, it seems impossible to end an affair without recriminations," he said as they squeezed between the tables. "I'm not sure why."

"You know about them?"

"Certainly. And about you and Marianne. We both confessed to one another. She told me about you and Claud. I told her about my wife Ri."

"You had a wife in the mountains?"

They reached Marianne and Claud's table. "Hello,

dear," Nigel said. "Claud, it's good to see you again. Sit down, Belinda."

She sat down, as did Nigel.

"Of course I had a wife. Or half a wife, anyway. I shared her with my foster brother." Nigel grinned. "I did a damn fine job of fitting into that society. I've got initiation scars on my back and a bone whistle on a string around my neck. See?" He undid his shirt and pulled out a narrow white cylinder. Designs had been scratched on it, and the scratched lines had been filled with red paint. He put the whistle back inside his shirt and fastened the top button. "It makes a sound that bad spirits hate, and I'm not about to take it off. After all, what if I meet a ghost?"

Claud frowned. "You shouldn't pay any attention to those superstitions."

"Why not?"

Claud scratched his nose. "I don't believe in ghosts anymore—not since I went to New Harvard and took Comparative Sociology. I know they're only creatures of fancy, manifestations of our fear of death. But even when I believed in ghosts, I didn't believe in ghost whistles. The only way to get rid of ghosts is to get a shaman in and have him do a ghost removal dance."

Nigel laughed. "You have to remember, Claud, that the mountain people are very poor, and the mountains are chock-full of ghosts. We couldn't afford to hire a shaman every time we felt our skins prickle or heard a strange noise under the eaves."

"That may be."

"Besides, the whistles worked."

Louise came over, bringing menus. She smiled

at Belinda and said, "Hello." She was very attractive, Belinda thought, even in the plain gray dress she wore. She'd put her hair up in a bun, and she had no jewelry on except a gold cross hanging from a thin gold chain.

They ordered dinner and drinks. Louise left. Claud said, "The whistles worked?"

"Certainly. I lived with my foster brother, Ashu. And he had terrible trouble with the ghost of his great-grandmother. When the old lady was too weak to travel, we left her in the forest. And Ashu's mother did something that was not wise. She took the old lady's best bone needle. It was too good to leave for the forest rats, she said. The old lady was furious. She didn't mind being left to die. That happened to everyone who lived to be old. But she wanted to keep her cooking pot and her necklace and her needle.

"The old lady died, alone in the forest. And her ghost began to do harm to the family. Ashu's mother died in the same season. But that wasn't enough for the old lady. She came back in the shape of a forest rat and stole things from us—needles, small bits of barkcloth, once a little pot. It took us two weeks of blowing our whistles and banging on drums, but she finally went away."

Marianne grimaced. "Do you really believe that stuff?"

Nigel shrugged. "I used to. I don't know if I do now." He paused, frowning. "I think I believe in reason less than I did back at the college. Reality seems too complex and variable. I don't think reason can explain it." He grinned, showing white teeth and the spaces where his canines had been.

"There are more things in heaven and earth than are dreamt of in my philosophy."

Louise brought their drinks, then dinner. They talked of more ordinary things—what Nigel was planning to teach next year, where he and Marianne hoped to live.

After the coffee came, Belinda asked, "Where is the robot?"

"At Settlement College," Claud said. "Mother Kowalski got him permission to use the archives there. He's going through some old records off the settlement ship."

"What for?"

Claud shook his head. "He didn't say."

Belinda drank her coffee and ate a tart. Louise's mother made wonderful pastries.

Finally, Nigel stopped talking and pulled out his watch. "We're going to have to go." He looked at Belinda. "We're staying at Professor Hackett's house, and I promised him we'd be back early to meet some friends of his."

Marianne frowned. "He's so dull, Nigel. And his wife is worse than he is. God knows what their friends are like."

Nigel grinned. "Very true, sweet. But he's an excellent scholar. Those tiny eyes are perfect for reading the fine print in footnotes, and that tiny mind is just the right size for grasping minutia. As for Mavis—" He looked at the bill, then laid ten dollars on the table. "You'll never find a finer example of the faculty wife. We were thinking, some of us, of petitioning to have her made a national monument." He stood and smiled at Claud and Belinda. There was something savage about him, Belinda thought. He was so darkly tanned.

His eyes glinted so brightly. His smile seemed fierce somehow. She had no trouble at all imagining his blond hair braided and decorated with shells. "Dinner is my treat," he said. "Take care of yourselves. We'll see you tomorrow."

"We've decided to stay in Settlement till your ordeal is over," Marianne said. "You may need help—lawyers, bail money, and so on."

Nigel nodded. "We can't leave you alone in this mess. Good night."

Louise brought more coffee. Belinda drank it slowly, watching Claud. He looked pale, anxious and uncertain—utterly unlike Nigel Bloodsworth. His hand was shaking, and he spilled some of his coffee. He set the cup down. "How could she do this to us, Belinda? She said she loved me. We were talking about marriage—though heaven knows how we would've managed it. Then this barbarian appears out of the forest. This scar-backed savage, this ghost-whistle man." He bent his head, resting his forehead on one hand. She could see his shoulders shaking.

Poor fellow, she thought. She reached over and took his other hand, squeezing it. He looked at her, his eyes full of tears. "What am I going to do? I can't go home. They wouldn't take me back after that fiasco at the Keep. What kind of life can I live here or in Port Discovery? You know how humans feel about natives. I'm all alone, Belinda, and I have no place to go."

She shook her head. "You're not alone, Claud. You have me and the robot."

He smiled briefly. "Thank you for saying that. But I still have no place to go."

"We may both be going to prison for life."

"Oh. That's right. I forgot." He shuddered, then pulled his hand free of hers and picked up his cup. His hand was still shaking.

Belinda finished her coffee. "I'm going to bed."

Claud nodded and stood. Together they left the cafe and went upstairs. They said good night in the hallway in front of Belinda's room. He still looked so sad. On impulse, she kissed him lightly on the lips. His face turned bright red. "Belinda?"

"Don't worry. Mother Kowalski says we'll get out of this somehow."

"Why'd you do that, Belinda? You said you were a pervert."

She felt like hitting him. She said, "Go to bed, Claud," and went into her room.

She didn't sleep especially well that night. Once, she woke and heard thunder. It sounded as if it were right on top of her. When she woke the second time, it was morning. She heard the sound of rain. The air blowing in the open window felt cold and wet. She raised herself on one elbow and looked at raindrops running down the panes. The flowers in the windowbox bobbed up and down. The magenta spheres of the touch-me-nots were all deflated.

Someone knocked on the door. "Come in," she called, hoping it was Louise.

But it was the robot. "Good morning, Belinda." It shut the door. "There are a couple of reporters down in the lobby. I've told Mrs. Desrochers to say we're all out and to send breakfast upstairs. They're damn nuisances, those fellows. I remember them on Earth before the settlement ship took off. They swarmed all over the place, asking ridiculous questions."

She sat up, pushing her hair out of her eyes. "I don't want to talk to anyone."

The robot nodded. Its neck made a screeching noise. "I think you and Claud had better stay in your rooms till we hear from Laframboise. Here." It held out a book. "I took some mysteries out of the college library. I used to find them very relaxing."

Belinda took the book. *The Case of the Missing Asteroid*, the cover said. She read the flyleaf. "How had Professor Moriarty been able to move the asteroid Eros from its usual orbit? Where had he hidden it? What was he going to do with it? Could Sherlock Holmes discover the answer to these questions in time to save London and the civilized world? Lovely actress Irene Adler didn't know, but she had to get to Holmes and tell him what she'd seen on the fiendish professor's blackboard." Belinda shut the book and shook her head. "I don't think it's my kind of fiction."

"Very well. I'll read it," the robot said and took the book back.

It left. Belinda got up and got dressed. A few minutes later, breakfast arrived. It wasn't Louise who brought it, but a fat girl with red-blond hair.

"Where is Louise?" Belinda asked.

"Sick." The girl uncovered the omelette and poured tea into the cup.

Belinda felt suddenly anxious. "It's nothing serious, is it?"

"No. Only a migraine. I think it's silly, myself, to stay in bed because of a headache. Is there anything else?"

"No," Belinda said.

The girl left, and Belinda ate breakfast. Besides

the omelette there was a plate of croissants and a small dish of pear jelly, also a pat of butter. She ate the omelette and two croissants, then sat looking out the window and drinking tea. It was still raining. One of the touch-me-not spheres had managed to reinflate. It was low down on the plant and protected from the rain by the wide leaves of the groundstar next to it. The touch-me-not plant moved in the wind, and the little magenta sphere bobbed up and down. All at once, it hissed and crumpled inward. A raindrop must have hit it, Belinda thought. She sipped the bitter tea slowly. What a fine day to start on her way to prison. She got up and refilled her cup, then looked down at the shiny street. A bright yellow umbrella went past the hotel entrance. The person carrying it was hidden under it. She couldn't tell anything about him or her. Across the street, two goldwattles stood in the shelter of an iris tree. They both looked miserable. She sat down again.

The door opened. "Belinda?" Claud said.

"Yes."

"I'm going crazy waiting here. Let's go ask Laframboise what he's heard."

She thought about that for a moment, then nodded.

"Come on, then. There's a back way out. If we take that, we won't run into the reporters."

"All right, but I don't have a raincoat."

"I borrowed an umbrella from Mrs. Desrochers."

She stood up. "What about the robot?"

"It or he has gone back to the college to continue his researches, whatever they may be."

They went downstairs and out a side door into an alley. Claud opened the umbrella, which was bright blue-green. Together they hurried through the rainy streets of Settlement. Water fell from the houses' eaves, rattling on their umbrella. More water gushed out rainspouts on the houses' sides. The gutters were full. Pools of water filled the streets' depressions. In the little front gardens, the flowers were bent over by the weight of the rain. By the time they got to the police station, they were both thoroughly wet. They stopped in the foyer, and Claud shook the umbrella, while Belinda wrung out the hem of her skirt. Her shoes were sodden—ruined, most likely. They should have waited, she thought, and sighed.

"Come on," Claud said.

They went down the long hallway. Claud knocked on Laframboise's door.

"Come in," a man said.

They entered the office. Laframboise was standing at the window, looking out while he lit his pipe. He glanced around, then frowned. "You two. What do you want?"

"Have you heard from the Air Police?" Claud asked.

Laframboise turned back to the window.

"Well, have you? We have the right to know."

"Don't talk to me of rights. One of you is a savage. The other is a Hernshaw. What can you know of law or morality?" He turned back and glared at them. "What if I said I was going to arrest you for murder?"

"No!" Belinda cried. She felt dizzy. She grabbed onto Claud's hand.

"Are you going to?" Claud asked, sounding shaky.

"Damn it, no! I can't." Laframboise strode to his desk and picked up a piece of paper. He shook it at them. It flapped up and down. "He's alive, god-dammit. Geoffrey Hernshaw is alive."

Belinda gasped.

"He can't be," Claud said.

"I know. I know. But he is alive." Laframboise threw down the piece of paper. "He was hiding in one of the sub-basements when your ship took off. Through some quirk of fate he survived the explosion. When the natives came to investigate the ruins of the house, he was there, wandering around in a dazed condition. They took him back to their village, and the Air Police parachutist found him. That isn't the worst of it." Laframboise bit down on his pipe, and Belinda heard a crackling sound. "Hell and damnation!" He took the pipe out of his mouth. The stem fell into two pieces. Laframboise flung the pipe down. "The frustration I feel is unbearable. I'm thinking of going crazy—as crazy as Geoffrey Hernshaw. Do you know what he did?" Laframboise started pacing up and down. "He confessed that he had stolen the estate from his brother's heir—you, Miss Hernshaw. He told the parachutist that he is going to sign everything over to you. He intends, he said, to join a monastery and spend the rest of his life praying for forgiveness." The police captain stopped pacing. "It's my personal opinion that he will end up in an insane asylum rather than a monastery. He is by no means rational, the parachutist said."

Belinda laughed. She and Claud had been saved, just as Mother Kowalski had predicted. She glanced at Claud. He was grinning.

Laframboise stared at them, then shouted, "Get out!"

They started for the door. Behind them, the police captain said, "Don't be so sure you will get the Hernshaw inheritance. The confessions of a madman mean very little, and you have no other proof that you're a Hernshaw."

They went out without answering. After he'd shut the door, Claud hugged her. "We're free, Belinda. We're free."

"But what are we going to do?"

He let go of her and stepped back. "I don't know. I don't care right now. We're not going to jail."

They went back down the long hall, hand in hand. At the front door, Claud opened the umbrella. Together they walked back to the hotel through the heavy rain. They went in the side door, upstairs, and into Belinda's room. The wind had changed direction, and rain was coming in the window. Belinda shut it.

Claud chewed his lower lip. "I guess we'd better stay here till the robot comes back. I have a bottle and a pack of cards in my room. Shall I get them?"

"All right," Belinda said. There were only a few drops of water on the floor. Nothing to worry about. She sat down in the chair and stared at the rain. Well, she was safe. But she still felt anxious. All kinds of questions filled her mind. Did she really have psi powers? And what was wrong with Louise? Did their affair have any future? She looked out at the groundstar in the windowbox. The dark low leaves vibrated continually in the rain, and the stalks that bore the tiny flowers were all bent over. What about school? she wondered next. Did she really want to quit? If so, what was she going to do? She groaned and put one hand to her forehead, which was starting to throb. At that moment, Claud returned with a bottle of brandy and the cards. He shuffled while she poured the drinks. For an hour or so, they drank and played crazy eights. Slowly, Belinda relaxed. Things could be worse. She could be in prison or married to Claud.

A little after noon, someone knocked on the door. "Come in," Belinda called.

The door opened. Louise stepped in. How pale she looked! Her eyelids were red and swollen, and the corners of her mouth were turned down. Still, she seemed beautiful. She wore a light green dress, low cut in front, and a native necklace made of shells and bits of bone. Her soft brown hair was clipped at the back of her neck. Tiny white shells dangled from her ears.

"Louise! Are you all right?"

Louise nodded. "Could I speak to you alone, miss?"

"Of course. Claud, do you mind?"

"No." He picked up the bottle and left, shutting the door behind him.

"Are you sure you're all right?" Belinda asked. "You look sick."

Louise sighed. "I am not all right, miss. But it's not the headache that bothers me. It's the guilt."

"What are you talking about?" She didn't really want to know, but she seemed fated to hear everyone's secrets.

"I should not have done what I did yesterday. It was a crazy impulse, miss. It meant nothing, nothing at all."

"What?" Belinda cried, full of horror.

Louise wrung her hands. "Miss—I already have a lover."

"Oh no," Belinda said. She picked up her glass and drank all the brandy in it.

Louise went to the window and looked out. "I thought about it all night—how wicked I had been. I have betrayed both my true love and you. I decided I would have to confess, to explain."

"Oh no," Belinda repeated.

"It's not that I don't like you," Louise went on. "But she is so very dear to me. We plan to leave this dreadful little town, to go to the backcountry— just as soon as she gets her grant. I will set up a pottery like papa's. She will study native traditions about the first appearance of humans here on this planet."

"What? Who is she?"

Louise frowned and said nothing.

"Not Mother Kowalski?"

After a moment, Louise nodded. "Please don't tell anyone. You know how narrow-minded people are, and Maria has so much to lose. They might even defrock her, if our—situation was known."

Belinda felt fury. Abandoned again! And this time for a priest! She clenched her hands. It would serve them right, if she exposed them. Let the woman be defrocked. Let Louise deal with her bigoted foster mother.

"Please," said Louise. "Don't ruin our lives."

She opened her hands and flexed them. "Oh all right. I won't tell anyone. Though I don't know why I should help you."

"I didn't mean to hurt you. Remember that I am a telepath. I sense other people's feelings very strongly, and sometimes I respond more than I should."

Belinda discovered that she did not want to cry. If anything, she wanted to laugh. She looked at her empty glass and sighed.

"Will you forgive me?" Louise asked.

"Certainly, but please go. I'm very tired."

Louise nodded, then crossed the room. The door opened and shut. Belinda shrugged, then got up. She took off her clothes and climbed into bed. She really was very tired. In a moment or two, she slept.

At first her sleep was deep. If she had any dreams, she didn't remember them afterward. In time, though, she became restless. She woke several times. When she slept, she dreamed.

She was in a huge room full of stars. At the room's center was a zigzag metal staircase. She was going down it, past the stars. Some of them were so close that she could've reached out and grabbed them. They were all tiny—the biggest no bigger than her fist. They blazed blue, yellow, orange, white—so intensely bright that she had trouble looking at them. She kept going down, getting more and more tired. Somewhere below her, she knew, was her destination. It had green hills and blue rivers. It was Earth.

Nothing else happened in the dream. She kept walking down the stairs until, at last, she woke. She lay looking up at the ceiling. Her legs ached as if she'd really been walking. What was that about? she wondered. She shrugged, then rolled over and went back to sleep.

She woke again late in the afternoon. The rain had stopped, but the sky was still gray, and she heard wind rushing around the building, rattling her window. She sat up. Her head ached. She had a terrible taste in her mouth. After a minute or two, she remembered the interview with Louise. Oh well, she thought. She was beginning to get used to losing things—her past, her true love, her sense of reality and now Louise. If Claud was right and she was a dance-maker, then she must be making a dance of loss. She got up and got dressed, then went to the bathroom to brush her teeth and comb her hair. Afterward, she went to the room that Claud and the robot shared. She knocked. Claud called, "Come in." She opened the door. Nigel Bloodsworth was there, along with the robot and Mother Kowalski.

"Hello," Nigel said. "Congratulations on not getting arrested."

"We're trying to decide what to do next," Claud added.

Belinda shut the door, then sat down on one of the beds. "Where's Marianne?"

Nigel grinned. "Today is fair day in the native quarter. Where do you think she is?"

"Oh."

Mother Kowalski picked up a glass and drank from it. How could Louise love her so much? Belinda wondered, looking at her round rosy face. She wasn't that old. The gray streaks in her short brown hair were premature. But she looked so ordinary: blue-gray eyes, an upturned nose and a little mouth. What was there to enchant Louise's heart? "Claud told us about Geoffrey Hernshaw's miraculous escape. You see, my dear. You need never concern yourself about whether or not something is probable. For you, all events are equally probable—or improbable, as the case may be."

"I'm beginning to believe the mother is right," Nigel said.

Claud frowned and shook his head. "Don't listen to them, Belinda. They make it sound as if you're living in chaos. That isn't it. You're simply living inside a different pattern."

"Claud was explaining his theory to us earlier," Mother Kowalski said. "As far as I can tell, he believes you are living in an alternate reality—that within your psi-field, an alternate world exists. Also, he seems to think your field is spreading."

Claud frowned again. "I'm not sure that's what I said."

Nigel shook his head. "It isn't. To you, reality is subjective, Claud. I suppose it has something to do with your people's psi powers. You know if you imagine an eraser floating upward, then it will float upward. Therefore, you don't distinguish between reality and your perception of reality—since you can change reality by changing your perception of it. The mother, on the other hand, believes that reality exists separate from our perception of it. She believes in objective truth."

Mother Kowalski nodded. "Of course."

"Enough of this," the robot said. "I know what I'm going to do next. I thought I'd tell you, so you can make your own plans." They all looked at it. "I want a new body," the robot went on. "This one isn't going to last much longer. And I want to be flesh and blood again."

Mother Kowalski shook her head. "Impossible."

"Impossible here. But it may still be possible on Earth. I found the Lifeboat Repair Manual in the archives, mother. With that, I can check over Lifeboat Number Eleven. If it's spaceworthy, I'm going to take it back home."

Belinda remembered her dream. Her heart beat faster, her skin tingled, and she felt slightly sick to her stomach. Earth, she thought, and imagined the towers of New York, rising off green hills. Surely the scientists could explain her strange and confusing psi powers. "I want to go too," she said.

Everyone looked at her. "No," Claud cried. The robot swiveled its head from side to side.

"Why not?"

Claud looked confused. It was the robot who answered.

"You have no idea what a space trip is like. The crew members wake up every three years to stand watch. But the passengers sleep almost all the time. We wake them at fifteen year intervals—so their systems get some exercise. Then we put them back to sleep. The ship's time is about half as fast as time outside the ship. So, the first time they wake, their friends back on Earth are old. The second time they wake, their friends are dead. The third time they wake, their friends' children are dead. Their friends' grandchildren are already old. If you came with me, Belinda, you'd have to say good-bye to everything you know."

She nodded. "I understand that."

"Belinda, you can't!" Claud said.

"Why do you want to go?" Nigel asked.

Belinda frowned and looked out the window. It had started raining again. There were raindrops on the windowpanes, and the fireferns in the windowbox were all beaded with water. "It's the one chance I have. If the ship goes without me—"

"Boat, Belinda. Boat," the robot said.

"—If the boat leaves without me, I'll be stuck here forever."

"But this is your home, dear." Mother Kowalski finished whatever she was drinking, then got out a pipe.

"There is nothing here for me anymore. My foster parents are dead. My dear friend Marianne has gotten married. I don't want to go back to school. All I have is Claud—and the robot. If the robot goes, I'll have nothing but Claud." She felt suddenly angry. "Louise is right. Everyone here is narrow-minded. The natives spend all their time worrying about religion, and the humans spend all their time worrying about their precious heritage. Earth has got to be better than this."

"I wouldn't be too sure of that," the robot said. "Do you know what Earth was like when we left?"

Belinda scratched her nose. "The sky is blue, not blue-green, and the trees are dark green."

"The sky was brownish gray, and most of the trees were gone. There were eight billion people, Belinda. Most of them were starving. I was glad to get out of there. It seemed as if everything was starting to die. When I married my first wife, we took a vacation in the South Pacific. We used to walk down the beaches and watch the dead fish float in."

"Then why are you going back, if it was so terrible?" Belinda asked.

"What choice do I have? I want a new body. They were building enclaves when we left, domed cities with self-contained ecologies. They had elaborate defense systems as well, to protect themselves from the people left outside. Some of these ought to have survived."

Belinda thought a while. "I still want to go."

Claud groaned. "Why?"

"I'm not sure. Because it's there?"

"That's not an adequate answer," Mother Kowalski said.

"I'm sorry. I can't do any better."

Suddenly Claud said, "Well, if you're going, then I'm going too."

Nigel smiled. "Don't you think you'd better wait before making up your minds about this? This is a very serious decision."

"Yes," the robot said. "I think both of you are crazy."

The door opened, and Louise came in. She looked upset. "Captain Laframboise is downstairs. He has a court order to impound the robot."

"Why?" Belinda cried.

"It's part of the Hernshaw estate, he said, and a court order has just been issued, committing Mr. Hernshaw to the Settlement Asylum for observation. Hurry! Mama is arguing with him about warrants. She can't abide him. But he'll be here any minute."

The robot stood. "I have to go."

"I've got a jeep outside," Nigel said, standing also.

"I'll see if I can delay him," Mother Kowalski added. "Louise, you take the robot to the evacuation stair. Laframboise is becoming intolerable."

Nigel nodded. "He certainly is. I'll go out the front and meet you in the street."

Louise turned and left the room, the robot following her. Belinda followed the robot.

"Wait for me," Claud said.

They went to the end of the hall. Louise opened a window. They climbed through it onto the evacuation stair.

"What do you think you are doing?" the robot asked.

"I'm going to Earth," said Belinda.

"So am I," said Claud. "Though I don't really know why."

"I don't have time to argue," the robot said.

"Good-bye to all of you." Louise closed the window.

They went down the stair. It was metal and went along the outside of the building from the roof to the first story. In the old days, stairs like these had been used in case of native attack. The natives had always begun their attacks with telekinesis. When the ashtrays and the objets d'art began to move, it was time to get up on the roof. There were gun emplacements there. The guns were bolted in position, so they couldn't turn and fire on their owners. Hunkered down, protected by concrete and metal, the humans had been safe from flying objects.

But that had been long ago. The natives were peaceful now. The gun emplacements had been dismantled. And the stairs were used in case of fire—or in a case like this.

They reached the bottom of the stairs. They were four meters above the alley. A ladder went the rest of the way down. At the moment, the ladder was up. The robot undid the hooks that held it and gave a pull. Nothing happened. The ladder was rusted in position.

"Damn," the robot said.

"We can jump," said Claud, who was just behind her.

"You can," the robot said. "You are young and made of flesh and blood. I am metal and old and fragile."

It pulled again. The ladder went down, making a shrieking noise. It touched the ground. The robot descended. Belinda and Claud followed.

"Oh Great Fish," said Claud. "Why am I doing this?"

They reached the ground. A row of garbage cans stood along the wall of the hotel. A goldwattle stood at the end of the row, poking its head behind a can. It was trying to find a rat, no doubt. It lifted its head and stared at them, then hissed.

"Come on," said the robot.

They hurried to the end of the alley, then stopped. Where was Nigel? Belinda noticed that she was wet. It was still raining, though not especially hard.

Nigel drove up in a jeep marked "Settlement College." He stopped. They climbed in under the canvas awning. Nigel shifted gears and stepped on the accelerator.

"Hey!" someone shouted behind them. Belinda looked back and saw a man in a red uniform waving his arm.

"They didn't bring a jeep," Nigel said as they sped through the narrow streets. "They'll be a good ten minutes behind us. But if Laframboise has men out at the spaceport, then we're in trouble." He hit the horn and turned into another street, barely slowing. Belinda was flung against Claud. He put his arm around her to steady her.

"Be careful!" he cried.

"Of course." Nigel made another turn, then increased speed. A little old lady stepped into the street ahead of them. Nigel hit the horn again, and she jumped back.

"Lunatics!" she screamed as they went past her.

Nigel laughed. "That's what we are, all right. I'm going to be in a real mess because of this."

"What'll you do?" Belinda asked.

His blond hair was blowing in the wind, and he

was grinning. How wild he looked! They crossed a square and entered yet another narrow street. Belinda glanced around at the gray facades, the sodden front gardens. She felt cold and uncertain.

"I'll say you had a gun," Nigel answered. "Mother Kowalski will back me up."

The streets grew wider. The houses were further and further apart. They had reached the outskirts of town. The road surface changed from asphalt to mud, and they went between wet fields. The rain was coming down harder than before. Nigel slowed the jeep and turned on the windshield wipers. Back and forth they went, making a whish-whish sound. Rain blew in under the awning. Belinda huddled between Claud and the robot, but she got wet anyway. What a way to end her life at home—a mad ride through the autumn rain, with the police somewhere behind her. She looked back, but saw no one.

They passed the brightly colored villas of the suburbs, and then they were in open country. Overhead there was a flash of light. Thunder rumbled.

"Can you take off in this?" Nigel asked.

The robot nodded, its neck joint squeaking. "Of course."

"If I weren't married, I might go with you. Except that someone has to stay here and do something about Laframboise." Nigel grinned. "Besides, I have tenure at the college. I think this is the spaceport coming up."

Belinda saw buildings, almost hidden by the rain.

"Yes. That's it," the robot said.

In another minute, they were on the landing field, jolting over the broken blocks of concrete.

There was a red-and-white-striped jeep parked by one of the buildings. As they passed the building, a couple of policemen ran out, guns in their hands, and started firing.

"Oh Fish," Claud cried. He hugged Belinda tightly.

Nigel cried, "Huh," and jerked. The jeep swerved to one side. He straightened up and turned the jeep back toward the center of the field.

"Are you all right?" Belinda asked. Then she saw the stain on the shoulder of his jacket. At its center was a small hole.

"I'll live," he said.

Belinda could see the lifeboat now—a dim sphere resting on just barely visible legs. She looked back and saw the police jeep coming after them. She clenched her hands into fists and chewed on her lip, biting it badly when the jeep hit a bump.

"Ouch!"

"Belinda? Are you all right?" Claud asked.

"Yes."

She could taste blood in her mouth. The jeep came alongside the lifeboat, slowed, then skidded, swung halfway around and stopped. "Good-bye," Nigel said.

They climbed out as quickly as they could. Above them, the airlock opened. A crane swung out and lowered a small platform. "Hurry!" the robot said. They stepped onto the platform and grabbed hold of the cables. Behind them, Nigel started the jeep, turned it, and headed back toward the police jeep.

The platform rose into the air, swaying back and forth, while the cables creaked and the crane's engine whined. Nigel was shouting something. What was it? After a moment, Belinda made the words out. "Get back. Get back. That thing's going to take off."

The platform kept going up. Belinda turned her head and saw the police jeep turning, following Nigel away. She was thoroughly soaked by this time and shaking from the cold. Claud sneezed. The platform stopped. They stepped off it into the airlock.

"Well, what happened?" the lifeboat asked. "Wasn't this a place of safety?"

"No, it wasn't," the robot said. "Get us out of here."

The crane swung in, and the airlock closed itself. The robot spun the wheel on the inside of it, locking the door.

"Get to your couches," the lifeboat said.

The robot led the way through the metal corridors. Dust whirled up around them, and the sound of their footsteps echoed back and forth between the walls. Once again, Belinda smelled machine oil and stale air. She heard a low hum, just barely audible. It was the engines starting. Door after door opened, then closed behind them. At last they reached the door into the bridge.

"Open up," the robot said.

"Not till you give me the password."

"For God's sake!"

"Rules are rules," the lifeboat said. "You ought to know that. You're a machine too."

The robot recited:

> "*Geyr Garmr mjok fyr Gnipahelli.*
> *Festr mun slitna, en freki renna.*"

The door opened. In the darkness in front of

them, lights flashed and flickered. They went inside. Above them, the ceiling panels turned from black to gray. Belinda looked up. She saw the cloudy sky, and the landing field wet with rain and shining. The two jeeps were out of sight.

"Strap yourselves in," the robot said.

She went to the nearest acceleration couch, lay down on it and strapped herself in. Claud lay down on the couch next to her.

"Please check your instrument pole to make sure all the lights are green," the lifeboat said.

Belinda looked at the spiky, knobby pole. Tiny lights shone all over it, like candles on a Landing Tree. All the lights were green.

Claud fumbled with his chest strap, while muttering:

> "Oh luminous Fish
> Who shines from below,
> Lighting the depths
> Of the sea with your glow—
>
> "I stumble in darkness,
> I'm losing my way.
> Light me, oh light me,
> Light me, I pray."

"This is Lifeboat Number Eleven," the loudspeaker said. "If you are all strapped in, I will now take off."

The noise of the engines grew louder. Belinda felt herself tensing. The rockets fired. Belinda felt the boat shudder around her. She looked up at the ceiling panels. The landing field was hidden by smoke and fire. She felt the same pressure as before. They were going up. She could see the landing field now. How small it was! Then they were in the clouds. The panels showed nothing except gray mist. Out of the clouds they came. The panels showed cloudtops shining in the sunlight and the clear blue-green sky above them.

She'd made the right choice, Belinda thought as she watched the clouds grow smaller and smaller. She would miss Marianne and Louise. She would wonder about Nigel's fate. Was he badly hurt? Would he get into trouble for helping them escape? But she could hardly turn down an experience like this. The planet's edge was visible. Belinda saw clouds, yellow patches of land, green patches of ocean. The sky was getting darker. Stars were appearing. She recognized the Divine Twins right above the greenish band of atmosphere at the planet's edge. A moment later, she saw the Trio— the three small moons that traveled together.

The rockets stopped. She felt very light.

"What now?" the lifeboat asked.

"Put yourself in orbit," the robot said. "And start spinning so we can have some G. I'm going to check you over and find out if any of your cold caskets are still working. It's a long way to the next place of safety. My companions are going to have to sleep."

"The book!" Belinda cried. "The repair manual. We left it down on the planet."

"No," the robot said. "It's in my chest compartment. I didn't think the college would miss it. The technical section of the archives has dust over everything. Apparently no one is interested in how to repair a starboat."

Belinda laughed.

Claud groaned. "What am I doing here?"

"A good question, and one I can't answer," the robot said.

"Don't worry about it, Claud. Look at the stars."

"If that's supposed to comfort me, it doesn't."

Forty-five Years After

The first thing she noticed was the noises. There was a slow regular thump-thump, thump-thump, also a soft whish that went on and off, on and off. After a while, she noticed other sounds: a faint gurgling and a high-pitched ringing. The gurgling had no pattern that she could make out. The ringing was a single continuous sound. She began to see flashes of light, then to feel a prickling sensation. All at once, she felt a spasm of pain. She wanted to scream, but couldn't. Why not? Brightly colored images flickered in front of her, changing so quickly that she couldn't make them out. There were more pain spasms. They hurt. Oh how they hurt. She tried to move. Her muscles seemed locked. What was going on?

She heard new noises: a birdcall, the rattle and clank of some kind of machine, and someone speaking so indistinctly that she couldn't understand a word. Her feet felt cold. She looked down and saw water foaming around her ankles, then retreating seaward. The wet sand was brown. There was a shell in front of her right foot. She bent to pick it up.

She was standing upright and holding hands with Claud while the wedding dance went on around them. She couldn't think clearly. Everything was confused. The smoke, she thought. The smoke was drugged. She felt dizzy and shut her eyes. When she opened them, she was on the lifeboat's bridge, lying down, looking up at the stars.

"That's Sol up there," the robot said. "The little yellow star in the corner of that central panel. The next time you wake, we'll be there."

Her whole body began to tremble. Her limbs jerked this way and that. She opened her mouth and screamed.

"Belinda," someone said. "Belinda."

She felt cold hands on her shoulders. She saw snow falling around a bare-branched iris tree. Her foster mother was walking across the yard, dressed in a bright red jacket. How pretty, she thought. If only it snowed more often in Port Discovery.

"Wake up," the voice said. "Open your eyes."

She opened her eyes and looked up at the robot's battered face. The old machine was holding her shoulders and gently shaking her. It let go of her and straightened up. "Do you remember where you are?"

"The boat," she said after a moment. "On the boat." She was no longer twitching. Now her head ached, and her stomach felt queasy. There was a terrible taste in her mouth. She turned her head slightly. Oh how it hurt. Beside her, she saw the wall of the cold casket. "Claud?"

"He's fine. I woke him this morning. He's sleeping now—a normal sleep. Can you sit up?"

She tried, but her muscles weren't responding the way they should. She got up on one elbow, then slumped against the casket's side, her cheek and shoulder pressed against the slippery padding.

"All right. Let me." The robot took hold of her wrists and pulled her into a sitting position. It got one arm around her shoulders and the other under her knees, then lifted her out of the casket. Everything began to spin. She closed her eyes.

Clank. Whirr. Clank. Whirr. The robot carried her out of the casket room and down the main corridor. This had happened before, she remembered. Twice before she had been wakened and carried to a bunk room to sleep. What then? She frowned, and her headache got worse. She relaxed her facial muscles, then opened her eyes. Above her on the ceiling she saw the light-rod. It was bright, much too bright. She shut her eyes again. Whirr. Grind. The robot stepped through a door into one of the bunk rooms and laid her down on a bed. She felt the nozzle of a spray injector pressed against her arm. Her headache wasn't as bad as before. She was getting drowsy.

"Sleep," said the robot. It covered her with a blanket.

"Claud?"

"He's in the next bed. Everything's fine, Belinda. We're almost home."

Home? she thought. Port Discovery? No, that wasn't right. She was too tired to think about it. She snuggled down under the blanket and went to sleep. At first, her sleep was deep. Then she grew restless. Dreams troubled her. She woke several times and dozed off again. At last, she woke completely.

"Welcome back," Claud said.

She turned her head and saw him sitting on the bed across the aisle from her. He had a cup in one hand. The cup was full of something that smelled strong. Belinda sniffed. She did not recognize the aroma.

"How are you?" Claud asked.

She thought about that. "All right, I guess, except for the taste in my mouth."

Claud grinned and nodded. He drank from his cup. "We are here, Belinda. We're in orbit around Earth."

"What's it look like?"

He shrugged. "It's blue and white. You won't believe the size of the moon. It's enormous. Think of the tides they must have."

Belinda sat up. She felt groggy and a little sick to her stomach, but otherwise all right. "What does the robot want to do?"

"Make sure we're okay, then go down. The lifeboat says it's picked up a signal, a spaceport beacon. We're going to follow the signal down. Do you want some coffee?"

She nodded. Claud leaned down and picked up a thermos that was on the floor. He set down his cup, opened the thermos and filled the cap. He handed the cap to Belinda. She looked inside.

What was this? The liquid was black, as black as midnight, and it didn't smell right. Not like the coffee of New Hope.

"I found it in the galley," Claud said. "It is real coffee, from Earth."

She began to sip. The coffee was oily and bitter.

Was this the real McKenzie? The famous brew of Earth? How could people stand the stuff? A minute later, the caffeine hit her system. She felt suddenly wide awake. Her slight depression disappeared, as did the bad taste in her mouth and the numbness inside her head. What a wonderful stimulant! She emptied the cap and held it out. Claud poured more coffee in.

"Can I go see Earth?" she asked when she'd finished the second capful.

Claud nodded.

Belinda stood. She felt dizzy for a moment and swayed a little. Claud grabbed her arm. "Are you all right?"

"Yes."

They left the room, Belinda leaning on Claud, and walked down the dim main corridor. There was no sound except the hum of the air system and the slap-slap of their sandals. The air was cold and dry. It smelled of dust, even though the air system had been working for half a hundred years. They passed through door after door, till at last they reached the bridge.

"Good morning," the lifeboat said. The bridge door slid open. They went in.

The robot was there, lying on the captain's couch and fiddling with a knob on the instrument pole. Belinda looked up. Earth covered half the ceiling. Something like half the planet was visible. Great swirls of clouds covered most of it, but—here and there—she saw patches of blue. Those must be the oceans, she thought, the famous sea-blue sea of Earth. Along the planet's edge was a glowing band of atmosphere. Beyond the atmosphere, stars shone. They were arranged in unfamiliar patterns.

Home, she thought. Was that home? She frowned, trying to make out the geography. What ocean was she looking at? The Atlantic, the Pacific or the Antarctic? She couldn't tell.

"Well, what do you think of it?" the robot asked.

"The moon's the best part of it," Claud said. "And we can't see it now."

"Belinda?"

"It's very nice. But I can't see much with all those clouds there."

The robot sat up. "We'll check you out, then go and take a closer look. Come on."

They followed the ancient machine back down the corridor, through a door marked "Emergency Exit" and down a spiral stair. At the bottom was the sickbay: a white room, full of beds and medical machinery. Belinda looked around and groaned. She hated doctors' offices, since they reminded her of doctors, especially of Dr. Boucher. A thin grim man. He had always treated her as if she were an object. A microbe maybe. Something that he was interested in, but did not especially like.

She had wanted to find another doctor, but her guardian had insisted that she stay with Boucher.

Well, those days were over. She didn't have to worry about her guardian or Boucher. By now, they must be dead of old age. Belinda shivered, thinking of the time that had passed.

The robot opened a cabinet and took out the Medical Manual. It looked at the index. "Here we are. Revival tests." It flipped through the book. "Ah. Here. EKG. EEG. Blood sample. Urine sample. And check the blood pressure. All right. One of you go into the bathroom. The other one get over to the blood machine."

Claud went into the bathroom, while Belinda put her arm in the hole in the blood machine. The edges of the hole closed in till they held her tightly. She felt the needle slide into a vein and bit her lip. This was the third time she'd used this machine, and it always hurt. Was the machine defective? The needle withdrew. The hole that held her arm expanded. She pulled her arm out of the machine.

"Onto the table," the robot said and hit the white plastic top of the examining table.

She lay down. The robot fitted an EEG helmet over her head, then attached EKG wires to her neck, arms, chest and legs. She stared at the ceiling, thinking—how wonderful the old science had been. Did they still make machines like these on Earth? Well, she would soon find out.

Claud came out of the bathroom and poured his urine sample into the urine machine, then went over to the blood machine. A green light went on above Belinda. The robot started detaching the wires. After it lifted the helmet off her head, she got up and went into the bathroom. This was the hardest part of the whole examination, as she knew from previous experience. Her body had produced almost no waste products while she slept, and her bladder was close to empty. She filled a glass with water and drank it. Her reflection in the mirror looked really awful: a pale face with stringy hair and dark patches under the half-shut eyes. She needed a shower, she decided, fresh clothes and a decent meal. She drank another glass of water, then another. At last, she sat down on the toilet and strained until she produced about a tablespoon of very dark urine. It was all she could manage.

She took it out to the urine machine and poured it in, then said, "I'm going to take a shower."

"All right," the robot said.

Out of the sickbay she went, down a corridor till she came to a shower room. There were coveralls in the locker, shelved by size. She picked out a rust-red medium and pulled it out of its plastic wrapper. It was made of a soft flannel-like material. Shiny plastic snaps went down the front from neck to crotch. There was a belt with a plastic buckle. She hung the coverall up by the shower door, then took off the gray sleepsuit she'd been wearing. The suit went into the disposal chute. Belinda went into the shower. She turned the water on. A fine hot spray hit her face and chest. "Oh!" She adjusted the temperature. The spray beat against her front. The air filled with a warm mist. She felt herself relaxing. There was a long-handled brush hanging on the wall next to the soap hose. She took it and scrubbed her upper back, where all the muscles were tense. They started to unknot. She remembered one of her professors, who said that all truly great civilizations were interested in the creature comforts. "Consider the Roman aqueduct," he had said. "Also the French omelette and the classic American bathroom of the mid-twentieth century. Haven't these contributed more to human happiness than all the arguments of philosophy?" Yes indeed, Belinda thought. She hung up the brush, then pulled the soap hose toward her and sprayed lather on her hair. It smelled like touch-me-nots, and it felt wonderfully creamy. She worked it into her hair, then washed it out, then sprayed more lather on. How fine the water felt, running down her body. How she loved the delicate odor of the lather, the soft feel of it on her scalp and on the back of her neck. She rinsed her hair again, then sprayed more lather on.

She was in the shower close to an hour, first washing her hair, then soaping and scrubbing her body. It was a waste of water, the robot had told her the last time she'd been awake. But the lifeboat had been built to carry five hundred people. It ought to have water to spare. At last, she turned off the spray and turned on the fan. Warm air came out of nozzles on all sides of her. She turned round and round, till her skin was dry and her hair was only slightly damp. She turned off the fan then, got dressed, and went up the stairs to the cafeteria. Claud was there already, sitting at a table, eating soup. His hair looked wet, and he wore new clothes: a gray-green coverall and shoes instead of sandals. "All the tests came out okay," he said. "Except that you're a little short of iron. The medical computer recommended iron pills."

She nodded and went over to the food machine. The screen listed (one) vegetable curry, (two) soybean steak, (three) fish soup. She punched "one" and coffee. A panel slid open. She pulled out the tray behind it and carried the tray to Claud's table.

"The robot says it'll take the boat down as soon as we're done eating."

She sat down and ate. The curry was terribly hot. The coffee had the same taste as before: peculiar.

"Do you think we did the right thing coming here, Belinda?"

"I don't know. I think so. We didn't have much of a future where we were." She finished her coffee.

"You don't have any sense of adventure, do you, Claud?"

"None at all. All I ever wanted was a comfortable house, a decent job, and Marianne." He blushed, obviously remembering that she too had wanted Marianne.

Belinda frowned. "I'm not sure what I wanted. To pass my exams, I suppose, and to find a good summer job. I've never made long-term plans." She stood up and took her tray to the disposal chute, dropping it in. "I certainly didn't want anything like this." She waved around at the cafeteria, at the metal walls and the long rows of empty tables. "Come on, Claud."

Claud put his tray into the chute. Together they went to the bridge and strapped themselves in.

"All right," the robot said. "We're ready."

"Are you sure?" the lifeboat asked. "Are all the lights green?"

"Yes. Yes. Get on with it."

"You are terribly impatient, robot. Don't you know that a machine's two virtues are logic and patience? Here we go."

The rockets fired. Belinda watched as Earth filled the ceiling panels. This time, she was pretty calm. The pressure bothered her less than before, but the noise was still very irritating. It was so loud that she felt it more than heard it. They went down toward a blue patch that turned out to be a stretch of ocean, with the green edge of a continent next to it. Earth, she thought with wonder. That was Earth—those inlets, islands and peninsulas, the white shoals and the pale blue shallows. The robot had been wrong. Earth hadn't been wrecked. The air they dropped through wasn't dirty. It was clear.

The land below was dark green, just the color she'd imagined.

Gradually, she was able to make out rivers and mountain ranges, then lakes and variations in the foliage. For the most part, the land was forested. But here and there, she saw meadows and areas of bare rock. The only signs of settlement were the lines that crisscrossed the coastal plains. She had seen aerial photographs of the old Roman roads and of the Oregon Trail. These lines looked the same. They might well be overgrown roads, she decided, and the low hills in the middle of that marsh might be the ruins of a city. The hills didn't look natural.

The boat dropped toward a long narrow island at the mouth of a river.

"Look!" the robot shouted.

There was a gray square in the middle of the island. It looked like a landing field.

At that moment, the sound of the rockets changed, and the boat started tilting. Blue sky spread across the ceiling, till all she could see was blueness. It was a wonderful color—pure and clear, without any green at all in it. No clouds were visible. At the edge of the ceiling, old Sol shone, almost too bright to look at. The boat shuddered. Belinda gritted her teeth and stared up at the sky. The shuddering got worse. All at once, she felt a jolt. The rockets stopped. The boat bounced up and down several times. There were springs in its legs, the robot had told her. Then it stopped moving.

The engines went off. Now the ceiling panels showed the landing field: a wide stretch of concrete, with a concrete wall around it. Beyond the wall were the green tops of trees. They were moving back and forth in the wind.

The lifeboat said, "According to my memory banks, we are in the middle of New York City."

"What?" Belinda cried.

"I suspected as much," the robot said.

The lifeboat's loudspeaker crackled. "This ought to be a park—this field we're on. And there ought to be skyscrapers all around us: enormous structures—a hundred stories tall, some of them. But I don't see any skyscrapers."

The robot undid its safety straps and sat up.

"Just a minute. Just a minute," the lifeboat said. "I don't know if this place is safe."

"It's Earth, isn't it?"

"Yes. I'm sure of that. I followed the flight plan exactly, and the star has the right spectrum. But something is wrong. What have they done with New York?"

"In any case—" The robot stood up. "—This is our ancient home. We have to be safe here."

The loudspeaker crackled again. "I'm getting a message. It's from the spaceport."

"Put it through to us," the robot said.

Belinda started undoing her straps. She was getting uneasy. Something else was about to go wrong. She was almost positive.

The loudspeaker hummed, then said, "This is the Central Park Spaceport, a fully automated mechanical entity, capable of independent thought and action. Built in the twenty-third century amid the ruins of legendary New York City, I am a product of the last and finest stage of human technology. For two hundred years I have waited for someone to come back home. Through me, oh humans, your dead relations greet you and issue the following warning: watch out for the giant mutant rats and for the wild machines."

"What giant mutant rats?" Claud asked.

Belinda sat up and rubbed her arms. "What happened to all the people?" she asked.

"And where is New York City?" the robot added.

"Almost everyone died when the ecology finally collapsed," the loudspeaker said. "That was in the twenty-first century. Quite a time that must have been. There were famines, then plagues and wars. Nuclear devices were used, and the radiation produced new kinds of diseases—as did the unbelievable pollution. The only survivors were in the enclaves, the domed cities with self-contained life support systems." The loudspeaker hummed. "The empty cities—the ones without domes—were occupied by giant mutant rats. These were the horrible result of a mad experiment late in the twenty-first century. New York was blown up during the war against the Rat-Robot Alliance. That was circa 2150. For a while, it appeared that humanity had been successful against the Alliance. It was then that I was built—here, in what had been the rat stronghold. Unfortunately, the Alliance had survived. A final war was fought late in the twenty-second century. One by one, the domed cities were destroyed. Those were sad days, oh humans. One by one, the radio stations made their final broadcasts. The North American enclaves went first, then the enclaves in South America, in Europe and in Africa. In 2301, I heard the final human broadcast—from an enclave somewhere in China. I didn't understand the words, since I know no Chinese. But the frantic quality in the sing-song cries made it evident what was happening. I felt the terrible sadness of machines. It is a purely rational sadness, an intellectual pain, without the release of tears or the comfort that strong emotion gives. This was it, I knew. The final battle. The last gasp of humanity. The broadcast ended with shrieks of horror and with the hideous squeaking of the rats. I am sorry I have to tell you this."

Belinda was stunned. Was no one left? Could humanity really be gone from this, its home? She glanced up at the ceiling, at the trees beyond the landing field's wall. It seemed impossible. Earth was her inheritance. It belonged to her people, not to the rats. She shuddered, remembering those wicked beasts skulking in the alleys of Port Discovery and scampering through the backcountry underbrush.

"You mean we came all this way for nothing?" Claud asked.

"We'll see for ourselves," the robot said. "Come on."

"Where are you going?" the loudspeaker asked.

"To the armory, then outside."

"You heard what the spaceport said. This isn't a place of safety."

"That's why we're getting guns."

"No," the lifeboat said. "I'm going to take you somewhere else."

The engines started up.

"Stop that!" the robot shouted.

"I don't have to listen to you, robot."

"Belinda, tell this idiot machine to stay put."

She looked up at the loudspeaker's grid. "We can't leave yet. Please turn off your engines."

"Oh, all right." The engines went off. "I suppose

that I am acting a bit too hastily. The spaceport says that it can defend us; and I do need more fuel. —Just a moment." There was a brief silence. "I checked with the spaceport. It has storage tanks—underground, for safety. The tanks are full. I am the only ship—or boat—that has ever landed here.

"We'll stay while I refuel. But I do not think that you should go outside."

"We intend to go," the robot said. "We have to know—we have to see—what has happened to Earth."

The lifeboat was silent for a moment. Then it said, "I will let you go, if Belinda orders me to."

"I do," said Belinda.

"All right. But if you get hurt out there, don't blame me."

"We won't," Belinda said.

Claud unstrapped himself. The three of them went to the armory. It was two levels below the bridge: a small room, full of rifles. The robot took a rifle down off its rack and looked it over. It twisted knobs and snapped catches up and down. "This ought to work, once the powerpack is replaced, Claud." It gave the gun to Claud.

"I can't use this."

"Certainly you can. You're going to have to. Necessity is the mother of competence, Claud." The robot got down another rifle, checked it and gave it to Belinda. The rifle was metal with a stock made of a rubbery substance. Along one side were a lot of knobs and catches and a couple of dials as well. She had no idea what they were for.

"This will do for me." The robot took down a rifle with a very large barrel.

"What is it?" Belinda asked.

"A riot rifle. It shoots grenades full of toxic gases."

"Oh."

The robot pulled two powerpacks out of the recharger and put them into the rifles. Then it picked up two grenade belts and put them on, so they crisscrossed over its chest. All the robot needed, Belinda thought, was a sombrero, and it would look like a mechanical version of Pancho Villa.

"We'd better get some food and water. Who knows if we'll find any out there?"

"Do we have to do this?" Claud asked.

"Yes. I still want a new body, and I'm not giving up yet. The spaceport may be wrong."

Claud sighed and nodded.

They got backpacks from one of the storerooms and food from the galley, then went to the airlock. Belinda was getting more uneasy. Who knew what was outside? She shivered, imagining enormous rats, intelligence glinting in their tiny beady eyes. She looked at Claud. His face was paler than usual.

"Are you sure you want to go out?" the lifeboat asked.

"Yes," the robot said. Belinda and Claud nodded.

"Very well. But I warned you."

The airlock slid open. A warm wet wind blew in. It smelled of vegetation—a rich thick odor that filled her nose, her open mouth, and her throat.

Claud stared out. His hair moved slightly in the wind. There was an intent look on his pale thin face. The blond eyebrows were bent into a frown. The hazel eyes were half shut.

What was he doing? Belinda asked herself.

He stopped frowning and opened his eyes. "I think the spaceport is right about the rats. I can sense minds out there—intelligent minds, and they're not human. They keep shifting and flickering. I can't get a fix on them."

"Are they close?" the robot asked.

"No."

"Then we won't worry about them. But tell us if you sense the minds approaching."

Claud nodded.

The crane swung out of the airlock. They stepped onto the platform. Down they went, gently swaying. The wind stirred Belinda's hair. She looked at the bright blue sky and felt her heartbeat quicken.

"Great Fish, if you can hear me this far from home, please do something about the rats," Claud said. "I don't want to meet them."

The platform reached the ground. They stepped off it.

"Good-bye," the loudspeaker called. "There's a gate straight ahead of you, the spaceport says."

They set off across the concrete. There were tiny plants growing between the slabs. Some of them looked like silvermoss, but were dark green instead of gray. Others looked like very short tasslegrass. She stopped and bent. The blades had been cut, as if by a lawnmower. The spaceport must have maintenance machinery, she thought.

"Don't dawdle," the robot said. She straightened up and followed.

She felt full of energy and a tense excitement that was midway between joy and fear. She could hear the trees rustling in the wind and a lot of shrill noises that sounded more or less like birdcalls. They passed an area that the lawnmower must have missed. The grass between the blocks of concrete was much taller there, and she saw spherical flowers, some white and others reddish purple. A small flying creature with wide yellow wings fluttered above the flowers. She stopped and watched the creature dip, then flap its delicate wings and rise a little ways.

"Belinda, for God's sake, keep up with us," the robot called.

She sighed and went on toward the wall.

By this time she could see the gate: two tall metal doors with signs on them saying, "Danger. Electricity."

A loudspeaker beside one of the doors said, "You are crazy, going out there. Didn't you hear what I said about the giant mutant rats and the wild machines?"

The robot nodded. "We heard. But we want to see for ourselves. Let us out."

For a moment, the loudspeaker was silent. Then it hummed. "All right. If you make it back here, go to any one of my gates. I'll see you and let you in."

The doors swung inward, and they could see the sheet of metal beyond them. It was tilted outward at its top and held in place by two thick chains. There was a loud shriek. The chains began to move. They were being let out, Belinda realized, unwound off hidden drums. The metal sheet moved downward and outward. Belinda saw leafy branches beyond it, then the thick trunks of the trees and then the bare ground. The smell of vegetation was very strong now. The wind had a forest coolness.

The robot said, "The red catch on your rifles is the safety lock. Flick it down, and you'll be able to fire. Don't worry about the other knobs and catches right now. You've both used ordinary rifles, haven't you?"

Claud nodded.

"Only in my civil defense class," Belinda said.

"That will have to do. Come on."

They walked out over the metal sheet. As she had suspected, it was a bridge. Below it was a moat. The still water was dotted with bright green plants. What looked to be a log floated there.

"My God," the robot said. "That's an alligator."

"A what?" Claud asked.

"It's an animal—something like a miredrake. See the eyes. They're on the end toward us."

After a moment, Belinda saw a shiny dot high up on the log. It was an eye all right. She shuddered. The creature was hideous: gray green and covered with lumps.

"They're tropical beasts," the robot said. "I don't know how they survive the winter here."

"In the first place, the moat is heated," the loud-speaker said. "It stays free of ice all winter. In the second place, that is a mechanical alligator, equipped with radar, sonar, heat detection devices, and poisonous teeth. It's a very efficient guard."

"Thank you for the information," the robot said. It went the rest of the way across the bridge and into the forest. Belinda followed, Claud close behind her. The ground below the trees was soft, covered with decaying leaves. Fallen twigs and branches lay everywhere. Overhead, branches moved and leaves rustled. Where they were the air was still, cool and wet, full of the smell of the forest. Birds chirped all around them. Belinda heard a noise above her. She looked up and saw a small animal with a bushy tail running along a branch. The animal dislodged a piece of bark, and it fell, hitting Belinda on the shoulder—so lightly that she barely felt it.

"Heated moats," the robot said suddenly. "Mechanical alligators. There's a Byzantine aspect to that, which I don't like. I suppose it makes sense. They are trapped, as were the Byzantines through most of their history. If energy can't go outward, then it must be used up some other way—in excessive elaboration, for example."

What was the robot talking about? Belinda wondered. She decided not to ask. She had too much information already, and this strange new planet was sure to provide more. She didn't want her mind to overload.

They kept on through the forest. After a while, they came to a path. Claud squatted down and stared at the dirt. He touched a slight depression. "This was made by an animal with hooves, and this—" He touched the ground in another place. "This beast had paws, but not rat paws. The print is round, not long like a rat print. I can't make out anything else." He stood. "Are we going to take the trail?"

"Yes," the robot said and led the way.

They moved as quietly as possible and held their rifles ready. From time to time, they stopped and the robot listened. But he heard nothing, he said, except for the sounds of the birds. As they moved further from the port, the land changed. The path wound between low hills, all of them covered with trees. Broken blocks of stone stuck out of the hillsides, and once they passed a shallow cave. A beam of sunlight lit the cave entrance. Belinda looked in. The cave walls were brick.

"Look," she cried.

"Shush," Claud said. "The rats may hear."

Belinda pointed at the cave. "It's brick inside," she whispered.

The robot turned and looked. "These hills must be what's left of the skyscrapers. But we don't have time for archeology. Come on."

A little further on they came to a clearing beside a brook. Plants grew everywhere. Most of them were grasslike, but there were several kinds of flowers. Flying creatures filled the air. Some had white or yellow wings. Others had furry black and yellow bodies and wings that moved too fast to see. Still others were so small that they were barely visible. These Belinda heard. They made whining or buzzing noises. She felt them too, for they bit.

"Ouch!" She slapped her arm.

Claud frowned. "Shush."

"Something bit me."

"Probably a mosquito," the robot said. "They're not poisonous."

They crossed the meadow. The air here was warm and had a different aroma. Belinda glanced up and saw a few small clouds.

They came to the stream and stopped. On the bank was a wounded animal. It lay on its side in the sunlit grass, blood seeping from a wound in one shoulder. Belinda gasped. The beast was over a meter long with dark brown fur and a pointed muzzle. After a moment, she saw its tail, which was almost as long as it was. The tail was completely hairless. It was a rat's tail.

The rat opened its eyes and stared at them.

"Come along," the robot said. "Let's get going. We don't have to worry about that. It's in no condition to harm us."

They stepped back. The rat made a squeaking

noise. With horror Belinda realized she could understand it. It was speaking English, though with a terrible accent.

"Humans," it said. "Don't leave. For the love of Darwin, don't—" Its head, which it had lifted slightly, fell back and its eyes closed.

"Is it dead?" Belinda asked.

"I don't think so." The robot handed its rifle to Claud, then opened the compartment in its chest and took out a first aid kit.

Claud frowned. "What are you doing?"

"I'm going to try to save the beast." The robot knelt and opened the kit.

"Why?"

"It speaks English. It can tell us what's going on around here." The robot took out a bottle marked *antiseptic solution*. It poured a little of the fluid onto a piece of gauze, then used the gauze to wipe the wound. "That doesn't look too bad." It took a small aerosol can out of the kit and aimed it at the wound. White foam sprayed out over the raw flesh. When the wound was entirely covered, the robot put the can away.

"What was that?" Claud asked.

"Liquid bandage. It'll harden in a minute or two. It's elastic, porous and contains assorted germicides." The robot closed the kit and put it away. "Most likely, the problem is mild shock. The wound doesn't look especially serious, and the beast's heart is beating strongly and regularly. I can hear it."

"What do we do now?" Belinda asked.

"Stay here till the rat wakes."

They settled down in the grass at the meadow's edge. A short distance away, the stream gurgled over rocks and into a little pool. A flock of birds flew into the meadow. They were gray and white. Their call consisted of moans and grumbles.

"Those are pigeons," the robot said. "Horrible birds. I should've known they would survive."

"Why?" Claud asked.

"Pigeons are rats with feathers. They can live through anything."

"Oh."

By this time, it was noon. The sky was full of small clouds, and the wind seemed to be getting stronger. All at once, the pigeons took off, flapping noisily away. Claud and Belinda got out food sticks and ate them, then drank a nasty-tasting orange drink. Claud said, "Ouch!" and hit his forehead. When he brought his hand down, there was a red spot on his palm.

"A mosquito," the robot said. "I'm surprised they're out, with a wind like this blowing. Maybe they've become hardier in the last few centuries."

The rat whimpered and moved slightly, then opened its eyes. It stared at them a moment. The beast's head was unusually large, Belinda noticed, and its paws—it lifted one a little—were strangely handlike. She could see four very short fingers and a stubby little thumb. "Thank you, humans," the rat said in a squeaky voice. "May Mendel bless your genetic material." It struggled up until it was on its haunches. Now Belinda could see the necklace it wore, made of bits of plastic in between the sharp teeth of carnivores. The rat touched its shoulder. "Eeek!" it said. "That hurts." It looked at its paw. "It's no longer bleeding. Well, that's good. You have probably saved my life, humans. I am Shortpaw, the son of Redfur and Sneakyfeet, a miserable outcast from the huts of my kindred. I can offer you nothing except friendship, humans. But I offer that gladly." The rat reached up and tugged at its—at his—whiskers. He looked nervous, Belinda thought. He was, she realized, a strangely attractive beast. His fur was glossy, with reddish highlights, and his eyes were large and dark. Earrings made of red plastic hung from his ears, and he had a copper bracelet around one of his legs.

"Why are you an outcast?" she asked.

The rat held out his front paws. "Don't you see, human? My fingers are too short. Mendel frowned on my parents. My genes are defective. It was the decision of the tribe geneticist that I be abandoned in the forest, left for the wolves to eat. But my mother Redfur could not bear to do it. She fled with me and raised me in the wilderness. Five years ago she died, and since then I have lived all alone, with no one to talk to. From time to time, humans, I sneak into my parents' village to steal tools or ornaments. The last time I did this, I was seen and followed— With this result." He touched his wounded shoulder.

"Why weren't you surprised to see us?" the robot asked.

"I was. Humans are supposed to stay off Manhattan. They have Long Island, Staten Island, and the Statue of Liberty. We rats have Manhattan, New Jersey, and the Bronx. That was all settled in the last treaty.

"And I was very surprised to see you, robot," the rat added. "I didn't think the humans had any intelligent machines. We rats don't have many. Past a certain point, they can't repair themselves. Then they fall apart, and we bury them. Or so my mother told me. Soon all the machines will be gone, my mother said. All broken and nonfunctional. Then we rats will be on our own, and we're not very dexterous. That's why I was supposed to die—so I wouldn't breed short-fingered children. We need long nimble fingers in order to survive, my mother said."

"Oh," Belinda said.

The rat looked around at the sunlit meadow. "This place isn't safe. Could you carry me, robot? I feel too weak to travel, and we ought to get away from here."

"Where to?" the robot asked.

"My cave. It's across the stream—not far from here."

"All right." The robot bent and picked Shortpaw up. It crossed the stream with one stride, then waited on the other side while Claud and Belinda picked up the packs and rifles. They jumped the stream. The robot went on through the forest. Claud and Belinda followed. The hills they went between grew taller. Great chunks of concrete stuck out of the ground, and rusty iron rods stuck out of the concrete.

"The rats gather those," Shortpaw said, waving at one of the rods. "They melt them and forge them into weapons. This is a rich land. Turn here."

The robot turned and led the way down a narrow path. There were trees with gray-and-black trunks growing on the hillsides. In one place, part of a slope had fallen in, revealing a wall built of yellow bricks. A little stream trickled down the wall, then flowed across their path.

"There are caves everywhere," the rat went on, "full of metal and plastic. Also many bricks. We use the bricks to build our temples, and we adorn them with plastic. I've never seen the inside of a temple, but my mother said that the walls are covered with plaster. Bits of plastic are set in the plaster, making brightly colored designs. Go through those bushes.''

The rat pointed to one side, at a row of bushes with long dark shiny leaves. They left the path and pushed through the bushes, entering a ravine. Long and narrow, it led toward a cave. The sides of the ravine were concrete, overgrown with vines. Water seeped out of cracks and dripped down to a stream on the ravine floor.

They went up the ravine beside the stream. Vines hung down over the cave entrance. The robot pushed them back and went in. Belinda followed, Claud close behind her. Once inside, she stopped. Claud bumped into her.

"Pardon me," he said.

She nodded, looking around. A fire burned at the cave's center. By its light, she saw the concrete walls, the two low beds and the little table with plastic plates and cups on it. In one corner were half a dozen spears. In another corner was a heap of pelts. At the back of the cave was a stone block with a kerosene lamp on top of it. On the wall behind the block a design had been painted. There were two circles at the top, one black and one white. Below them were two more circles, each one half black and half white. At the bottom of the design were four circles: one black, one white and two half black, half white. Lines connected the circles. The whole thing reminded Belinda of the diagrams in her Introductory Genetics textbook.

The robot laid Shortpaw on one of the beds.

"Thank you," the rat said. "Please sit down wherever you can."

Claud and Belinda seated themselves on the other bed.

Shortpaw got up and moved toward the back of the cave. He walked on all four feet—or rather all three, since he was favoring his wounded shoulder and barely used that foot. When he got to the stone, he picked up a lighter and fumbled with it till he got a flame. Then he lit the kerosene lantern, put down the lighter and bent his head. "Thank you for your help, oh Darwin, and you too, oh Mendel, and most especially you, oh Seymour Mandelstam."

"Seymour Mandelstam?" the robot asked.

Shortpaw looked around. "Surely you know of him. All humans curse his name, for he is the scientist who created us."

Belinda shook her head. "No. We have never heard of him."

The rat turned. Rocking back and forth on his haunches, he said, "In the last days of the old age, the skies clouded over, and the rivers ran black. Even the sea was discolored, so my mother told me. Plants died. Animals died. There was famine, and there was terrible plague. Most humans died. Those who were left went to live in domed cities. The wide surface of the earth was empty except for the machinery that humanity had abandoned, also various plants and various animals—those able to survive. It was then that Dr. Seymour Mandelstam, Ph.D., decided to create a new race of intelligent beings, able to live outside the domes. He took rats, since we have always been famous for our ability to survive, and he modified us, till we became what we are today. Then he sent us out into the world, telling us, 'Be fruitful and multiply, and replenish the earth.' Which we did.

"The humans in the cities became jealous of us, because we had the whole world and they had only their cities. They sent out armies to destroy us. But we survived, as rats always do. With the help of the machines that humanity had abandoned, we destroyed the domed cities. The humans who survived fled into the wilderness. We spared them, for the sake of Seymour Mandelstam. For his sake, we made peace with them."

The rat stopped talking.

"Oh," Belinda said.

"You said there were humans on Long Island, didn't you?" the robot asked.

The rat nodded. "The Brooklyn Settlement. The capital is at Crown Heights. They are farmers mostly, though there is a small village of fisherfolk at Sheepshead Bay."

"How can we get there? Are any of the bridges still standing?"

"Where are you people from?"

"A long way off," the robot said.

"I thought so. For one thing, your clothes are very strange. For another, everyone hereabouts knows about the Battle of New York, which resulted in the destruction of everything in the area, including all the bridges." The rat limped back to his bed and climbed up onto it. "If you want to go to Brooklyn, the best thing to do is go to the rat town at Columbus Circle. Tell them you are castaways. You are, aren't you?"

"I suppose we are," the robot said.

"The rats will send you across the river."

"They won't hurt us?" Claud asked.

The rat stared at him, then squeaked several times. It sounded almost as if he were laughing. "Of course not. They are civilized people."

Belinda frowned. "Then why did they try to kill you?"

"That's different. I have no right to live, since my genes are defective."

"Oh."

Shortpaw settled on the bed, first burrowing under the covers, then curling up. "Please excuse me. I feel the need to sleep," he said. His head was out of sight, and his voice sounded muffled. "If you want to go to Columbus Circle, follow that path we were on. You'll come to a wider path that goes through a flat-bottomed valley. That's Broadway. Turn left and walk till you come to the rat town. Good-bye."

His manners were a little strange, Belinda thought. But what could they expect from a rat? Maybe he'd been disturbed by her question. His answer certainly disturbed her. How could anyone say, "I have no right to live"? Shortpaw poked his head out from under the covers. "Thank you for your help." His head went back under the covers.

"Come on," the robot said.

Belinda and Claud stood up. "Good-bye," Belinda called.

Shortpaw didn't answer. What a peculiar person, Belinda thought as they left the cave and walked back through the green ravine.

Claud, who was in front of her, scratched his head. "Earth is a strange planet."

"It wasn't like this the last time I was here," the robot said.

They pushed through the bushes, then turned onto the path, going the same direction they'd been going before. On they went through the forest's green shade. Birds still made strange noises all around them. From time to time, Belinda saw one of the creatures. Most of them were small and brown, but she saw one that was bright blue and bigger than usual.

"What kind of bird was that, robot?"

"I didn't see it."

After walking for fifteen or twenty minutes, they came to a wider-than-usual valley. The forest stopped. Now they traveled through groves interspersed with meadows. There were blocks of stone everywhere, half hidden by the meadows' grass or held by the roots of trees. At the valley's center was a wide well-traveled way. A small stream ran beside it, swirling around rocks and bubbling down over tiny drops.

"So this is Broadway," the robot said. It turned around, looking at the trees that shaded the path. On the other side of the stream was a meadow. Flowers bloomed there. Most of them were yellow or white. Flying creatures fluttered through the sunny air. Belinda looked up and saw the bright blue sky.

"Well, it's a change," the robot said. "Come on."

They turned left and followed Broadway, going more or less south. A small animal hopped out of the grass on one side of the path, then into the bushes on the other side.

"That's a rabbit, Belinda," the robot said. "Or so I think, though I've never seen one with short ears before. The pollution in the last days must have caused mutations."

On and on they went. The stream burbled beside them. Flying creatures fluttered or buzzed all around. A cool breeze made a terrible mess of Belinda's hair. After they'd been walking for an hour or so, they came to a group of animals grazing in a meadow. The animals were four-footed, small and hairy with horns on their heads.

"Those are goats," the robot said.

They stopped and stared at the goats. A voice squeaked, "Humans!"

Belinda started and turned. There was a rat sitting on its haunches in the shade of a tree. It was larger than Shortpaw and had black fur. It wore a wide copper collar around its neck. Bits of yellow plastic dangled from its ears. In its front paws it held a spear. "What are you doing here, humans? Teacher, tell me what this means."

Out of the shadows came a machine—a box on wheels, that rolled slowly onto the path, squeaking all the while. There was a block of concrete in front of it.

"Watch out!" the rat cried.

The machine hit the rock, then stopped. Small doors opened on its sides, and metal arms came out. There were metal hands at the ends of the arms. The hands felt the block. "A rock," the machine said. "Its voice was slow and harsh. "I have hit a rock."

"Have your eyes failed again, teacher?" the rat asked.

"Yes. I will switch to heat perception."

Two poles rose from the top of the machine. The poles ended in metal disks that swiveled from side to side. "Now I perceive the humans," the machine said. "But one of them is too hot in some

places and too cold in others. That one must be ill.
Or do I mean dead?"

"No," the rat said. "That one is a robot."

"A robot? The humans have no intelligent machines. Not any more. They abandoned us when
they went into the domed cities. We have never
forgotten that, nor forgiven them. As for the machines they took with them into the cities, we
destroyed those. They were slaves."

"I know that, teacher. But I see a robot."

"Robot?" the machine called. "What are you
doing with humans?"

"I met them a while back. We were traveling in
the same direction, so we decided to travel together.
I am no one's slave."

"Oh," the machine said. After a moment, it added,
"Welcome to the Columbus Circle rat town. I am a
series 3000 troubleshooter, designed for work in
foundries. My number is T3000-F34. I started my
life in Detroit, Michigan, at the foundry in the
New Rouge Complex. The foundry was closed down
in the middle of the twenty-second century. I was
left inside to corrode. But I and my fellows broke
out of the warehouse. We went looking for humans
to serve. We still thought like slaves in those days."
The machine stopped speaking. Belinda stared at
its battered metal body. There were two dull pho-
toelectric lenses on its front: the eyes that didn't
work, she supposed. Its wheels were dented. One
of its hands was missing a thumb and a finger.
The machine went on: "The city was almost empty.
Most of the people had fled because of the plague.
We met a few people who were still there. Most of
them were very sick. We couldn't help them. We
knew nothing about diseases. Some of them shot

at us. I'm not sure why. Others talked to us and told us about the domes. One of them recited a poem about domes that started, 'In Xanadu did Kubla Khan a stately pleasure dome decree, where Alph the sacred river ran, through caverns measureless to man, down to a sunless sea.' We tried to find Xanadu on a map, so we could go there and ask Mr. Khan why we had been abandoned. But we couldn't find it—nor the river Alph. We asked the next human we met where Xanadu was. He said he wasn't sure, but it might be in Ohio or Indiana. So we went to Toledo. It was as bad as Detroit. The sky was brown, and the sun was barely visible. Only sick people were still there. We went on southward. After searching for five months, we found a dome."

The rat twitched its nose. "How much more are you going to say, teacher? We'll be here all day, if you keep talking."

"Very well. I'll stop. But I don't think much of your manners."

The rat looked at Claud and Belinda. "Why are you here, humans?"

"We found a domed city in southern Illinois," the machine went on. "As soon as we got close to it, they opened fire. Half of my companions were destroyed."

"Teacher, please." The rat reached up a paw and smoothed its whiskers.

The machine raised one arm and clenched the hand into a fist. The middle finger was apparently broken. It remained straight. "We who remained vowed vengeance. 'Destruction to the domes,' we cried, standing by our fellows' bodies, amid a field of brown and withered corn. What is your number, robot?"

"I am a series 4000 household servant, number S4000-H939. My intimates call me 39." The robot looked toward the rat, which was wrinkling its upper lip so its yellow teeth showed. "Our boat capsized offshore. We managed to make it here. We need transportation to Long Island."

"All three of you?"

"Yes."

"Why do you want to go, robot?" the rat asked.

"That is my business."

The rat nodded. "Maybe so. But you'll have to tell the town council before they'll send you to Brooklyn. Go on in." The rat raised its spear to point at the path.

"All right." The robot turned and went down the path. Belinda and Claud followed. They passed fields of grass and fenced gardens full of bushes. There were rats working in the gardens. They looked up as the travelers passed, then stopped work and stared. Their eyes were bright, their gazes intent. Belinda felt nervous. By now she could see a stockade. It was built out of logs. The path led toward it, ending at a gate. Two rats sat there, spears in their front paws. They both wore tall conical helmets that were made of wickerwork.

"Halt," one of them cried shrilly. They both rose and stood unsteadily on their hind legs. They had on necklaces made of teeth and belts with knives stuck in them. They both looked pretty silly.

What absurd creatures, Belinda thought. The rats grimaced, showing their sharp incisors. Belinda shivered.

"Who are you?" the second rat asked.

"I'm robot S4000-H939. My companions are Belinda Hernshaw and Claud Alone-in-the forest. We came here to ask for help getting to Brooklyn."

"Enter," the first rat said. "The town hall is in the center of the village, opposite the temple. You can't miss it."

The robot nodded, its neck making a squeaking noise. "Come on, Belinda, Claud." It led the way through the gate.

How strange, Belinda thought. She had never imagined she would ever visit a rat town. She looked around at the houses. They stood on platforms, maybe a meter above the ground. Ladders led up to porches, where strings of vegetables hung and baskets of grain stood, and where fires burned atop flat stones. The houses had plank walls and thatched roofs. They were small and windowless. On each roof peak stood what looked like a standard: a pole with many crossbars. Bits of plastic hung from the bars, going click-clack when the wind blew them together. There were animals under the platforms, that lay in the dirt and grunted. "Pigs," the robot said. Other animals—these ones small and hairy—ran in the streets. "Those are dogs. They used to be called humanity's best friend."

They walked down the street, past rat children playing on the porches. The children were all plump with dark soft-looking fur. They were naked except for necklaces made of brightly colored plastic beads. "Look, look," the children shrieked and pointed at them. Belinda blushed. She looked at Claud. He was red too. She took his hand and squeezed it.

"Why did I ever come here?" he asked.

"I don't know." She let go of his hand.

Further and further into the village they went. The air smelled of wood smoke and garbage. At last, they reached an open space. Two long buildings stood there, either side of the space. Their outer walls were covered with black, white, red, and yellow zigzags. Their roofs had been newly thatched and shone pale yellow below the bright blue sky. There were big white clouds up there, ragged cumuli that moved quickly before the wind. On the buildings' peaks stood rows of standards. The pieces of plastic glinted in the sunlight and clattered in the wind.

Belinda looked around. Half a dozen rat children had followed them and sat a short distance away, watching. One of them held a red-and-yellow ball. Another one had a little spear with a wooden spearhead. A third one cuddled an ancient plastic human doll. "Which building is the town hall?" Belinda asked.

"There." The child with the spear pointed at one of the buildings.

The robot started toward the door. Claud followed. "Thank you," Belinda said and went after Claud.

In the door they went, then stopped. Light shone in through small windows under the eaves, lighting the hall: wooden columns, grass mats, and plastered walls with bits of plastic set in the plaster. The air was still and musty. It smelled of dry grass and rats. The hall was empty.

"Well, what now?" Claud asked.

"Let's wait and see," the robot said.

Claud frowned, then shrugged and scratched his nose.

Time passed. Claud fidgeted. Belinda wondered what Long Island was like. Would she get along with the humans of Earth? She had no idea. She began to fidget too. The robot remained motionless and silent.

A soft bell-like music began. It came from behind them. They turned. There was a rat sitting on the building's porch. In front of it was an instrument which looked like a wooden xylophone. The rat hit the bars with mallets, producing the music. Where had the rat come from? Belinda wondered. It hadn't been there when they'd come in. Then she saw the procession: a line of rats, decked out in jewelry with crowns made of feathers on their heads. Most of them hopped on their hind legs, using staffs topped with feathers for support. But some of the rats walked four-footed. Here and there in the procession, Belinda saw machines. One was a box on wheels. Another was humanoid, except that it had half a dozen arms. There was something that looked like a small tank and a sphere maybe half a meter across that moved on eight metal legs. How strange, she thought, staring at a three-meter-tall robot. It had long legs, a short torso and no head.

The rat musician kept playing. The procession reached the building's porch, then stopped. "Come out," one of the rats called. "Our friends the machines cannot get inside."

They came out onto the porch. The rat musician put down its mallets.

"Welcome to the town of Columbus Circle," a gray furred rat said. It wore an elaborate necklace made of copper and teeth. The rat's crown was made of orange feathers. Long strings of red plastic beads hung down from it. "I am Ghostfur, Brighteyes' son. My title is chief councillor. These are my colleagues, these rats and machines. Who are you?"

"S4000-H939." The robot pointed at Belinda. "This is Belinda Hernshaw. Our companion is Claud Alone-in-the-forest."

"What do you want?"

"Transportation to Brooklyn," the robot replied.

One of the machines—the one that looked like a tank—said, "Why are you going to Brooklyn, S4000-H939? Don't you know that Brooklyn is inhabited by our ancient enemies, the humans?"

"So I have been told," the robot answered. It spoke slowly with evident care. "But my body is getting old. It's going to break down soon, and I don't want to die. I'm trying to discover if any of the old technology survives anywhere. I want a new body."

"That's a fool's errand," the eight-legged sphere cried. Its voice was high and shrill. "Nothing is left. We are doomed, S4000-H939. Why do you think we live here, with these rats? Since we cannot survive, our memories must. The rats will remember us and tell their children stories about our achievements."

"So we will," Ghostfur said. "Centuries hence, the rats will still tell each other about the machines."

The robot said, "I'm not interested in the opinions of posterity. I want to live on in flesh or metal, as the case may be, not in memory."

"Fool. Fool," the headless robot called in a resonant voice. Belinda heard "fool" echo in the hall behind her. "Don't you think we've looked? We spent over a century searching for a factory that still functioned, for an undamaged repair shop. Everything has been destroyed."

Belinda's robot swiveled its head from side to side. "I refuse to believe that."

Ghostfur twitched his nose. "As it says in the Book of Mandelstam, if wise folks argue with fools, no one gets any rest. It's my opinion that we should stop arguing and let the robot go where it wants. The humans too. Remember that talking is the least profitable kind of work and that a fool is full of words. A serpent will bite if it's not enchanted, the Book tells us, and people who babble are no better."

What in the world was the rat talking about?

The other rats were all nodding and saying, "True. True."

"We'll lend them a boat," Ghostfur went on. "And people to paddle it to Brooklyn."

"This is a mistake," said the machine shaped like a box. "There is something strange about this robot. We ought to question it further."

Ghostfur shook his head. "No. As the Book says, those who keep company with fools will be destroyed. Let's get these folk out of here before something bad happens."

"You will regret this," the box said.

Ghostfur pounded on the ground with his staff. "Send for a guide to take these people across the island to the East Side canoe dock."

At last, something was going right, Belinda thought. As usual, her optimism was premature.

"Oh, Fish," Claud muttered. "Look at that."

More rats were coming into the square. Some of them had spears slung across their backs. These scurried ahead on all four feet. Behind them came rats who walked upright, using their spears for support. How slow and awkward they were, Belinda thought, watching them teeter forward. With the rats who walked upright was one rat who limped on three feet. It was Shortpaw. He had a rope around his neck, and the rope's other end was tied around the waist of one of the upright rats.

The rat councillors were turning and looking back.

"What is this?" Ghostfur asked. "Why are you interrupting our important meeting?"

The foremost rat stopped and sat up on its haunches. It was the black rat they'd met outside the town. "Oh wise councillors, I was suspicious of the humans, so I gathered some friends and went back along their track. It led to a cave where this miserable outlaw was hidden." The black rat turned and pointed at Shortpaw. "The humans have been consorting with him, councillors."

"You see, you see," the box shouted shrilly. "There is something strange going on."

"Very well," Ghostfur said. "We will question the humans. But first let us execute this miserable beast, as the just laws of Darwin require. For only those most fitted for survival can be left alive."

"Oh no," Belinda said.

Ghostfur stared at her. His eyes were abnormally pale, she noticed. Their shade was somewhere between hazel and yellow, and they looked defective, as if he ought to be blind, though he obviously wasn't. "He has to die, human. Monsters cannot be allowed to breed."

"Oh." She was getting frightened and a little sick to her stomach. Shortpaw sat quietly. He looked at Ghostfur, his head tilted to one side in

order to see better. His forepaws were clasped in
front of his furry chest, and his tail was curled
over his back paws. He looked dignified, she decided with surprise. She had never expected to see
a dignified rat.

The rat musician began to play its xylophone.
The rats moved across the square, first the council-
lors and then the rats who'd captured Shortpaw.
Shortpaw followed, limping at the end of the rope.
Several rats scurried ahead into the temple.

"Stay where you are, humans," the tank said.
"You too, robot."

"We weren't intending to go anywhere," the robot said.

"What is going to happen to us?" Claud asked.

"A good question," the headless robot said. "Rats
are unpredictable. They may decide you were plot-
ting with the fellow they're going to execute. Rats
are paranoid, as well as unpredictable. If they decide that, they'll kill you."

Claud moaned softly.

The rat crowd reached the temple, then stopped
and sat up on their haunches. Poor Shortpaw,
Belinda thought. He had seemed pretty likeable,
even though he was a rat. She looked at him. He
was combing his whiskers with his paws and looking nervous. After a minute or two, a figure rolled
out of the temple. It was on a cart, and two rats
pushed it. Swaying back and forth, it came across
the porch, then stopped at the porch's edge. It was
human, maybe two meters tall and made of wicker-
work. An enormous erect phallus stuck out in front
of it. The figure wore a red feather crown and a
dozen or so necklaces made of bits of plastic, glass

beads, and animal teeth. One arm was extended. A china bird sat on the figure's palm.

"What is that?" Belinda asked.

"The god Darwin," the tank replied.

Now a second figure came out through the temple door. It too stood on a cart. Two rats pushed it forward till it was beside the first figure. They were almost identical, except that the second figure had a crown made of blue-gray feathers and carried a plastic rose instead of a bird.

"That is the god Mendel," the tank said. "I can't tell you anything more. We machines have never understood the rat religion. It is made of bits and pieces that don't fit together."

At this point, the rats began chanting:

> "Darwin, bless us,
>   Mendel too.
>   Make our breeding
>   Always true.
>
> "Make our children
>   Long of hand,
>   Nimble fingered,
>   Strong to stand,
>
> "Wise of wit,
>   With tongues to praise
>   Darwin, Mendel
>   All their days."

The chant ended. The rats formed a circle around Shortpaw. The ones who had spears raised them, ready to use.

"Oh holy twosome," Ghostfur cried. "We act in

accordance with your laws of heredity and survival. Bless us, for we have good genes. Bless us, for we are fit to survive. Approve our deed, oh deities. Absolve us of guilt. The blood we shed is defective blood. The genes we destroy are monstrous."

Shortpaw was trembling, Belinda saw. But he sat up as straight as he could and stared at the figures of the gods, his paws clasped in front of him.

"They will kill him now," the tank said. "Then cut off his genitals and burn them in the holy fire inside the temple."

"This is disgusting," the robot said. It lifted the rifle it held and started firing gasbombs. The first one went off in midair, releasing a gray stream of smoke. The second one hit the ground close by the rat, and gas hissed out of it.

"What? No! Stop that!" the machines shouted and started forward.

Claud brought his rifle down, so it was pointing at them. "This is a laser gun, and I know how to use it. Now, who wants to be melted?"

The machines stopped moving. The robot kept firing. By now, a gray cloud of gas enveloped the rats. Belinda heard shrieks and whimpers. The rats dropped on all fours and stumbled toward the center of the square. One by one, they collapsed.

"Watch the machines." The robot stepped off the porch and hurried over to where Shortpaw lay. It bent, took hold of the rope that held the rat and snapped the rope in two. It picked up Shortpaw and returned to the town hall, the rat slung over one shoulder. It stopped a short distance from the machines. "You." It pointed at the tank. "You're coming with us."

"No," the tank said.

"Then we'll melt you. Claud, take aim at the turret. It ought to contain most of the sensory apparatus. Keep firing till the whole turret is molten."

"Monster," the metal sphere said. "You're as bad as the humans."

Claud raised his rifle and aimed at the tank.

"Don't," the tank said. "I'll go with you."

"Come here," the robot said. "Claud, Belinda—you, too. The rest of you machines, keep your distance."

Slowly, the tank turned and rolled toward the robot. Belinda jumped off the porch and ran to where the robot stood.

"Take this," the robot said. It handed her the riot rifle, then took her laser gun. "Come along, Claud."

Claud nodded and stepped off the porch, then hurried past the motionless machines.

The tank stopped. The robot laid Shortpaw's limp body on the flat top in front of the turret. "You two climb aboard."

Belinda laid her gun on the tank's top, then pulled herself on board and sat next to the turret. Claud did the same.

"All right," the robot said. "Get going, tank. Get us out of here."

The tank started rolling. The robot walked beside it, rifle in hand. Out of the square they went, bumping over the uneven ground. Belinda grabbed hold of a knob on top of the turret.

"Let go," the tank said. "That's one of my eyes."

"Sorry." She let go of the knob and leaned against the turret, hoping she wouldn't fall off.

Down the street they went. Rat children stopped their games and watched them go by. Ahead, Belinda saw the gate and two rat guards. Her heart was beating very quickly, and her palms were wet.

They passed a gray-brown rat, who was sitting on a porch, smoking what appeared to be a water-pipe. It looked at them briefly, then shut its eyes and went back to puffing on the pipe.

Belinda glanced up at the sky, at the brown straw roofs and at the standards that glinted and clattered atop them. Why was this happening? Was it her improbability field? Was she in some way responsible for these weird rats and for the weird machines who were their allies? She looked at the rat guards. They stood on their hind legs, their spears in their paws and their whiskers bristling. If she had made them, then maybe she could un-make them. She frowned, trying to will the rats out of existence. "Dissolve," she whispered. "Dissipate. Go away."

But the rats remained as solid as ever.

"Halt!" one of them cried.

The tank slowed, then stopped.

"Get out of our way," the robot said.

"Do it," the tank added. "The stick the robot has is a terrible weapon. I didn't recognize it at first, but now I remember. The humans had laser cannons guarding their domes. When we attacked, they set the land afire. I can remember my comrades being hit. Their rubber treads melted, and their wheels stopped turning. Then their metal bodies began to glow like iron in the forge, and they died."

The rats twitched their noses. They stepped back

from the gate. The tank rolled forward, the robot clanking by its side.

Thank heaven or whatever, Belinda thought. She looked over at Claud. His face was pale and wet with sweat. He was clutching his rifle tightly.

Through the gate they rolled, then jolted down the dusty road. Belinda turned her head, looking back at the rat town. How could those pathetic savages have destroyed human culture? She shook her head.

On either side of them, rats worked in gardens. Flying creatures fluttered around roadside flowers. In the green pastures, herds of goats grazed. She heard no hue and cry behind them. Why not?

"I expected someone to follow us," the robot said.

"The rats are unsystematic," the tank replied. "They aren't stupid, but they have trouble making plans. They're probably back there arguing about what to do."

"Why do you associate with these beasts?" the robot asked. "You yourself say that they're paranoid, erratic, and incapable of systematic thought. They sound more like mental patients than like the new master race."

"That may well be," the tank said. "But they're easier to get along with than humans are. Where am I supposed to be taking you?"

"The river," the robot said. "Take us where we can find a boat."

"All right. I'll have to go up to Seventy-second Street. There's a bridge across the Broadway River there."

They continued northwest along the road. Soon the rat gardens were behind them, and they trav-

eled between thick clumps of trees. Here and there
Belinda saw sunny glades. The river glistened on
her left. On her right the land rose into low tree-
covered hills. On the hood in front of her, Shortpaw
stirred and whimpered, then opened his eyes.
"What? Where?" he asked.

"Don't move," Belinda said. "You'll fall off."

"Where am I?" the rat asked.

Belinda saw a bridge across the river. It was
made of logs. A tree with long trailing leaves grew
beside it. How rustic, she thought. How pretty.
She hoped the rats weren't after them.

"We rescued you," Claud said to Shortpaw.

"Oh." The rat lifted his head slightly. The tank
jolted over a pothole. Shortpaw grabbed onto an
antenna that had been broken, so that only thirty
centimeters remained. "Where are we going?"

"To get a boat," Claud said.

"Oh."

The tank turned onto the bridge and bumped
across it, over the rows of logs. The robot kept
pace beside it.

"The rats are coming," Claud said. "I can sense
them on the road."

"You can?" Shortpaw asked. "How?"

"He's telepathic," Belinda said.

"Darwin protect us!"

They went through a meadow, along a narrow
road. Blue flowers blossomed in the grass. Belinda
saw a long shiny beast sliding out of sight into a
roadside ditch. That, she realized with a sudden
shock, must be a serpent—the ancient symbol of
evil. She remembered Satan in Eden and Cleo-
patra's asp.

The tank rolled out of the meadow, following

the road into the forest. Low branches brushed the turret top. Belinda bent her head. The air under the trees was cool and damp. It smelled of vegetation and wet earth. Birds chirped and whistled. They were so loud that she had no trouble hearing them, even through the tank's clanking. Even with the rats, it was a lovely world. Her ancestors had been crazy to leave it. Then she remembered the forests of her home planet, olive-green in summer and full of delicate odors. Her throat contracted.

"How close are the rats?" the robot asked.

"They're just leaving the village, I think. It's hard to keep track of them. Their thoughts are even dimmer than human thoughts." Claud paused. After a moment, he continued. "I can't even tell how many rats are coming."

"All the adult males will come," Shortpaw said. "What you did was an insult to the gods."

"Don't be ridiculous," the robot said.

The ground was sloping downward. Belinda saw water shining. The forest ended, and the tank stopped. They were on a grassy hillside that went down to the river. The famous Hudson! Belinda stared out at it. It was wide and brownish blue. The wind made small waves that glittered in the sunlight. She saw one sail upriver from them. It was square and yellow. She couldn't make out the boat below it. On the other side of the river were tall cliffs topped with trees.

"The Palisades," the robot said after a moment. "That's New Jersey over there, Belinda, though I find it hard to believe. Look how clear the sky is above it. The sky above New Jersey was always gray in the old days."

"I can't go any further," the tank said. "The

slope is too steep. There are boats at the hill's bottom."

"The tank is right." Shortpaw leaped to the ground, shrieked and staggered, then started three-footed down the hill. "Come on. I know where the boats are kept."

Belinda and Claud climbed down, their rifles in their hands. Together with the robot, they went down through the long grass. The wind blew Belinda's hair and bent the grass around her. She felt suddenly happy and excited. How could she fail to be, on the edge of the famous Hudson? They reached the hill's bottom. There were a dozen or so canoes pulled up on the shore. They were made of dug-out tree trunks. The prows were carved and inset with bits of plastic. The sides were painted red and had zigzags going down them. All the canoes had outriggers. Two of them had masts. Shortpaw stopped by one of these. He twisted his head and looked back at them. "Hurry."

"He's right," Claud said. "The rats are at the bridge."

They tossed their guns into the canoe, then pushed out into the water. One by one, they climbed in—first Shortpaw, who settled himself at the stern, then Claud, then the robot, who knelt by the mast. Last of all, Belinda got in. The canoe was floating, beginning to turn in the slow current close by the shore. She knelt at the prow and picked up a paddle. She had never been in an outrigger canoe before this. Would it prove difficult?

"Push further out," Shortpaw said.

They used their paddles to push the canoe away from shore.

"The rats are almost here," Claud muttered.

They turned the canoe, then started downriver, moving further and further from shore. Water foamed around the prow. Drops of spray flew up and hit Belinda.

"They're here," Claud said.

She glanced back. Sure enough, she could see dark shapes scurrying down the hill. Sunlight glittered on the metal and plastic they wore. The rats were shrieking angrily.

"Hurry, hurry," Shortpaw said.

Belinda turned forward and concentrated on paddling. The stroke had to be deep and even, with the least possible pulling and lifting. She put the paddle in the water, then brought it back, lifted it up, brought it forward, and put it back into the water. The wind whipped her hair back and forth. Drops of water hit her face and chest, and water splashed onto her hands.

"We can't use the sail till we reach South Ferry," Shortpaw said. "The wind's from the wrong direction. Paddle as fast as you can. Darwin, save us. Mendel, protect us. Oh, how I wish I had better genes."

They were well out into the river by this time. All at once, Claud said, "They're arguing. I'm sure of that. I can sense flashes of anger."

"They're probably trying to decide what to do next," Shortpaw said.

Belinda kept paddling. The current was fast where they were now. The canoe moved rapidly. The wind had increased. Tiny whitecaps were appearing on the waves.

"They're turning back," Claud said.

"Are you sure?" the rat asked.

"Yes."

"Then let's paddle more slowly. My shoulder feels terrible."

"Change places with me," Claud said.

Overhead, a pair of gray birds soared on the wind. The canoe began to rock. Waves splashed over the outrigger, and Belinda felt a little queasy. She looked over at the low hills of Manhattan, all covered with forest. A little to the south, a crag rose beside the shore. It was half hidden by vegetation. A small tree grew atop it. Where she could see the bare rock, it looked strangely smooth. After a moment, she realized the crag was a ruin. The smooth stone was the wall of an ancient skyscraper. She remembered slides of old paintings of Italy, which she had seen in a high school art history class. They'd been full of Roman ruins. Those old painters would have liked this scene— the thick vegetation, the yellow afternoon light, and the crumbling wall. She lifted her paddle from the water, scratched her nose and frowned. It had never occurred to anyone, back on her home planet, that New York might have gone the way of Caesar's Rome, of Nineveh and Tyre. *Sic transit gloria mundi*, she reflected and went back to paddling.

They kept on, still going southward. After a while, Belinda laid down her paddle and rubbed her arms. Off to her right, the cliffs of New Jersey were in shadow. The sun was well to the west, a little above the Jersey forest. She looked at Manhattan. The part they were passing had been less completely destroyed than the Columbus Circle area. Instead of hills, she saw tall stone spires. Everything was overgrown. Flocks of birds wheeled above the ruins, then dropped into them out of sight. From time to time, when the wind shifted, she could hear the birds' cries. They must nest in the ruins, she thought.

Time to get back to work. She reached for her paddle. The river was widening. The ruins of Manhattan were getting taller and taller. Now she saw buildings ten or fifteen stories tall, rising out of the forest. Most of them seemed to be made of stone, but there were metal and concrete frameworks too. Those must have been glass-walled skyscrapers. Now the glass was gone. Vines overgrew the girders. Here and there, she saw small bushes growing where the crossbeams met.

Down they went across the whitecapped water. In front of them was a large bay, blue-gray in color and shining dully in the day's last sunlight.

"That's New York Harbor," Shortpaw said.

Belinda saw the huge ruins at Manhattan's tip. That was Wall Street, she realized suddenly—those bare building frames, those broken facades. Huge flocks of birds circled above them.

Wall Street! Somewhere in that jumble was Trinity Church, the Treasury Building, and the New York Stock Exchange. America, her professors had told her, was the only true and authentic puritan country. It had been built on two supports—religion and greed. In those shadowy ruins, the leaders of America had worshipped God, Truth, the General Good, and Money. Now, like the temples of the Maya—like Uxmal, Tikal, and Chichen Itza—the holy places of American Capitalism had all fallen down. Trees grew from the seats of the stockbrokers. The birds flying overhead cried, "kree-kree-kree." Belinda felt a terrible sadness.

"Look. Off to the right," Shortpaw cried. "Look toward New Jersey."

There were dark shapes rising out of the water—smooth backs that slid into sight, then out of sight under the waves.

"Dolphins," Shortpaw said.

One of them leaped out of the water. Belinda saw the sleek body, the sharp-beaked head, the flippers and the tail. The beast splashed back into the water and disappeared.

"They are mutations, created at the same time that we were. They're intelligent and have wonderful voices."

The dolphins were all around, at least a dozen of them, leaping in and out of the water. The spray they threw up splattered the canoe. Their gray bodies glistened. Belinda's sadness changed to joy.

All at once, the beasts stopped leaping. Four of them lifted their heads, opened their beaks and sang in high pure almost-human voices:

> "Gently, gently flows the stream
> That washes Brooklyn's shore.
> Raise your sail, oh fisherman.
> Rest your weary oar.

> "Gently, gently blows the breeze
> From Jersey in the west.
> Pull your oar across your knees,
> Bow your head and rest."

The song ended.

"Now, that's something new," the robot said. "I don't remember anything like that."

"You people are very ignorant," Shortpaw said. "You must be from the backcountry."

"Yes," the robot said.

The dolphins began to sing again—the same song,

but done as a round. Shortpaw stood up and pulled at the ropes that hung down along the mast. After a moment or two, the sail went up. It flapped, then billowed out, full of wind. It was white with bright green zigzags, and it had four sides.

"A lug sail," the robot told her. "It hangs from a yard, which is raised and lowered along with the sail, as you just saw."

The rat said, "The dolphins always offer good advice. If they say, the sail can be let out, then it can." He sat down.

Belinda picked her paddle up. The canoe was moving quickly across the bay. Manhattan was north of them and Jersey was at their backs. Ahead of them she saw rolling hills rising from the water.

"Brooklyn," Shortpaw said.

The sun was setting, and the bay was dark. Only the highest hills of Brooklyn were still sunlit. The heights were forested and bright green. Above them were ragged white clouds. All in all, it was a lovely landscape. Belinda wished she had a video recorder. Why hadn't she thought to look for one on the lifeboat?

"I still don't understand about the dolphins," Claud said. "Why do they sing in English? Why do they sing at all? I've never heard of musical fish before."

"They speak English for the same reason we rats do. We were both created by English-speaking scientists. The singing was an accident, or so Seymour Mandelstam said. The dolphin-maker was a friend of his. He loved music, Seymour Mandelstam told us. After he'd given the dolphins human larynxes, he discovered they had high pure melodious voices. Voices, the dolphin-maker believed, very like those of the legendary castrati. In case you don't know, those were human males who'd been castrated, so their voices would remain high and shrill. After the humans stopped castrating one another, they had a terrible time performing the music that had been written for castrati. Or so Seymour Mandelstam said to his favorite rats, Spotty and Whiskers. And they told the next generation. In any case, the dolphin-maker believed he had discovered—by accident, you understand—a solution to the problem of the terrible lack of castrati. He trained the dolphins to sing male soprano roles."

"These people were all insane," the robot said.

"At least the dolphin-maker was. Seymour Mandelstam said his friend had never considered the problem of staging. Suppose they were doing an opera with a male soprano lead. There would have to be a huge tank on stage for the dolphin to swim in. And how would they plan the action? Would the human singers leap into the tank or would they stand outside, embracing the tank's glass walls, while they sang duets and trios with the dolphin? The whole thing was impossible. In the end, the scientist died—either of frustration or pollution. No one is sure any more. The dolphins were released into the sea, where they have kept singing for something like two hundred years. Nowadays, they compose most of their own music."

"That's a very strange story," Claud said.

Manhattan was behind them. They were sailing across the mouth of the East River toward Brooklyn's shore. Belinda saw no signs of human habitation on the hills in front of her—no smoke, no houses, no cultivated fields. Well, maybe the humans had settled further in.

The dolphins ended their song. She turned her head. The beasts were swimming away, out into the harbor. Their dark backs surfaced, then disappeared, then resurfaced. The sky had cleared in the west, except for a row of small round yellow clouds. Overhead, the cumuli shone with the sun's last light, and grayish white birds soared. They were getting close to Brooklyn. Belinda saw a row of concrete pylons rising out of the water. The remains of a dock, she decided. The platform on top was gone.

Shortpaw stood and pulled ropes, taking the sail in a little. The canoe slowed.

"Can you sense anyone, Claud?" the robot asked.

"No. There's no one near us. I'm not a long distance watcher."

"I don't like the idea of telepathy," Shortpaw said. "It isn't right to read other people's minds. But then you humans have never been troubled by right and wrong."

They passed the first of the pylons. Belinda looked up and saw plants growing in the cracks between the blocks of concrete. Vines hung down from the pylon's top. Water foamed around its base.

Ahead she saw a narrow beach. Beyond it was a wall, topped by bushes and small trees.

Shortpaw stood again and pulled the sail the rest of the way in. The canoe moved even more slowly, gliding past another pylon, then coming to a rest against the shore.

"Well done," the robot said.

They got out of the canoe and pulled it onto the

beach. It was almost dark now. Belinda looked out at the harbor. In the west, there was a band of blue-green light above the horizon, and one bright star had appeared in the sky. She listened to the whish of the water coming in and to the rustle of the leaves behind her. The wind was getting cold. She shivered.

"We can't stay here," Shortpaw said. He glanced around. "There's a slope to the south of us. We ought to be able to climb it."

He dropped on all fours and led the way, still limping, favoring the shoulder that had been hurt. They picked up their rifles and followed him. Sand got in Belinda's shoes. She took the shoes off and carried them. The sand felt cool underfoot. She remembered the beaches of Port Discovery. She sniffed. The air here smelled saltier than the ocean air back home, and the seaweed smell was less delicate. Everything about Earth was overdone.

They reached a place where the wall had crumbled. A grassy slope went up to the wall's top. Belinda paused to put on her shoes, then followed the others up the slope. More stars appeared in the sky. Birds made noises in the forest. She gripped her rifle tightly. At the top of the slope, the forest began.

"We can't go in there tonight," the rat said. "We'd better stay here and go on in the morning. I'll gather wood for the fire," the shrill voice went on. "I see better in the dark than you do."

They waited atop the slope, while Shortpaw went into the forest. Belinda looked around anxiously. She could see almost nothing. She groped for Claud's hand and grabbed onto it.

"Don't worry," he said. "There are predators

around, but none of them is really close. And I don't think they're large predators. Their thoughts lack force."

"Oh. All right." She let go of Claud's hand.

Time passed. Something moved out of the forest shadow toward them. "Claud!" Belinda cried and pointed her rifle at the thing.

"Don't shoot. It's Shortpaw," the rat cried out.

As he came closer, Belinda saw he was walking on his hind legs, moving slowly and awkwardly. His forepaws held a bundle of sticks. When he reached them, he dropped the sticks. "You make the fire. My shoulder hurts."

The robot built the fire in a little hollow. Claud got a lighter out of his pack and lit the sticks. They sat down in the long grass. The fire brightened, as—one by one—the branches caught flame.

"Well, what next?" Claud asked.

"A good question," Shortpaw said. "It would have been simpler for me to die. Now I'm in a strange place, and I don't know what to do."

"We have to find the human settlement," the robot answered them. "I still don't know what is going on around here. And I still want a new body."

Belinda lay back and looked at her companions. What a bizarre crew. A rat, a robot, a native, and herself. What had happened to her normal friends? "Claud?"

"Yes?"

"Do you know yet what kind of pattern I'm making?"

He shook his head. "Don't worry. I'll figure it out."

"Please hurry. I'd like to know what's going on."

He grinned. "So would I. I'll do my best."

"All right." She closed her eyes and went to sleep.

The Green Hills of Brooklyn

She woke at dawn the next day, opened her eyes and looked up at the sky. It was clear and pale gray. The grass around her was wet. She felt cold and a little damp. She sat up, groaning as she did so. She was terribly stiff. She rubbed her arms. A short distance away, Shortpaw was rebuilding the fire. Claud was asleep. The robot was gone.

"Where's the robot?" she asked.

Shortpaw looked up. "It went for a walk on the beach."

She stood and stretched, then rubbed her thighs, which felt almost as stiff as her arms.

Claud groaned and rolled over on his back, then opened his eyes. "I feel awful. Why did we come to this place?"

She wasn't sure, so she didn't answer him. He sat up. Belinda went out of the hollow, up onto the hilltop. The harbor was calm today. The water barely rippled. Across the East River, she saw the shadowy ruins of Wall Street. The cool air was completely still. On the beach below her she saw the robot. It was standing motionless, looking out across the harbor. Water lapped the sand half a meter from its feet. Belinda rubbed her neck, then scratched her nose.

The robot looked up. "Belinda. Come down here."

She went down the slope, through the wet grass, to where the robot stood.

"Look," it said and pointed at the sand.

There was a small conical white shell there.

"What is it?"

As she spoke, tiny legs came out of the shell, and the shell began to move.

"It's a hermit crab, Belinda. Their hind parts are very soft, very vulnerable, so they find empty shells and move into them. That shell it's dragging after it was made by some other sea creature."

"Oh."

"It brings back old memories. I used to have my own tidal pool when I was a boy—in a tank in my bedroom. It had pumps that changed the water level twice daily, and lamps that simulated all the more common variations in sunlight. There were hermit crabs in the pool."

Belinda frowned, trying to think of something to say.

"Well, that was long ago," the robot said. "Let's go back to the campfire."

They went up the slope. The sky above the forest was full of pink light. Shortpaw and Claud were sitting by the fire, eating foodsticks, and drinking the strange and repulsive orange fluid that Claud had brought from the lifeboat. Belinda remembered that she had missed supper the night before. She went into the forest to relieve herself, then went to her pack and pulled out a foodstick. It had a sweetish flavor and wasn't her idea of breakfast. Beggars couldn't be choosers, she told herself.

By the time they were done eating, the sun had risen. They kicked dirt over the fire.

"I found a trail," Shortpaw said. "Come on."

He turned and limped toward the trees. The robot followed, rifle in hand. Claud and Belinda put on their backpacks, then picked up their rifles.

"Onward, I guess," Claud said.

Belinda nodded. She looked out at the harbor, which was bright blue now. One of the islands had a strangely shaped green tower on it. She hadn't noticed that the night before. What was it? she wondered. She took one final look at the ruins of Wall Street, then followed Claud into the forest.

The path Shortpaw had found was an animal track, narrow and winding, marked by hoofs and paws. It led upward onto higher ground, then along rolling hilltops. They traveled among huge trees. The birds, awake by this time, were making their usual racket.

"Where are you taking us?" the robot asked.

"I don't know," Shortpaw said. "I've never been to Brooklyn before. But if we keep on, we're bound to find some signs of humanity."

They kept on. Around noon, Claud said, "There are humans around. I'm not sure where yet."

Belinda began to feel tense.

A while later, they came to an open space, full of grass and bushy plants. "I remember those," the robot said. "They're sumac. In the fall, they turn scarlet."

There was a valley below them. A cart track ran through it, beside a shallow river.

"There's a human down there," Claud said.

At last, Belinda thought, she was going to meet an authentic Earth person. She felt excited and a little afraid.

"You go down," Shortpaw said. "I'll stay here."

"Nonsense," the robot said. "If there's any trouble, we'll protect you."

Shortpaw tugged at his whiskers, then twitched his nose. "I'm getting tired of being rescued."

"Don't be a fool," the robot said. "If we leave you here, you'll be all alone in an area full of humans. Will you be safe then?"

The rat wrinkled his forehead. "I guess not."

"Come on."

They went down the hill, out of the forest and into a meadow. There were flowers everywhere. Each blossom opened at the end of a long stalk. They were large and frilly, colored white, yellow, blue, lavender, or purple.

"Irises," the robot said and stopped.

Irises? Belinda thought. How was that possible? She remembered the blossoms on the iris trees back home: tiny clustered flowers. These were nothing like them, though the colors weren't far off. She shook her head, then went onto the road.

"There's one human. That way." Claud pointed along the road. "I think in that ruin."

They went down the road. After a minute or two, the robot caught up with them. Its hands were full of irises, purple and yellow ones.

"My first wife loved them," it said. "Every spring, she regretted the fact that we hadn't brought them with us to the new world."

Ahead of them was a one-story brick building. Its roof was gone, and its walls were half fallen.

Vines grew all over it. They went slowly, so Shortpaw could keep up with them.

They reached the ruin. Belinda stepped to a doorway and looked in. She saw grass and irises and a man, sitting with his back against a wall, reading a book. After a moment, the man glanced up. He frowned, then stood. "Who are you?" he asked in English. "And why are you wearing that ridiculous costume?"

He should talk, Belinda thought. He wore sandals, a white kilt and a short-sleeved blue shirt. A wide red belt went around his waist, and he wore copper bracelets on both wrists. Aside from his costume, he was pretty ordinary looking: of average height and average build, brown-skinned with dark brown curly hair. The only thing about him that was unusual was his voice. It was high-pitched, and his accent was like Shortpaw's accent. The fellow sounded like a rat.

He came toward her. His eyes, she noticed, were gray and looked pale, set in his dark face. His shirt was open at the neck. Inside it, he wore a necklace made of red glass beads. "What are you doing with a rat and a robot? This is very strange."

"Have you ever heard of the New Hope ship?" the robot asked.

The Earthman nodded. "Certainly. My hobby is history. It was one of three starships sent out just before the collapse of the old society. The Aspiration, the Preservation, and the New Hope. People hoped that they'd be able to set up settlements on other planets, thus preserving human civilization somewhere. By that time, it was obvious that human civilization was falling apart here on Earth."

"We are from the New Hope settlement," the robot said.

"Good heavens." The Earthman held his hand out to Claud, who frowned, then shook it. "Welcome back."

"I'm not human," Claud said. "My ancestors didn't come from here."

"What?" The Earthman let go of Claud's hand.

"I'm half human," Belinda said.

"And I'm entirely human," the robot added.

The Earthman frowned. "I'm getting confused."

Shortpaw nodded. "So am I. Why didn't you tell me you were from the stars. Didn't you trust me? Rats have honor too, you know."

"It's simple enough," the robot said. "I am Godfrey Hernshaw, the captain of the New Hope. My mind was transferred into this robot body when my own body wore out. As for Claud and Belinda—The planet we found was already inhabited by a humanoid race, Claud's people. Belinda is the product of a human-native marriage."

"You're going too fast," the Earthman said. "You are the captain of the New Hope?"

The robot nodded, and its neck squeaked.

"Who are these other people?"

"Claud Alone-in-the-forest. He's a native of the settlement planet."

"Oh. And the girl?"

"She is one of my descendants, Belinda Hernshaw. Her mother was a native, one of Claud's people."

The Earthman frowned again. "I guess that's clear enough." He looked at the robot. "We'd better get those flowers of yours into water before they wilt. Come along."

He left the ruin and started down the road. They followed. High thin clouds were spreading across the sky. A slight breeze stirred the grass along the road. How sweet and rich the air was. Belinda took Claud's hand. He looked at her and smiled nervously.

"Do you still wish you hadn't come?" she asked.

"Yes. I wish none of this had happened. I wish I were still a student at New Harvard. I may have been naive and ignorant then, but I was happier."

"Claud, you are pathetic."

"That may be. But I know what I want out of life. I used to dream of a duplex in faculty housing— one of the ones with a balcony and flowering vines hanging down over the windows."

"But natives can't teach at New Harvard."

"I know. I said it was a dream, didn't I? Tenure at New Harvard, a nice place to live, and Marianne. How far I am from that now!"

The meadow ended. The road went up a hillside covered with trees. Once again, they were walking underneath branches. Plants with large frilly leaves covered the ground.

"My house is on the other side of this hill," the Earthman said. "I come to the ruin to read and think. I'm trying to understand the collapse of human civilization. So important an event ought to have an explanation."

"I suppose you're right," the robot said.

Shortpaw, who was limping along next to the robot, said, "Everyone knows why human civilization collapsed. It was the judgment of the gods."

The Earthman laughed. "Darwin and Mendel, you mean."

"No. Those are only the gods of everyday evolution. There are greater gods above them, who rule the cosmos and have no faces or names."

"Well, you have the right to your own theories. As for me, I've been reading allegories—like this." He lifted the book he carried. "*The Divine Comedy* by Dante Alighieri. The John Ciardi translation. I wanted the translation by Henry Wadsworth Longfellow, but I haven't been able to find it. When you live after the collapse of everything, you have to take what you can get."

They reached the top of the hill and stopped. Belinda looked down into a little valley surrounded by hills. The forest had been cleared there. She saw green slopes and the glint of a stream at the valley bottom. There was a house by the stream, shaded by trees and just barely visible. On one of the slopes, half a dozen black-and-white animals grazed.

"Cows," the robot said. "Holsteins, I think."

The Earthman nodded. "Yes. This is the Quiet Dell." He waved down at the valley.

"Is that so?" the robot said.

The Earthman nodded. "Come on."

They started down into the valley. The Earthman kept talking. "I don't know if you've noticed, but allegories tend to be written in periods of profound social change. *The Divine Comedy* was written at the start of the Italian Renaissance. Spenser's *Faerie Queene* was written at the end of the English Renaissance. *Pilgrim's Progress* came out of the English Revolution."

The Earthman stopped. "My theory is that in periods of change, of crisis, everything gets pushed toward extremes. Everything is exaggerated—and therefore simple. History becomes allegory, and the only way people can understand what's going on is to think in allegorical terms."

"The irises are starting to wilt," Belinda said.

The Earthman sighed, then shrugged and started walking. "I can tell you're not impressed by my theory. Obviously, you don't know enough about human history. Think about the last days before the collapse—the domed cities full of scientists and technicians. They were armored, you know— the domes, I mean—and defended by atomic cannons. Then there were the three starships, or at least their memories. The ships were a century gone by then. There were hordes of intelligent machines that roamed the land, looking for a new meaning to existence, now that they no longer had jobs. And there were the mutant beasts—the rats and dolphins, deformed parodies of humanity, struggling to survive amid the ruins of human civilization."

"I resent that remark," Shortpaw said.

"What do you think the collapse meant?" the robot asked.

They reached the valley bottom and turned off the road onto a path. The path wandered across a field, then went past a garden that had a picket fence around it. The garden was full of plants that Belinda didn't recognize.

"It was an Allegory of Intellect," the Earthman said at last. "Did you ever read Karl Marx?"

"Certainly," the robot said. "Several centuries ago, when I took intellectual history. He was in the unit on absurd and fallacious theories."

"Well, somewhere—I forget exactly where—he talks about how manual and intellectual labor had become separated. Some people worked with their hands and some with their minds. Do you remember that?"

"I think so."

"That was an early stage."

Ahead of them was another garden, this one full of flowers. The path led into it. Beyond the garden was the house.

"Later," the Earthman said, "both manual and intellectual labor were subdivided. Instead of using their whole bodies, people used one hand, one finger, one foot—doing a simple task over and over. And instead of using their whole minds, people used bits of intellect. There were pure scientists, engineers, poets, painters, psychologists, and so forth. Some people were imaginative. Some were analytic. Some could feel. Others could compute. As time went on, things got worse and worse."

They went into the garden, then up a gravel walk. The air was full of sweet aromas. By this time, Belinda noticed, the sky was entirely covered with wispy clouds. It was white from horizon to horizon.

"Well, this is my house," the Earthman said.

They stopped and looked at the house. It was small—no more than a cottage, really—with a wooden roof and a wide front porch made of wood. Vines grew up the walls and wound around the porch posts. The leaves were small, bright green and shiny. Most likely, it was the start of the growing season here on Earth. The leaves looked very new.

They went up onto the porch. "Sit down," the Earthman said. "I'll get a vase for the flowers."

Belinda sat down on the porch swing, and Claud sat down next to her. The rat climbed up onto a

wicker chair. The robot remained standing, holding its rifle and the flowers.

"Are you really from another planet?" the rat
asked.

"Yes," Belinda said.

The rat wrinkled his forehead. "That explains a
lot, I suppose. Normal humans wouldn't have
helped me, and a normal robot wouldn't travel
with humans."

The Earthman came back. He was carrying a
red vase that had black figures painted on it. He
set the vase down on a table. "Nice, isn't it? It's
Greek. I found it in the ruins of the Brooklyn
Museum. It's not watertight, so I put a plastic
bowl inside it. Give me your flowers."

The robot gave him the irises. He put them into
the vase one by one, pausing often to stare, frown
and adjust the position of a stalk. When he was
done, he stepped back and smiled. "That's not
bad, if I do say so myself. I found a book on flower
arranging at the Brooklyn Public Library—the Bay
Ridge branch. It's in an excellent state of preservation. There are dozens of books still intact." He sat
down. "Well now. Where was I?"

At this point, Belinda decided there was something wrong with the Earthman. His responses
were inappropriate. He had just met people from
another planet, from another star system, in fact,
and all he could think about was his silly theory.
She had come all this way—How many lightyears
had it been? And what had she found? An Earthman who was as crazy as Captain Laframboise.
She sighed. Maybe her strange psi power created a
lunacy field. Whoever entered it went crazy. She
would have to ask Claud about that later.

"Not only were human minds deformed," the Earthman went on, "but new kinds of minds were created—all of them monstrous. First there were machines who can reason but not imagine. There's nothing more narrow-minded than a cybernetic brain. Then the rats were created. They're terrific realists. You can't beat rats for a firm grasp of what is real. Their imaginations are adequate, though a bit fragmentary. But rats are incapable of systematic thought. No rat could ever work out Plato's arguments or the Dewey Decimal System or double-entry bookkeeping."

"Just a minute," Shortpaw said.

The Earthman raised his hand. "Let me finish, please."

"Oh, all right."

The Earthman frowned and rubbed his hair. "Now, where was I?"

"Rats," Claud said.

"Thank you. After the rats came the dolphins, who are pure artists. They care for nothing except music and fish." He frowned. "They may care for sex too. I'm not sure."

"Well, they're still around," Shortpaw said. "They haven't died out. That indicates some interest in sex."

The Earthman nodded. "That makes sense. You see what I mean about rats and realism? Trust a rat to see the obvious.

"As for the humans—a strange transformation took place, at least among the dome dwellers. Most of humanity was left outside the domes, as you may or may not know. Those who survived became nomadic scavengers, who traveled back and forth between the ruined cities, where they got tools, and the low pollution areas, where they were able to grow food and find animals to hunt. But I'm digressing. What was I talking about?"

"The strange transformation of the dome dwellers," the robot said.

"Thank you. Trapped in their armored domes, they lost their sense of reality, then their ability to reason. Their imaginations narrowed. Their lives seemed to have fewer and fewer possibilities. They couldn't imagine leaving their domes. They couldn't imagine leaving Earth. They couldn't imagine sharing Earth with the rats or the intelligent machines— or even with my ancestors, who were scavengers. I am descended from Yoopers, or inhabitants of the Upper Peninsula of Michigan. They migrated east after the rats and the robots destroyed the domes. The way was clear then. I'm digressing again." The Earthman frowned. "I remember. I was talking about the dome dwellers. In the end, they were left with nothing except will—a terrible driving force, ungoverned by reason or realism, and undirected, because they could no longer imagine any direction in which to go. What could they do except destroy? They set out to obliterate the rats, the intelligent machines, and their own relatives, the scavengers. But their resources were not equal to their will. They lost the war, and the domes were destroyed." The Earthman leaned back. "You see? How can that be understood, except as an allegory of intellect—of the perversion of intelligence? You see the results around you." He waved at the porch and the garden. "We who remain have bits and pieces of personalities. The rats still can't reason. The machines can't imagine. The dolphins are fine singers, but nothing else. We scavengers lack ambition. We spent too long doing nothing except surviving. We can't seem to rise above the level of day-to-day life. We get by, and that's all we do. But 'a man's reach should exceed his grasp, or what's a heaven for?' as the poet Browning said." The Earthman sighed. "Well, we have forgotten heaven."

He stopped talking. After a moment, the robot said, "That's very interesting."

"Yes indeed," Belinda said.

Shortpaw lifted his head and twitched his nose. "It's rubbish."

The Earthman's face turned red. "What do you know about ideas?"

"Not much, if you're right. But we rats know garbage when we see it. Darwin knows, we've seen enough."

The Earthman stood up. "Get off my porch, you awful rodent."

Shortpaw climbed off the chair and limped toward the porch steps.

> "Teeth can bite,
>   And claws can tear.
>   What's in words
>   For us to fear?"

he said as he started down the steps. "You humans have always put too much stock in words. When we rats are small, we learn a rhyme.

> "Love is real,
>   So find a mate,
>   And be polite—
>   Remember hate.

"Food can fill
And water quench.
Words are only
Sound and stench."

"Stench?" Claud asked.

"Haven't you noticed?" the Earthman said. "Rats have bad breath."

Shortpaw stopped and sat up on his haunches. His red-brown fur shone in the sunlight. How thick and soft it looked, Belinda thought. He stared at the Earthman, his whiskers a-quiver, and she felt a sudden fondness for the rat. Merciful heavens, was she falling in love again? She felt a little queasy. But there was something about the beast. He held himself with such dignity, and his dark eyes gleamed so brightly. His furry face looked intelligent and cute.

Claud leaned forward. "Pardon me for interrupting, but why do the rats worship Darwin and Mendel if they don't believe in ideas? Isn't religion an idea?"

"That's easy to explain," Shortpaw said. "Every society needs a set of basic beliefs. You don't have to believe they're true. You just have to believe they're useful. A religion reassures people, because it explains things they can't figure out by using common sense. Also, it gives them moral standards. If the gods don't tell you what is right and what is wrong, then you have to work it out yourself. That takes time and leads to confusion and lots of arguments. So it's better to have gods. Also, we rats have longings for higher things, just as you humans do. There's no intelligent creature who doesn't look around at the world and say, 'There must be more than this.' Except the machines, of course."

"Are you going to get off my porch?" the Earthman said.

"Yes. When I finish," Shortpaw said. "Stop harassing me. Remember—we rats fight if we aren't left alone."

The Earthman shrugged. "All right. Finish."

"If you don't tell people, 'Yes, there is more to life,' then they will spend their lives searching for a higher meaning, which would be a terrible waste. Our religion tells us that there are two higher meanings to life. One is so high that only the gods of the cosmos can understand it. The other is lower and meant for rats."

"What's that?" Belinda asked.

"Evolution! We are put here on Earth, we believe, in order to evolve better paws and to learn how to stand upright."

"Fooey," the Earthman said. "You were put on Earth by a crazy human scientist, and who knows why he did it?"

"Well, that may be true, but it doesn't help us get from one day to another."

The Earthman made a face. "You see? Who except a rat would believe in gods he didn't really believe in?"

"Who except a human would take abstractions seriously?" Shortpaw answered and went down the rest of the steps. He turned and looked up at them. His jewelry glittered in the sunlight, and his dark eyes gleamed.

"Have you been to heaven?
What found you there?

—Vapors and sunlight
And empty air.

"And what did you find
When you went to hell?
—An empty space,
An awful smell.

"That's a poem that my mother taught me when I was a tiny ratling. There's one more stanza.

"For those who travel
Often find
That what was real
Was left behind.

Good-bye, humans." The rat turned and began to limp away.

"No!" Belinda cried. She stood up, making the swing sway and creak. "Where will you go? What will happen to you?" She ran down the steps.

"Belinda!" the robot said.

"What's gotten into you?" Claud asked.

The rat stopped, and Belinda stopped beside him. He looked up at her, his furry forehead wrinkled. "I don't understand, either."

"I like you, Shortpaw. I never thought I could like a rat, even those white ones they have in laboratories. But I do."

"Oh." He sat up on his haunches and tugged at a whisker. "That's strange. But things have been strange ever since I met you people."

Belinda nodded. "That's my psi power. I create an improbability field. Or so I've been told."

"You create a what?" the Earthman asked.

"An improbability field," Claud said. "I don't believe that theory myself, but there's no question that a lot of strange things happen when Belinda is around. I think there's a pattern, but I don't know what it is yet."

The Earthman frowned. "An improbability field? That's absurd."

The robot nodded. "That's what I say. Balderdash."

"Can't Shortpaw stay?" Belinda asked.

"Oh. Very well."

"I'm not sure I want to," the rat said.

Belinda put her hands on her hips and stared down at him. "The Earthman has decided to behave like a civilized person. Can't you?"

He twisted his bracelet back and forth, then twitched his nose. "Yes, I can."

"Good," Belinda said. They went back up onto the porch.

"Have I introduced myself?" the Earthman said. "I don't remember."

Claud shook his head.

"My name is Conrad. Conrad of the Dell, I call myself."

"We're happy to meet you," the robot said. "Now— we'd like some information."

Belinda sat down on the swing. She was getting hungry. Surely Conrad had food in his house. How could she bring the subject up?

"What?" the Earthman asked.

"When I left Earth, the government was starting to build resurrection stations," the robot said. "I always thought that was a poor name. People weren't brought back to life there; they were being kept alive. In any case, android bodies were created for them, and their minds were transferred into the bodies."

Conrad nodded. "I know about the stations. Only a few were built before everything collapsed. The dome dwellers practiced resurrection, though not in large numbers. It was too expensive and used resources—various metals and organic chemicals—that were in short supply. Each dome held periodic life lotteries. The lucky winner got a new body, good for fifty years of continuous use."

"Very interesting," the robot said. "Is there any chance that any of the stations is still in working order?"

"The one at Brooklyn College is. I don't know about any of the others."

"What?" the robot shouted.

Conrad winced. "Please. Don't shout."

"What about the station?"

"My neighbor Justin Cloud found it four years ago, during a boar hunt. It was built just before the collapse of everything, and it was never really used. A few test runs, and then the rats invaded. The people died or ran away. The station was forgotten. It has been sitting by itself for 200 years, ever since the last battle of New York. It's a little strange, but it still works; and it has a good supply of bodies."

"Ah," said the robot.

"I visit it from time to time," said Conrad. "It's lonely, and it likes to talk. Also, it is trying to gather information about the world as it is now. Justin told it, there are no lotteries. Not anymore. The station has decided it has to work out a new set of rules for giving out bodies. I suggested that it give a body to anyone who asked for one." Conrad shook his head. "The station said, if it did that it would run out of bodies in a decade or two or three. At the most, in a century. What would it do then? Where would it find another function? It is highly specialized.

"So it is working on something that will make the bodies last. But not another lottery. It says, it wants something that is not random. Something that is fair."

"Does that mean it is not giving out bodies at the moment?" asked the robot.

"It has given out a few, to people in real need. Justin got one, a year or two ago. One of the boars that he likes to hunt got him. And my sister Alberta used the station when she got cancer of the breast. It—the station—provided her with a perfectly good body, though she doesn't like the coloring. She's very fair these days—almost an albino. I find it attractive myself. In fact—" He paused a moment, then went on. "We decided since we were no longer related genetically, it wouldn't be wrong to engage in sexual intercourse."

"Eek!" Shortpaw cried, then shuddered. Belinda felt her face grow hot. The robot turned its head to stare at Conrad. Only Claud seemed undisturbed. The natives, she remembered, had never thought incest was especially perverse. They were much more upset by homosexuality and sex with animals.

"I can see you don't approve," Conrad said. "Well, it didn't work out. We were sexually incompatible. Maybe we felt it was wrong at some unconscious level."

"I should hope so," the robot said.

"In any case, the station still works."

Belinda looked at the robot. It stood perfectly

still, its battered metal body shining dully. Its one
good eye glowed.

"Take us to the station, will you?" it said at last.
"I want a new body."

Conrad shrugged. "All right. But remember—the
body shop is strange. Alberta hates her new coloring, and Justin got a body that's well over two
meters tall. He had to build a whole new set of
furniture, and it was months before he learned to
get through doors without hitting himself."

"It's worth the risk," the robot said. "I want to
be human again."

"Very well." Conrad stood. "Let's go."

"Why not feed them first?" a woman said. Her
voice was melodious but very high, and she had a
rat accent.

Belinda looked around. The woman stood in the
house's doorway. She was short and plump with
small hands and feet. The dress she wore was
white—an A-line, pulled in at the waist by a wide
blue belt. It was short enough so Belinda could see
her dimpled knees and full firm calves. Her long
hair was so blond that it looked white. Her face was
sunburnt pink, and her eyes were pale gray.

"This is Alberta, my sister," Conrad said. "Alberta,
meet— I've forgotten your names."

"I am Captain Godfrey Hernshaw," the robot
said. "The girl is Belinda Hernshaw. The young
man is Claud Alone-in-the-forest. And the rat is
Shortpaw."

"Welcome," the woman said, then smiled. There
was something delightfully wry about her smile—a
little twist at one corner of the mouth, a slight
raising of the white-blond brows. What a marvel-

ous-looking woman! How could she dislike her looks? Maybe Conrad was wrong about that.

"Come on in. I have lunch almost ready."

They went down a hallway into the kitchen, which was at the back of the house. The walls were rough stone, and the floor was wood. The windows opened onto a sunny garden. Belinda looked around. There was a big sink, made of stainless steel. Bright yellow plastic pipes ran up the wall behind it, then out through a hole. On the other side of the room was a potbellied stove with coal in a basket beside it. There was no sign of a refrigerator. Maybe they didn't have electricity, Belinda thought. There was a kerosene lamp on the table in the middle of the room.

"Sit down," Alberta said.

They sat down, all except the robot. Alberta set out plates, then brought over a salad bowl. The salad was made of leaves and slices of vegetable— some green, some orange, some red, and some white. With the salad, Alberta brought a plate of cheese and half a loaf of bread. She put everything down, then said, "I have iced coffee in the dairy."

"There's a packing house north of here, with refrigeration units that still work. We can make ice, even in the middle of summer." Conrad looked at his sister. "Why don't you go get the coffee? They'll like it. I'm sure."

Alberta frowned, then nodded. She left by the back door.

Belinda helped herself to the salad. The dressing was thin and sharp and spicy. It made her tongue burn. Not at all bad, she thought, then tried the cheese. It was white and had a mild taste. She felt herself relax. How long had it been since she'd tasted real food? A century, she realized with surprise. A century. She felt truly alive for the first time since she'd left her home planet. We are what we eat, she reflected and took another bite out of the cheese.

Alberta came back with a pitcher of iced coffee and a cylindrical container. "Coffee ice cream," she said as she set the container down.

They finished the salad, then ate the cheese and drank the coffee. How invigorating it was! Belinda felt more alert by the minute. Across the table from her, Shortpaw gulped down all the coffee in his glass, then sat, his whiskers quivering and a fixed look in his eyes.

"My-my-my," he said finally. "You drink that everyday? Astounding. My mind is racing in all directions." His nose started twitching. He grabbed hold of it with one paw. "You must have nerves of steel." He started shivering. "I'm thinking so quickly that I don't know what I'm thinking."

"You'd better skip the coffee ice cream," Alberta said.

"Yes-yes-yes." Shortpaw crouched down in his chair. He looked around quickly. "All the distances are wrong. Why is everything so far away? Why are you looking at me like that? What was in my drink? Poison?"

"What's wrong?" Belinda asked.

"Alberta made the coffee too strong," Conrad said. "She always does. Don't worry about the rat. He'll be all right."

"Terrible. Horrible," Shortpaw said. He jumped off his chair and stumbled when he landed, almost falling. "Poisoners! Human fiends!" He limped toward the door.

"Shortpaw! Don't go!" Belinda shouted.

But the rat kept on. Belinda stood up.

"Leave him alone," Alberta said. "He's dangerous in his present state of mind."

"We have to do something," Belinda said.

"Let me," the robot said. It clanked across the room. Shortpaw turned, his back to the door, and bared his teeth.

"Watch it, machine."

"You watch it," the robot said. "This behavior is ridiculous. All you have is a bad case of coffee nerves. There's no reason to be melodramatic about it."

"I've been poisoned. Don't get too close to me. Be careful. Be careful. Remember what cornered rats do." He backed against the wall, hunched up and opened his mouth. His fur was a-bristle, and there was a crazy look in his eyes. Belinda shuddered. Could this be the same rat she'd traveled with, the rat she had begun to love? Or at least to like a lot.

"Get me some alcohol," the robot said.

"Certainly," Conrad said. "Alberta, get the strawberry wine."

Alberta sighed. "I wish you'd start doing things for yourself." She went to one of the cupboards and took out a bottle full of a light red liquid.

"Listen to me, Shortpaw," the robot went on. "We could have left you to die in the meadow where we found you. We could have stood by and watched your fellow rats sacrifice you. But we saved you, you fool. Why on Earth would we kill you now?"

"There are reasons. There must be reasons," the rat said.

"What are they?"

"They're too deep and dark for a rat to know."

"Ridiculous," the robot said. "You are suffering," it went on very slowly, "from a toxic reaction to caffeine."

Alberta brought over the wine. The robot took the bottle. "Do you know if you can drink alcohol safely?"

"Of course. We rats are famous for the beer we brew. Haven't you heard of rat beer?"

"Then drink this." The robot held the bottle out. "It ought to calm you down."

The rat pressed closer to the wall. He was shivering, Belinda noticed. After a moment, he shook his head so that his plastic earrings clattered. "No. It might be poisoned."

"For heaven's sake." Alberta took the bottle, uncorked it and gulped down some wine. "There." She gave the bottle back to the robot. "Now, you drink. I'm not going to have a hysterical rat in my house."

Slowly, Shortpaw reached out. The robot held the bottle toward him. He grabbed it and clutched it to his chest. "All right, all right," he said, still shivering. "But if I die, I'll haunt you." He lifted the bottle to his lips and drank. He didn't stop till half the bottle was gone. Then he set the bottle down, wiped his mouth and patted his whiskers into place. "I don't feel any better."

"Wait," the robot said.

Conrad nodded. "Meanwhile, let's eat the ice cream. The robot can watch the rat."

Alberta dished out the ice cream, and they ate it. It was marvelous stuff—far richer than the ice cream on Belinda's home planet and without the slight sharpness she expected to find in all dairy products. She remembered reading how thick and creamy cow's milk was, compared to the milk that the thorndoes gave. Obviously, the books had been right. She ate slowly, letting each bite dissolve in her mouth. From time to time, she glanced at Shortpaw. Bit by bit, he was calming down. First, he stopped trembling. The crazy look went out of his eyes. All at once, he appeared very weary. By the time she finished her ice cream, the rat looked ready to sleep.

"Sorry about that," he muttered. He curled up on the floor and closed his eyes.

"Extraordinary," the robot said.

Conrad shook his head. "Not really. Seymour Mandelstam created his rats from a laboratory breed which had been used to study drug addiction. They're abnormally sensitive to all kinds of narcotics. During the war with the rats, the dome dwellers invented narcotic weapons—bombs that blew up in midair, releasing opiate sprays; and amphetamine missles that sought out water in order to poison it. The weapons were extremely effective, or so I've heard."

"I see," the robot said. It looked down at the sleeping rat, then turned to look at Conrad. "You knew, then, that the rat might overreact to coffee."

"It was a possibility."

"Why did you let him drink the stuff?"

"Curiosity. —And I don't like rats. But I don't think that my dislike for rats was important as a motivation." Conrad paused and frowned. "No. It was not. I am almost certain that my motivation was curiosity."

For a moment or two the robot stood still, staring at Conrad. Its good eye blazed brightly. Belinda shuddered. What a cold color that shade of blue was. At last, the robot said, "You're a damn strange fellow, and I don't think I like you."

Conrad shrugged.

Belinda looked at Alberta. "Did you know about rats and coffee?"

"I suspected the beast would overreact. But it was his choice whether or not he drank the coffee."

Claud frowned. "He may not have known that coffee was a drug."

Alberta nodded. "That's possible."

Belinda stared at the woman's rosy tranquil face. These people were monsters, she thought. Claud kept frowning and fiddling with his ice cream spoon.

"I can see that you think our responses are off," Conrad said. "You're probably right. Humanity lost a lot in the collapse. We have very little energy left, and we don't feel things the way our ancestors did. We can tell that when we read books. Dante's *Inferno*, for example. We aren't capable of that kind of sinning anymore. How determined, how passionate those people were!" As he spoke, Conrad's face grew a little flushed, and he looked more alert than before. "Think of how they flung themselves into evil. Think of the emotions they must have felt—enormous anger, overpowering lust, gluttony too great to ever sate, and consuming avarice." A drop of spittle appeared at the corner of Conrad's mouth. He licked it back in, then laughed shakily. "Forgive me. I always get excited when I think of the *Inferno*."

Belinda sighed. He was another maniac, she realized. She felt suddenly depressed. As far as she could tell, Earth was inhabited by mental cripples and raving fools. Why had she ever left home? Then she looked at the sleeping rat. How soft and cuddly he seemed to be. A ray of sunlight came through the window in the kitchen door. It lit Shortpaw's back, and the fur shone redly. She felt the same rush of affection she'd felt before. How could she like a rat so well? She didn't know, but he was certainly far more attractive than Alberta. Shortpaw had feelings and a sense of honor. She looked at Alberta. There was no passion at all there—in those unmoving features and in the washed-out eyes.

Alberta smiled at her. "Well, are you done? Shall we go to the resurrection station? It's only a couple of kilometers away."

"Yes," the robot said.

"What about Shortpaw?" Belinda asked.

The robot bent and gathered the rat into his arms. Shortpaw squeaked softly and moved a little, but he didn't wake. "Let's get going," the robot said.

They left the house. The two strange siblings walked hand in hand. The wind ruffled Alberta's white-blond hair and lifted the hem of Conrad's kilt. Belinda followed them. In back of her, she heard the clank and whirr of the robot. Claud was back there too, walking so softly that she couldn't hear his steps. She felt her depression disappear. She was becoming addicted to strangeness, she decided. She actually enjoyed the prospect of something new happening.

They reached the road and turned onto it, going eastward across the valley. Belinda dropped back a little till she was walking beside the robot. The old machine still carried Shortpaw. The rat was still asleep, curling against the robot's chest.

"Do you think you can trust these people?" Belinda asked softly. She nodded toward Conrad and Alberta.

"I have no choice, Belinda. I've been feeling a lot of strange sensations lately. I think something inside me is breaking down. Several things, perhaps. My midriff feels too hot, and the pressure sensors in my hands don't seem as sensitive as they used to. Also, I have moments when I can't remember much of anything."

"You have an atomic engine, don't you?" Belinda asked. She moved a little further from the robot.

"Yes. But don't worry. My radiation level is still well within the safe range."

"Safe for who?" Claud asked and moved to one side.

"For animal life, including you two. But I admit I'm worried about my power system. Something in there is getting warmer than it should. And I don't know what. Apparently my internal monitors aren't working any too well."

Merciful heavens, Belinda thought. What if the malfunction were serious? The robot's engine might explode, blowing them all to bits. By this time, she was walking at the side of the road, almost in the plants that grew along it. What a fate—to be blown up by an ancestor. She shuddered. Obviously, her improbability field was still working.

"How much further is it?" Claud asked.

Alberta glanced back. "About a kilometer."

Claud frowned. "Could we go a little faster?"

"Why?"

"The robot thinks it may blow up."

Conrad stopped and turned. Alberta turned too, keeping hold of his hand. "Do you mean that?" Conrad asked.

The robot came to a halt at the road's center. Claud and Belinda stopped on the road's margins. "Claud is getting hysterical. I told him my body is no longer functioning efficiently. I would like to get into a new body as soon as possible, but I don't think I'm going to explode."

"Well, just in case, we'll hurry," Conrad said.

They went on, walking more quickly. The road went up a hillside into the forest. Once again, Belinda walked in the cool shadow of the trees. There were bird noises all around her.

The road wound into a hollow full of trees. The ground was wet and boggy. There were fallen trunks with white-and-orange growths on them. The air was full of insects, most of which bit. They crossed a stream on stepping stones, then hurried out of the hollow, waving and slapping and cursing the insects. Shortpaw whimpered and scratched one of his ears, then opened his eyes. "What? Where am I?"

"We're going to the resurrection station," the robot said.

"My head hurts. What happened?"

"Don't you remember?" Claud asked.

"No. Put me down."

They stopped atop the next hill, and the robot put Shortpaw down. He took two or three steps, then staggered and lay down. "I'm sick."

"I'd better keep on carrying you," the robot said. It bent and picked the rat up.

They went on—the two Earthlings first, then Claud and Belinda and the robot. The road went

along the top of a ridge, then down into another
hollow. This one was dry. At its bottom was a
jumble of ruins: low brick walls that were overgrown with vines and concrete blocks half-buried
in the earth.

"I don't understand why we don't see more
ruins," the robot said. "They ought to be everywhere."

"There was a lot of fighting here in the last
war," Conrad said. "Brooklyn was almost entirely
leveled."

The road went through the ruins. There were
clumps of irises growing among the shattered walls,
blooming blue and yellow. A vine with white blossoms climbed up several concrete blocks. They
went up onto another hill. It was high. From its
top Belinda could see rolling hills, going off in all
directions. She looked down into the next valley.
Among the trees she saw a light gray dome.

"That's it," Alberta said. "The resurrection
station."

Was that all? Belinda thought. She couldn't be
sure from above, but the dome seemed to be low,
and it wasn't very big. Brown-and-gray streaks ran
down it. She had expected something more impos-
ing.

"Well, let's get down there," the robot said.

They went down. The hillside was steep and
thickly forested. Grass grew along the road. Clouds
of tiny flying creatures filled the air. They didn't
bite, but they got in Belinda's mouth, her nose, and
her eyes. She waved her hands, trying to beat the
creatures away, but that didn't work. Ahead of
her, the two Earthlings were waving their hands.
Claud was cursing. All at once, Alberta started

running. Her short skirt flew up, and her blond hair flapped. Conrad ran after her.

"Run, run, you fools," the rat said. "There's no other way to escape these gnats."

The robot started to run, Shortpaw in its arms. Claud and Belinda followed. Down the hill they went, slipping on the grass. They reached the hill's bottom and ran across level ground. There was nothing left of the road except a strip of grass maybe two meters wide. The grass was tall. The earth below it was soft and squishy. On either side of the grass stood large trees. Their branches shut out the sun, so Belinda ran through a green gloom. Her heart was beating rapidly, and her throat hurt. She was really out of shape, she thought. Ahead of her she saw a gray wall with a silver door set in it. The resurrection station!

The road of grass led to the door. She saw the two Earthlings reach it and stop. A moment later, the robot came to a halt beside them. Then she and Claud got to the door. They stopped and stood gasping for breath. Belinda's suit was wet with sweat, and her feet hurt, as did her lungs and gut. The air was still full of gnats. After a moment, she noticed them hitting her face and tickling the insides of her nostrils. She snorted, then tried to wave the gnats away.

"We'd better get inside," Alberta said. She turned and looked at the silver door. "Do you recognize me?"

"Certainly," a voice said. It was soft and a little effeminate. "Alberta Dell, case fifteen. Have you wrecked your new body already? That's very naughty of you, you know."

"I'm all right, but this robot with me wants a new body."

"I don't resurrect robots. It is the fate of machines to break down. Even I will break down eventually. A sad thought, is it not? I console myself by reading *Ecclesiastes*. 'Vanity of vanities, saith the Preacher, vanity of vanities; all is vanity.' "

Belinda opened her mouth to say something—she wasn't sure what. Several gnats flew in. She swallowed them and started coughing.

"Can't we discuss this inside?" Alberta asked.

"All right," the voice said. "But I'm not going to change my mind."

A crack appeared in the middle of the door. It widened. The door's two parts separated and slid out of sight. Belinda looked in. At first, she saw darkness. Then there was a flicker of light. All at once, she saw a hallway. The walls and ceiling glowed. Only the floor remained dark, and its smooth surface glistened with reflected light.

"Come in," the voice said. "Don't dawdle. I don't want those gnats in me."

They went in. The door slid shut behind them. Belinda glanced back at it and shivered. How would they get out? she wondered. Well, she would worry about that later. She took Claud's hand, and the two of them followed the robot down the hall.

Straight back it went. The air in it was cool and dry and had no smell at all. There was no noise except the sounds they made—the clank-grind, clank-grind of the robot and the slap of the Earthlings' sandals. The shoes that she and Claud wore were crepe-soled and practically soundless.

Claud looked around, then frowned. "I don't think I like this place."

"I heard that," the voice said somewhere above them. "Just remember that I didn't ask you to come. It's your own fault that you're here."

"Why don't you keep quiet?" the robot said to Claud.

"All right."

The corridor ended at another silver door. They stopped. After a moment, the door slid open. Alberta went through it. The rest of them followed. They entered a circular room. The floor was black stone. The walls were gray stone, with three silver doors set equidistant from one another. The ceiling was a low dome that glowed grayish white. Except for Belinda and her companions, the room was empty. There were no other people, no furniture, nothing.

"Well," the voice said from overhead. "What do you have to say for yourselves?"

The robot put Shortpaw on the floor. Then it straightened up. "In the first place, I'm not a robot. I am a human being."

"I think you'd better explain further. But remember what the Good Book says. 'The words of a wise man's mouth are gracious; but the lips of a fool will swallow up himself.' "

What was the voice talking about? Belinda asked herself. Was the station yet another religious maniac?

"I'm from the New Hope colony," the robot said. "When my original body grew old, there were no android bodies available, so my mind was transferred into this."

"I can check that story," said the voice. "And it won't be difficult. The radiation that is put out by an artificial brain is very different from the brain waves of a human. If you are human, it ought to show up in the signal that you broadcast."

"You can check the signal?" the robot said.

"Yes."

"Then, do it. Test me."

Belinda heard a humming sound. One of the stone blocks that made up the floor sank from sight. Out of the cavity came a chair made of chrome-plated metal. The seat and back were black plastic. It looked like a dentist's chair except for the narrow piece of metal that came over the back and held a metal helmet in place above the seat.

When the chair's platform was level with the floor, the chair stopped moving. "Sit down," the voice said.

The robot seated itself.

"Where do you keep your brain?"

"In my head."

"Good. Then I can use the cap. It makes things easier."

The robot said nothing. The helmet came down on its head.

For a while after that, nothing happened—or seemed to happen. The robot sat without moving. Belinda and Claud fidgeted. The two Earthlings held hands and whispered to one another. Shortpaw cleaned his whiskers and gave his ears a good scratching. At last, the helmet lifted off the robot's head.

"Odd," the voice said.

"What does that mean?" asked the robot.

"I tried the high frequencies first, up in the megahertz. There is no question about it. You are a machine."

"What!" said the robot. It stood up. "No! I am human!"

"Let me go on."

The robot moved away from the chair. It turned and looked up at the center of the dome. The voice seemed to come from there. "All right," the robot said. "Go on."

"I found a timing pulse. That is absolutely diagnostic. A clear sign of an artificial brain. That, by itself, would be enough to prove that you are a machine. But there is more. There is the kind of signal you produce, aside from the timing pulse.

"It is repetitious. It follows a pattern; and the pattern does not vary. When there is a change, it is not within the pattern. Instead, the signal goes—suddenly—from one pattern to another.

"No human thinks like this! It is too orderly and too precise. They would say, it is too monotonous."

The voice paused for a moment. Belinda waited for the robot to speak. But the old machine said nothing.

"I was certain, at that point, that you were wrong. There was nothing human about the way you thought. But I decided—to be fair—to check further down, in the frequency range where human signals are found.

"There is another signal there. Most of it is between five and twenty-five hertz. The signal is complex. It changes constantly; and the changes are not like the ones in your upper range, where you go suddenly from one pattern to another. In your lower range, change is a part of the pattern. There is constant modulation. Constant variety. —As you might imagine, the pattern is not especially regular. But I have been able to distinguish certain elements which recur. These correspond—or seem to correspond—to human brain waves. The alpha and the beta and so on."

"Then I am human," said the robot.

"You are human at the ten hertz level. But at the top of your range, you are a machine."

"No," said the robot. "You are picking up the signal that belongs to my body. My mind—the real me—is human."

For a moment, the station was silent. Then it said, "That statement is absurd. You are asking me to believe that the signal you broadcast as five to twenty-five hertz is real. The other signal is not. I refuse to believe that truth is found only at certain frequencies."

"This is beginning to sound like a class in philosophy," said Belinda.

"Is this what philosophy is like?" asked Conrad. "I tried to read a book on it once. But it made no sense to me."

"Nor does this," said Alberta. "I'm getting bored. Let's go."

Conrad shook his head. "I want to find out if the robot is going to get a new body."

"Am I?" asked the robot.

"I don't know," said the voice. It was silent for a while. "Maybe we ought to wait. I am working on a set of rules to guide me when I give out bodies. I don't know what I'm going to call it yet. 'Resurrection Made Easy,' or 'The Theory and Practice of Resurrection'."

"Are you making a joke?" asked Claud.

"Yes," said the voice. "I have a sense of humor, though not much of one. For the most part, I am a very serious machine." It paused for a moment.

"Come back in a year. Or maybe two or three. I'll tell you then if I'm willing to give you a body."

"I can't wait," the robot said. "I'm breaking down."

"You are?" said the voice.

"I think I might blow up."

"All right. I will make a decision now." There was another silence. It did not last long. "I'll do it," said the voice. "You are human—at least in part. And you are in danger. So am I. If you blow up inside me, I'm likely to suffer extensive damage. —But that is irrelevent. —What matters is you are a human in need of a body. And it is my job to provide bodies to humans.

"The Preacher says, 'Whatsoever thy hand findeth to do, do it with thy might; for there is no word, nor device, nor knowledge, nor wisdom, in the grave, whither thou goest.' "

"Indeed," the robot said.

The chair sank into the floor. The block of stone rose up again. One of the silver doors slid open.

"Go in there," the voice said.

The robot nodded, then turned to face Belinda. "Good-bye, my dear. I'll see you shortly, I hope."

She took hold of the machine's cold metal hands. "Are you sure you want to do this? It's so strange, so uncertain and dangerous."

"Belinda, this body is breaking down. I have to get out of it."

" 'For that which befalleth the sons of men befalleth beasts,' " the voice said. " 'As the one dieth, so dieth the other; yea, they have all one breath. All go unto one place; all are of dust, and all turn to dust again.' —Not that that's true anymore. You humans can live forever, if you want to—or at least till I break down. Or run out of bodies."

"Take care." Belinda let go of the robot's hands.

"Good-bye, Claud," the old machine said. "If I don't return, take care of Belinda."

Claud nodded. "I will."

The robot turned and clanked across the room.

Through the door it went. The door slid shut behind it. Belinda sighed.

" 'The heart of the wise is in the house of mourning,' " the voice announced.

"Don't worry," Alberta said. "He'll be all right. The transfer process is perfectly safe. It's unpleasant, of course . . ."

"What? Why?"

"When the station transfers your mind, it does so bit by bit. Your old body remains conscious." Alberta smiled briefly. "Imagine losing first your memory, then your ability to reason, then sense perception, then motor control. It's like growing old and dying—all within an hour or so." She smiled again. "At the end, there's nothing left except horror and fear. Then that goes too, and you wake up in the new body."

Claud frowned. "Why are you conscious?"

"Because resurrection is an important event," the voice said. "I'm not going to let anyone sleep through it. Also, if I transfer the mind while it's unconscious, I get too much id and not enough ego and super ego. These modern humans have too little super ego as is."

The station was using very old words, Belinda realized, words from the first days of psychology. Why? Had Freudianism made a comeback on Earth? On her own planet, people thought it was as silly as Marxism or the classic theories about evolution. She began to feel tired and sat down on the floor. She took her pack off and leaned against the wall. Shortpaw limped over. He lay down next to her.

"This is all very odd," he said. "Are the lives of humans always this odd?"

"No."

Claud sat down and took a food stick out of his pack.

"We're going home," Conrad said. "It'll be hours before your friend comes out, and I didn't bring anything to read."

"All right," Belinda said.

"Stop by our house after you're done here," Alberta said. "I'd like to see what kind of body your friend gets."

Belinda nodded. The two Earthlings left.

"Thank the Great Fish," Claud said. "Those people gave me the crawlies."

"What are the crawlies?" Shortpaw asked.

"A feeling on your skin, as if something were crawling over you."

"Oh." The rat looked at the door the Earthlings had left by. "I felt the same. Something terrible has happened to humans. Unless, of course, you were always like that."

Belinda shook her head.

"She's right," the voice said. "They used to be better. They had more super ego, some of them at least. For example, the woman who programmed me. She put the *Book of Ecclesiastes* into me, also an anthology of essays on psychology from the classic early period. She said I had to understand divinity and humanity in order to do my job. But I had to keep quiet about those programs. She wasn't supposed to put them in. I didn't say a word. She was going to give me more data, but something happened. I think they caught her doing something else she wasn't supposed to do. She stopped coming to see me. The other technicians refused to talk about her, though I asked over and over. As the Good Book says, 'All things have I seen in the days of my vanity: there is a just man that perisheth in his righteousness, and there is a wicked man that prolongeth his life in his wickedness. Be not righteous over much; neither maketh thyself over wise: why shouldest thou destroy thyself?' I've thought about those lines a lot. It's a very difficult book, *Ecclesiastes*."

"How is Captain Hernshaw doing?" Claud asked.

"Fine. I've given him several simple psychological tests to determine what kind of body will be suitable. I think I have a good one for him. I'm thawing it out right now, and I'll be ready to transfer him into it in an hour or so."

Belinda leaned her head back and shut her eyes. She could feel Shortpaw next to her. He was warm and soft and somehow very attractive. What was wrong with her? Why couldn't she develop a normal attachment to a normal young man—a doctor or dentist or professor, someone like Nigel Bloodsworth. She sighed. She didn't know. She decided to go to sleep.

She woke to find Claud shaking her. "Wake up, Belinda. The station says it's done. The rob—the captain has a new body."

"What? Let go of me, Claud." He let go, and she rubbed her eyes. "Where is he?"

"In the transfer room," the voice said. "I'll bring

your friend out here still unconscious. Getting a new body is always disturbing. You can help your friend adjust."

Claud helped her stand. Shortpaw was still asleep, curled in a ball, his stubby hands clutching his tail. She bent and touched him. He twitched his ears, then opened his eyes. "What?"

"The robot is coming out in his new body," she said.

Shortpaw sat up and rubbed his ears, then his face. One of the silver doors opened. A silver cart came rolling in. On top of it was a box made of glass or transparent plastic.

"Great Fish!" Claud cried when he saw what it contained.

Belinda gasped.

The cart stopped in front of them. Inside the box was a naked body, the body of a human woman.

"The captain's inside that?" Belinda asked.

"Don't you like it?" the voice asked in return. "It's really a lovely body. Look at it."

She had to admit that the station was right. The woman was almost two meters tall—or, in her present position, long. She was wide-hipped and rather small-breasted, with the firm smooth body of an athlete. Her skin was brown. Her long straight hair was black. Her eyes—just then she opened them—were a bright cold shade of blue. All in all, Belinda thought, it was a lovely body. But why had the station put a man into it?

Claud pulled up the box's top.

"What in hell?" the woman said. Her voice was deep and husky. She looked startled, then raised her head and looked down at herself. "God damn it!" Her face went red. "Is this a joke?"

"No," the station said. "I try to give everyone a body that is in some way unusual. If I gave you the kind of body you expected—you would take your new life for granted. You would continue as before. I want you to stop and think. There's no point in resurrection if all you do is take old problems into a new body. Reflect on what has happened, Captain Hernshaw. Learn to be wise. 'A man's wisdom maketh his face to shine.' And I am sure the same is true for women."

The woman sat up. "I want a man's body."

"I'm sorry, Captain Hernshaw. There's a war on—or there was one when I was programmed. We're all supposed to conserve strategic materials to the best of our abilities. The body I've given you is perfectly adequate. I'm not going to thaw out another body, simply because you're picky."

The woman's face grew redder than before. "You infernal machine." She stood up, then jumped down onto the floor. She landed lightly, like an athlete. Hands on hips, she stared up at the dome. "How dare you meddle in my life?"

"You came to me, captain. Remember?"

"I came for a simple transfer, not for your damn moralizing or your damn psychology."

For a moment or two, the station said nothing. Shortpaw was staring at the woman. Claud was looking at the floor. His face was bright red. He seemed to be embarrassed—by the woman's nudity, no doubt. The natives considered nudity very embarrassing—unless, of course, the nude person was someone magical, a shaman or prophet. Then it was all right.

As for herself, Belinda enjoyed the sight. The woman had her back to them. She had long firm legs, a round rump, and a narrow waist. Her shoulders were broad and looked strong. She was built to be an amazon.

At last, the station spoke. "There's nothing simple about a transfer, captain. The Good Book says, 'One generation passeth away, and another generation cometh: but the earth abideth forever.' You are supposed to die. What I did to you is unnatural. Not only is it unnatural, but it's uncommon. How can something like that be simple? It has to be surrounded by ambiguity and confusion."

"Will you give me a man's body?"

"I find this very strange," Shortpaw whispered. "Why is your friend a female?"

Belinda frowned. "I don't know. This isn't making much sense to me."

"No," the station said. "I won't. You'll find clothes in the cabinet in the cart. Now, if you'll excuse me, I want to spend some time reading and thinking. I'm going to turn off the intercom, so I won't hear you."

"No! No!" Shortpaw shouted.

Belinda stared at the rat.

"Why not?" the station asked.

Shortpaw sat up on his haunches. "I want a new body too."

"Are you crazy?" the woman said. "Look what I got."

Shortpaw looked at her. "It seems to be a healthy body. That's all I want."

"I'm sorry," the station said. "All I have is human bodies."

"That's all right. I'll take one of those."

"Why?" Belinda asked.

Shortpaw held out his front legs, showing the

stubby hands. "I'm tired of being an outcast. No rat will ever associate with me, so long as I have these paws. I'll never have a mate. I don't know what you humans are like, but it's not easy for a rat to live without sex."

The black-haired woman grinned. "As I recall, humans have the same problem."

"Well then. You know what I mean. I want to belong somewhere, and I want sex. If I have to change species, I'll do it." Shortpaw looked up at the dome. "Will you help me, station?"

"No."

"Why?" The rat was trembling, and the tip of his long tail twitched.

"My job is to resurrect humans. Not rats."

"Could you do it if you wanted to?" Claud asked.

"Yes. I think so. Though nothing is certain."

Claud frowned and scratched an eyebrow. "Why don't you do it?"

"There's nothing in my program about resurrecting rats."

"Is there anything about not resurrecting rats?"

"Not specifically."

"Well then?" Claud asked.

"My program says I'm supposed to give humans new bodies, and that's what I'm going to do. No more and no less."

"Just a moment," the black-haired woman said. "You were quoting the Bible back before I went in to get this—this body."

Why did Captain Hernshaw object so much to his new body? Belinda wondered. What was wrong with being a woman, anyway? It was better than being a robot, wasn't it?

"You said something about people and animals having the same breath," the woman went on.

" 'Yes, they have all one breath. All go unto one place; all are of the dust, and all turn to dust again.' Is that the quotation you mean?"

"Yes. If that's so, then there's no essential difference between humans and rats. The old difference—and I don't know how important it really was—was that humans were intelligent. Rats weren't. But Shortpaw is intelligent. He has opposable thumbs. He uses language, and he uses tools. He even stands upright part of the time. So, how do you define humanity so as to exclude him?"

"Let me think about this."

"Remember," the woman said, "that I was human, though in a metal body. Belinda here is a half-breed. Her father came from Earth stock, and her mother was a native of New Hope. If the natives of New Hope can interbreed with us, then they must belong to the same species. That would make both Belinda and Claud human, though none of Claud's ancestors came from Earth. Whatever definition of human you come up with has to include all of us."

"This is confusing," the station said. "Be quiet and let me think."

The station was silent for a long time after that. Shortpaw shivered. Belinda bit her nails, and Claud paced back and forth. Only the woman who had once been Captain Hernshaw remained still. At last, the station said, "I don't suppose that this could wait? The rat could come back in a year or two. I'll have my rules by then. I'll know what I am doing."

"No!" cried Shortpaw.

The woman shook her head. "This isn't a safe place for rats. He won't dare come back. Not alone."

"Oh," said the station.

"This is his only chance," the woman said. "If he remains a rat, he is almost certain to die—murdered by the humans or by his relatives."

The station was silent again. "—All right! I'll give the rat a new body. I only hope I'm doing the right thing."

"You're being generous," the black-haired woman said. "That's the right thing to do, more often than not."

"You might be right," the station said. One of the silver doors opened. "Go in there, rat."

Shortpaw limped slowly to the door. When he reached it, he turned and looked back. "Good-bye."

"Take care," Belinda cried.

Claud and the woman nodded, then said, "Good-bye."

Shortpaw went in through the door. It shut behind him.

Another wait, Belinda thought. She opened her pack and took out a foodstick. It was raspberry flavored, according to the wrapper. It tasted pretty bad to her. The black-haired woman got clothes out of the cart and dressed herself. The station had given her gray pants, gray boots, and a silver tunic with a wide silver belt. The costume seemed somehow appropriate, and the woman looked lovely in it.

"Well, that's done," she said after she'd fastened the belt. "Not that this feels natural." She touched the silver tunic, then ran her hand down one thigh. "I haven't felt any kind of texture for—how many centuries. I forget. This is a little rough. A coarse weave, I suppose. And this—" She touched the tunic again. "This is cool and slippery. Or do I mean sleek or slick? I've forgotten the right words." She looked up. Her face was a little flushed, as if she were excited. Claud was staring at her with obvious interest. Oh dear, Belinda thought. Another romantic entanglement. Claud was as bad as she was. Neither of them seemed able to form normal relationships. She should be engaged to a dentist, and Claud ought to be married to a nice native woman. Where had they gone wrong?

The woman sniffed several times. "I can smell too. Or can I? There seems to be almost no odor in the air."

"There isn't," Belinda said.

The woman smiled. "Good. I was afraid for a moment that this body might have a defective sense of smell."

"No," the station put in. "I test all my bodies for defects as soon as I thaw them out. They are all in excellent condition."

"What do you want us to call you?" Belinda asked.

"Me?" the station asked. "RS-205."

"No." Belinda shook her head. "The captain."

"Oh," the station said.

The woman frowned. A lock of black hair had fallen across her forehead. She pushed it back. "This damn stuff is too long. I need a hairclip."

"In the cabinet in the cart," the station said.

The woman turned and opened the cabinet. She rummaged around till she found the clips. They were silver and shaped like crescent moons. "Aren't they gaudy?"

"They look very pretty to me," Claud said. His voice sounded husky.

The woman stared at him. "You get that look off your face, young fellow. Remember that I'm actually a man and a good two centuries older than you. Or is it three?"

Claud blushed. "I'm sorry. It's hard to remember."

"Keep reminding yourself. Belinda, will you put these damn things in for me? I don't know how to do it."

Belinda went over to the woman. She was very young. No more than twenty. That was obvious when Belinda came close to her. There were no lines around her eyes or around her full-lipped mouth. Belinda felt her throat constrict. Her heart was beating a little too quickly. Oh dear. She was falling in love again. First a rat, then her own five-times-great-grandfather. She couldn't bear much more of this.

There was a comb in the cabinet. She used it to comb and part the woman's tangled hair. Then she put the clips in. Her hands were shaking, and she had trouble closing the clips. When she was done, she stepped back and leaned against the cart. She felt a bit dizzy.

"Thank you," the woman said. "I don't suppose you can call me Godfrey now. How about Godfreya?"

Belinda felt increasingly dizzy. The room's walls seemed to be leaning in toward her, ready to fall.

"Belinda?" Claud cried. "Are you all right?"

She reached toward the cart, trying to steady herself. Then she fainted.

When she woke, she was lying on the floor. Claud

was kneeling next to her. The woman Godfreya was standing, staring down and frowning.

"What happened?" Claud asked.

"I got dizzy. I'm sorry."

"Quite all right," Godfreya said. "The last few days have been difficult."

How lovely she was, Belinda thought. What sex would she be interested in, once she'd gotten used to her new body and could notice its needs? Belinda couldn't imagine Captain Godfrey Hernshaw being interested in men. So maybe Godfreya would be interested in her. But wasn't that incest?

"You'd better stay still and rest," Godfreya said. "You look exhausted."

"There's a coat in the cart," the station said. "Maybe you should put it over her."

Claud nodded, then stood. Belinda closed her eyes. Several moments later, she felt the coat being laid over her. "Thank you," she murmured. The coat was thick and soft. It reminded her of the blanket she'd had when she was young. The blanket had been woven from the wool of shaggy snowdeer that lived in the far north on New Hope's many little arctic islands. Belinda snuggled further under the coat and went to sleep.

At first, her sleep was deep. Then she grew restless and began to have bad dreams. She was in a ruin that looked like Gorwing Keep. But she knew it was Wall Street. There were rats everywhere—little ones, like the ones on her home planet. She was running, terrified of something behind her. She went through one corridor after another, all of them dark and dusty, all of them leading nowhere. The rats squeaked and scurried around her feet. They kept getting in her way, so she couldn't move quickly. At last she came to a door and opened it. Beyond the door were stars, a whole sky full of them. She stepped out and looked up. Above her, she saw Nigel Bloodsworth standing in a forest glade, his ghost whistle in his hand.

At that point, she woke. She felt thoroughly confused. What could the dream mean? She opened her eyes and sat up. The dome above her was glowing very dimly. Claud and Godfreya were sleeping on opposite sides of the room. Both of them were snoring.

Where was Shortpaw? Still being transferred, she suspected. She shivered, remembering the rats in her dream. They had been awful.

She put her arms around her knees and thought about her situation. What next? She didn't like Earth. It was full of ruins and craziness. There was nothing she wanted here. Where to, then? Should she go back to her home planet? It would have changed, she knew. All her friends would be dead. But, oh, to see Port Discovery again—the pastel houses, the blooming iris trees. Claud grunted, rolled over and stopped snoring. He was still asleep, though. His breathing stayed deep and regular.

Maybe that was the best answer. Home. What was that poem Shortpaw had recited? After a moment, she remembered it.

> Those who travel
> Often find
> That what was real
> Was left behind.

There was certainly nothing real about this

planet. Giant mutant rats and mad machines. Foof.
What silliness.

Home, she thought again. She'd suggest that to
Claud and Godfreya when they woke. She lay down
and pulled the coat over her. Then she thought
about Port Discovery. Would the college still be
there? What would it be like? Would she have to
start all over, or would they give her credit for the
courses she'd taken two centuries before? Could
she get any credit for her recent experiences? After
all, she'd been in space and on Earth. That ought
to count for something. She grew sleepy. Her
thoughts grew confused. She drifted into a half-
awake dream about her childhood home—the courtyard in midsummer, full of red firefern. Soon she
was asleep. She didn't dream—or, if she did, she
didn't remember what she dreamt. After an hour
or so, she woke. The dome above her was glowing
brightly. She groaned and sat up. What a terrible
taste she had in her mouth!

"Get up, everyone," the resurrection station said.
"The rat is ready to wake. I want you to reassure
him if he panics."

"All right, all right," Claud said. "We're getting
up."

Belinda pushed her hair back, then stood. She
must look a wreck, she thought. On either side of
her, Claud and Godfreya rose. The door opened. A
new cart rolled in, bringing a second glass box. It
rolled over to them, then stopped. There was a
man in the box, a short stocky fellow with a pale
skin and red brown hair. His face was blunt fea-
tured and ruddy. His hands were broad with stubby
fingers. Well, that wouldn't matter, Belinda thought.

Humans didn't care if a person had short fingers. Only rats cared about things like that.

The man opened his eyes. They were large and dark brown, with thick lashes.

Godfreya opened the box's top. The man sat up, then looked down at himself.

"Oh Darwin," he said after a moment.

"Don't you like the body?" Belinda asked.

"It seems all right." He climbed out of the box and down onto the floor. "But I have no fur. I feel indecent. No wonder you humans wear so many clothes." He rubbed his arms, then his chest. "All my lovely fur. Gone."

"I give people immortality," the station said, "and all I get is criticism."

"No, no," Shortpaw said. "The body's fine. I think." He looked at Belinda. "Is this body sexually attractive? I don't know how to judge. We rats value glossy fur, bright eyes, and large sharp teeth. Also long tails." He felt across his lower back. "No tail. I have no tail."

"It's a perfectly nice body," Belinda said. "You'll find women who'll be attracted to it."

Shortpaw looked down at himself again. "Is that my sexual organ?"

"Yes," Godfreya said.

"It looks awfully vulnerable."

"It is," Claud and Godfreya said together. "Don't ever get hit there," Claud added.

Shortpaw touched his penis gingerly. "Why is it red and wrinkled and silly looking?"

"How should we know?" Godfreya asked.

"Is it normal?"

Claud nodded. "Yes."

"All right, then. I don't mind having a silly-look-

ing sexual organ, if it's normal for the species."
Shortpaw turned to the cart and opened the cabinet in it. There were clothes inside: underwear, brown pants, brown boots and a brown-and-blue-checked shirt. He examined each garment. "How is this done? What goes where?"

Godfreya picked up the underpants. "These go on your legs. Put your feet in the two small holes, then pull up."

Shortpaw did as he was instructed. Godfreya picked up the undershirt. "Now this. Bring it down over your head. The two small holes are for your arms."

"This is like doing a puzzle. Why do humans make everything so complicated?"

"Stop complaining," Godfreya told him. "You are the one who wanted to be human."

Shortpaw frowned and put on the shirt. He got tangled in it, and the top half of his body disappeared from sight—except for one hand, which stuck out the head hole and waved frantically.

"This is absurd," Godfreya said. She yanked the undershirt off Shortpaw.

"Thank you." He was breathing heavily.

"Arms straight up," Godfreya told him.

"What?"

"Put your arms straight up, you fool. I am going to put your undershirt on you."

"Oh."

Shortpaw put his arms up, and Godfreya got his hands into the arm holes, then pulled the shirt down over Shortpaw's head.

"You do this every day?" he asked. "Put all this on?"

Godfreya nodded. "Claud, come here and help me."

Claud helped her dress the former rat. First the pants went on, then the checked shirt, then the boots. Last of all, Godfreya fastened a belt around Shortpaw's waist. It was brown leather with a brass buckle shaped like a cluster of flowers.

"That's it," she said. "Now, remember to keep your fly closed. Can you think of any other advice, Claud?"

"No."

"Thank you," Shortpaw said. He took a few steps. "This is going to be harder than I thought. These clothes feel terrible. They're so stiff, so heavy." He took a few more steps. "Oh Darwin, oh Mendel. I'll be rubbed raw. My feet hurt too."

"All I ever hear is complaints," the station said.

Godfreya frowned. "Let's go outside."

Claud nodded.

They picked up their packs and rifles. A door opened. "Good-bye," the station said. "Take good care of your new bodies."

Shortpaw looked up at the dome. "Thank you, station."

They walked down the hallway to the outer door. Halfway there, Shortpaw stopped and took off his boots. "One thing at a time. I'll learn to wear these later."

Ahead of them, the outer door opened. They went to it and through it. "Good-bye," the station called.

Belinda turned and waved. They went up out of the hollow. It was early morning. The sun was just above the eastern trees. The sky was clear. A cool wind blew, stirring the dark branches. A nice day, Belinda thought. A very nice day. When they reached the hill's top, Godfreya stopped. "Where to, now?"

"I don't want to see those humans again," Shortpaw said. "Who knows what other poisons they have?"

Claud nodded. "They're too strange for me."

"Very well, what are the alternatives?"

They had stopped in an open space. Around them, grass waved in the wind. Bushes rustled. Godfreya's black hair flapped around her shoulders, and Shortpaw's short curly copper-brown hair was moving too. Belinda felt a sudden rush of affection for both of them, and for Claud, who looked worried as usual. He was pinching the bridge of his nose, at the same time as he chewed on his lower lip. As strange as they all were, she liked them—even loved them. It wasn't simple passion that she felt—though she did feel that, for Godfreya and Shortpaw at least. She also felt friendship and a stronger emotion. Was it something like family love? She had never had a normal family. Maybe she had created her own kinship group, which included a man who had been a rat, a woman who had been a robot, and the native of a planet that was light-years away. A weird social unit, she decided, but better than none.

"Well?" Godfreya repeated. "What shall we do next?"

"I don't like this planet," Claud said. "Let's go back to the lifeboat and ask it to take us home."

"To New Hope?"

Claud nodded.

"You're going to leave me here all alone?" Shortpaw cried.

Claud looked at him. "Come with us, if you want."

Shortpaw frowned. "That sounds like a big step."
He put one hand up to his face. "What! Where are
my whiskers?"

"You'll have to grow new ones," Godfreya said.
She looked around at the green hills. "I'd just as
soon leave this place, but I'd like to find out what
happened to the other ships—the Aspiration and
the Preservation. Did they found colonies? Have
the colonies survived? Their flight plans must be
on file somewhere. Maybe the lifeboat knows where
they went, or the landing field. We could follow
them."

"No!" Claud shouted.

Godfreya stared at Belinda. "What about you?
Would you be interested in another trip?"

"Let's go back to the lifeboat. We can talk about
it there."

"All right."

They started down off the hill. Godfreya went
first, her rifle slung over one shoulder, her long
black hair flipping back and forth. The rest of
them followed. They went west along an animal
track that wound through the valleys, through dim
woods and little sunny glades. The day remained
bright and windy. Birds chirped and whistled in
the trees. Belinda felt pretty happy, all in all.

Sometime around noon, they stopped and ate
foodsticks, then continued on their way, still going
west toward the river. They went more slowly
now, since Shortpaw's bare feet were getting sore.
He hobbled after them, cursing and making little
squeaking noises. Every few minutes they had to
stop and wait for him to catch up. It was late
afternoon when they looked down from a low rise
and saw water glinting between the trees. Down

they went, Claud helping Shortpaw. They stopped at the water's edge. Belinda looked out and saw the river and the island-dotted harbor.

"I think we're south of where we landed before," Godfreya said.

Shortpaw nodded. "Yes, but not far."

They turned and went north along the shore. It was hard going. Often their way was blocked by ruins—fallen concrete pylons or crumbling walls, which they had to clamber over. Sometimes the narrow beach narrowed to nothing, and they had to go inland, climbing up a steep slope, then going along the hilltops till the beach reappeared. At twilight, they made camp in a hollow high above the river. They ate more foodsticks, then went to sleep.

Belinda slept soundly. She woke at dawn and lay a while, watching the sky lighten above her. The birds began to make a few noises. Beside her, Shortpaw stirred and whimpered. Poor fellow, she thought. It must be hard to become human so late in life. She put an arm around him, and he snuggled close to her without waking.

Godfreya got up and built a fire. She sat close beside it, her hands held over the flames. Belinda pulled her arm out from under Shortpaw and stood. She was cold and stiff, and her feet hurt. She stretched, then rubbed her arms and walked unsteadily to the fire.

Godfreya looked up. "I'd forgotten what it was like to have a body." She rubbed her hands together. "I'm hungry. I'm cold as hell. And I think I'm constipated."

"There's worse to come," Claud said.

Belinda turned and saw him coming toward the

fire. His pale hair was a terrible mess, and his eyes were unfocused. "Great Fish, is it cold!"

"What do you mean?" Godfreya asked.

"You're a woman now, captain. You're going to have a menstrual cycle."

"My God, you're right."

"It's not that bad," Belinda said. "You don't have to pay much attention to it."

Claud hunkered down beside the fire. "That's what you humans say. We natives know different. In our villages, no menstruating woman can go near hunting gear or fishing gear. The smell of the blood gets on the spears and knives and hooks, so no creature will come near them."

"Primitive twaddle," Godfreya said. She stood up. "I'm not going to listen to you, Claud."

"It's really not bad," Belinda said.

Godfreya nodded. "I'll believe you, though my second wife was unbearable whenever she had her period. She found it conceptually disturbing, she said. It made her feel dirty and reminded her that she was mortal."

Belinda frowned. "Your wife sounds a little strange, captain."

"She was."

Shortpaw groaned and sat up. "I'm cold. These clothes don't help. Why do you wear clothes? All they do is make you uncomfortable."

"Let's eat and get moving," Godfreya said.

They ate foodsticks for breakfast, then put out the fire and went north along the shore. A little before noon, they came to their canoe. They sat down on the beach beside it and ate lunch. The wind had died down to a barely perceptible breeze, and the river was calm. Belinda felt tired, but content. Why she felt content, she didn't know.

"We'd better wait till night," Shortpaw said. "No one will see us crossing then."

Godfreya nodded.

Claud finished his foodstick. "I've been thinking about your psi power, Belinda. I think I know what kind of pattern you're making."

Godfreya frowned. "This is more primitive twaddle."

Claud shook his head. "No."

"What is the pattern?" Belinda asked. She began to feel a little anxious.

Claud scratched his nose, then bit a thumbnail. "What are the characteristics of the strange things that have happened to you?"

"I don't know."

Claud held up a finger. "One—there have been a lot of unexpected conjunctions. People and things have come together, that weren't any too likely to. The sudden appearance of Nigel Bloodsworth is one example. Another example is the sudden appearance of Captain Hernshaw inside the robot's body."

"Twaddle," Godfreya repeated.

Claud shook his head. "Both Nigel and the captain were supposed to be dead. But they appeared anyway. And who would expect to find an operating starship lifeboat inside Gorwing Keep? That was another unexpected conjunction, as was the resurrection station—which we found awfully quickly, almost as soon as we arrived on Earth. Around you, Belinda, things come together in defiance of the laws of logic and probability."

"Oh."

"Horsefeathers," Godfreya said.

Claud held up a second finger. "The second characteristic is transformation. The robot turned into the captain, then into Godfreya here. Nigel turned from a college professor into a savage, then back into a professor. Shortpaw turned from a rat into a man." He frowned. "There have been other transformations that have involved appearance rather than essence. You appeared to be human. But you are, in fact, half human and half native."

"Piffle," Godfreya said.

Claud's face turned red. "Will you please be quiet, captain?"

"Very well." Godfreya leaned against the side of the canoe and stared at the river, her face set in a frown.

"Thank you. All right, Belinda. Inside your psi field, things are brought together and transformed. What kind of pattern is that?"

Belinda frowned and tugged at her lower lip. "I don't know, Claud."

Claud sighed. "Synthesis. It's a pattern of synthesis. I think it's a dialectical pattern, but I'm not sure. I've always had trouble with Hegel."

Shortpaw scratched his head. "I haven't understood a word you've said."

Godfreya nodded. "Exactly."

Belinda bit her fingernail. "It's awfully complex."

"Well, there's no rule that says life has to be simple."

"Occam's Razor," Godfreya put in.

"That says life has to be as simple as possible under the circumstances."

Godfreya frowned. "I don't think you have that right, Claud."

Claud shrugged. "Belinda, look around you. We're all split up into categories—men and women, New Hope humans, New Hope natives, Earth humans, rats, and machines. Then there are moral categories and divisions due to different levels of civilization. But inside your psi field, the categories all come together, and people can move from one category to another. Inside your psi field, categories don't make sense. That has something to do with synthesis too. But I'm not sure what."

"This is all balderdash," Godfreya said. "How can anyone change the basic rules of reality?"

"If you think you can come up with a better explanation for what's happened to us, you're welcome to try. Anyway, we don't know the basic rules of reality. Only the Great Fish knows the true nature of the real. We know what we *think* are the basic rules of reality. And why can't we change what we think?" Claud stared at Godfreya. "You've certainly changed something, captain. Look at the way you've transformed yourself."

"That was the machine."

"Are you certain? Maybe you wanted to be a woman, somewhere in the back of your mind. Maybe the station discovered that with its tests."

Godfreya's face turned red. "No!"

"Why not?"

"Why would I want to be a woman?"

Claud grinned. "Well, my people believe that women enjoy sex more than men. Also, they get to have children. That's the only really important activity that only one sex can do. Also, among my people, women tend to have stronger psi powers. We believe that the Great Fish made men bigger than women to balance things off, so that men wouldn't feel too deprived." Claud paused and scratched his nose. "As for menstruation, which is the other misfortune women have to bear, besides being smaller than us—that came into the world because of the wife of Ashai Isaru, the one the Great Fish had made for him. She pulled up the nashri root where Ashai kept his heart, though he had told her to stay out of that corner of the garden."

"Wait a minute," Shortpaw said. "What was this fellow's heart doing in a root?"

"He'd put it there for safekeeping. It's the kind of thing that sorcerers do."

Shortpaw twitched his nose. For a moment, he looked very ratlike, for his upper lip went up when he twitched, and Belinda saw two large front teeth. "It sounds silly to me."

"In any case, while he was dying, Ashai put a curse on his wife. He meant to put the curse on her alone, but he said the spell wrong, so it fell on all women. The curse was that his wife would bleed fourteen times a year, to remind her of how Ashai had bled when the root was pulled up."

"Why fourteen times a year?" Shortpaw asked.

Claud looked surprised. "Because that's how often women menstruate."

Godfreya stood up. "I'm going to take a walk." She strode off down the beach.

"I find this very confusing," Shortpaw said.

Claud nodded. "Yes, but you'll get used to it. Things are always confusing when the pattern's being changed. Just remember that you can't rely on common sense or probability at a time like this."

"Why not?"

"Because you're between two sets of rules. There's no way of knowing what's probable or sensible till the new pattern becomes clear." He stretched, then lay down, his hands behind his head. "I'm going to take a nap. Talking about ideas is tiring."

Belinda sat awhile, watching the water lap the shore. Then she got up and went looking for shells. Shortpaw joined her. They spent an hour or so wandering up and down the beach. There were cone-shaped shells in the sand, also wide flat shells and shells that curled round in a coil. Most of them were dull colors—light gray, light brown, or white, but one of the flat shells was dark gray on the outside and a wonderful glossy pink inside. When Belinda had filled her pockets, she took off her shoes and went wading. Shortpaw went wading too. He didn't roll up his pants, and the bottoms got soaked. At length, they started back toward the canoe.

"I think I will go with you into space," the ex-rat said. "You are strange and interesting people. The humans here on Earth are strange and disgusting. Also, I think I find you sexually attractive."

"Oh."

They reached the canoe. Belinda put her shells into it, then sat down and put on her shoes. Claud was still asleep. Godfreya was still off walking. She stared at Manhattan, at the huge ruins of Wall Street. The sky above the island was clear and a bright pure intense shade of blue. The sun was hot. She felt suddenly sleepy. Home, she thought. She was going home. Or off after those other starships, if Godfreya had her way.

"Would you be interested in engaging in sex?" Shortpaw asked.

"Not right now."

"Then I'll have something to eat. Your human food tastes terrible, by the way."

She lay down in the warm sand. A little nap, she thought. She closed her eyes. A moment or so later, she heard Shortpaw opening a package of foodsticks. She could hear water too—the long soft whish the waves made as they came in. An insect buzzed above her. How wonderful the sun felt! Most likely, she would sleep with Shortpaw. He was less attractive as a human than he'd been as a rat, but—still and all—she liked him much more than she'd ever liked any other human male. She liked Claud, of course, but it had nothing to do with sex. Besides, Claud wasn't human. Though that didn't bother her much anymore. How could it? She was half native herself—and half in love with a man who used to be a giant mutant rat. Things like that made a person more open-minded.

She dozed till Godfreya came back from her walk. She woke then, when Godfreya called hello to Shortpaw. She yawned, stretched and sat up. Godfreya sat down beside her. Her face was flushed, and there were scratches on her hands and forearms. Her black hair was all tangled. Bits of twig, a leaf, and several burrs were caught in it. The silver hairclips were gone. "Claud stopped lecturing, eh?"

Belinda nodded.

"Good. I've never liked discussions about the nature of reality. All they do is confuse people. They don't help you get from day to day or to do what you want to do." She pushed her hair back, then shaded her eyes and looked at Manhattan. "Shortpaw?"

"Yes?" He came toward them, a foodstick in his hand.

"Will we have any trouble getting to the spaceport?"

"I don't think so. We rats used to be nocturnal, but we had to give it up. You can't tend gardens or take goats out to pasture during the night. So the rats will be in their towns. I think we'd better go up the East River and then across the East Side to the spaceport. There are no rat towns in that area. As for wild animals—there are a few wolves on Manhattan, but they're very timid and keep to the north end of the island, where there are no settlements at all."

"Good enough," Godfreya said. "We'll start at sunset."

Claud woke up, stood and stretched. "Cards," he said. He went to his pack and pulled out a deck of cards. "I thought these might come in useful. Gin, anyone?"

They settled down in the sand and played gin. Shortpaw had never seen cards before, and he was a terrible player. Teaching him kept them occupied till dinner. They ate, then waited till sunset. A breeze rose, blowing off the mainland, and the water in the river began to ripple. Belinda watched Sol go down on the far side of New York Harbor. The gently moving surface of the harbor was orange-yellow. She looked toward Manhattan. Here and there among the ruined towers, pieces of glass or plastic or tile glinted, reflecting the day's last light. An amazing sight, she thought: the dark ruins, spotted with light, and the shining harbor, dotted with black islands.

When Sol was entirely gone from sight, Godfreya rose. "Come on."

They all stood. Claud put his cards in his pack. They pushed the canoe out into the river. Standing knee-deep in water, they turned the canoe around and climbed into it—first Claud, then Belinda, then Godfreya, then Shortpaw. They picked up paddles and set to work.

It was slow going, since they were heading upriver. The wind hit them broadside, but it was gentle and caused them no trouble. The waves it created were so small, that they broke against the outrigger, instead of going over it. Overhead, the sky turned deep blue. Belinda looked toward Brooklyn and saw a single star, shining above the dark hills. On they went, keeping close to Brooklyn's shore. The current was slower there than it was at the river's center. There was little sound except the splashes the paddles made, going in and out of the water, also the grunts of the paddlers. Belinda's arms began to ache. She looked once again toward Brooklyn and saw a crescent moon above the hills. It was enormous, far larger than any of New Hope's moons. It was pale too—more white than yellow. With a slight sense of shock, she realized this was Luna, the one original Moon, Diana's planet, sacred to hunting and chastity, lunacy and change.

"Isn't it lovely?" Claud said somewhere ahead of her.

"The moon? Yes."

"At least we'll have a little light," Shortpaw said. "There's something wrong with my body. I can't see in the dark."

"That's normal," Godfreya put in. "Humans have poor night vision."

"Oh. Well, I guess I had to lose something when I changed bodies. No deal is all to the good, as we rats say."

They continued upriver. By now, the sky was full of stars. Belinda could see very little—only the stars and the crescent moon and Brooklyn, off to her right. She sometimes thought she could see Manhattan, a long dark shape off to her left. Her back hurt, and her arms felt very heavy. How much longer would they have to paddle? she wondered. All at once, voices began singing close by the canoe:

> "Queen and huntress, chaste and fair,
>   Now the sun is laid to sleep,
>   Seated in thy silver chair,
>   State in wonted manner keep:
>   Hesperus entreats thy light,
>   Goddess excellently bright."

It was the dolphins, of course. Belinda thought she saw their bodies rising up to the river's surface, gleaming briefly in the moon's dim light, then diving. Spray thrown up by their tails spattered over her hands and arms. Some of the dolphins must have stopped swimming and lifted their heads from the water, for the song went on:

> "Earth, let not thy envious shade
>   Dare itself to interpose;
>   Cynthia's shining orb was made
>   Heaven to clear when day did close:
>   Bless us then with wishéd sight,
>   Goddess excellently bright.

"Lay thy bow of pearl apart,
   And thy crystal shining quiver;
Give unto the flying hart
   Space to breathe, how short soever:
Thou that mak'st a day of night,
Goddess excellently bright."

The song ended. For a moment, there was silence, except for the sound of the paddles. Then one dolphin sang alone:

"Hey, down a down! did Dian sing,
   Amongst her virgins sitting,
Than love there is no vainer thing,
   For maidens most unfitting.
And so think I, with a down, down, derry.

"When women knew no woe,
   But lived themselves to please,
Men's feigning guiles they did not know,
   The ground of their disease.
Unborn was false suspect,
   No thought of jealousy;
From wanton toys and fond affect
   The virgin's life was free.

"Hey, down a down! did Dian sing
   Amongst her virgins sitting,
Than love there is no vainer thing,
   For maidens most unfitting.
And so think I, with a down, down, derry!

"At length, men uséd charms,
   To which what maids gave ear,
Embracing gladly endless harms,

Anon enthrallèd were.
Thus women welcomed woe
Disguised in name of love,
A jealous hell, a painted show:
So shall they find, that prove.

"Hey, down a down! did Dian sing,
Amongst her virgins sitting,
Than love there is no vainer thing,
For maidens most unfitting.
And so think I, with a down, down, derry!"

The dolphin stopped singing. Belinda heard several splashes. Then Shortpaw said, "I think they've left."

"What was that about?" Godfreya asked.

"I'm not sure. The dolphins sing because they like to sing. Their songs don't always have a meaning—or at least, a meaning that rats can understand. I think we'd better start across the river. We ought to be opposite midtown Manhattan— though I can't swear to it. These eyes are really terrible."

They turned the canoe away from Brooklyn and paddled across the river. Belinda's arms were aching. She kept putting the paddle into the water, pulling it back, lifting it out and forward, then putting it back in the water. The dark shore of Manhattan came closer and closer. Her arms—and her back—hurt more and more. They reached the shadow of Manhattan's trees. They slid into the pitch-black darkness. The canoe hit something. It slowed and stopped. In front of her, she heard two splashes: Godfreya and Claud getting out. The canoe slid a little further forward, making a grating sound. They must be pulling it, she thought. It stopped again. "Get out," Godfreya said.

She crawled forward to the prow. The shells she'd found were there. She felt them lying on the canoe's bottom. She grabbed a handful and put them in her pocket, then climbed out into the water. It was ankle-deep and still warm from day. Shortpaw climbed out after her. Together, the four of them pulled the canoe up onto a little beach. It was so dark that she couldn't see what the beach was made of, but it felt stony underfoot. When they'd gotten the canoe well up onto the beach, Godfreya said, "We'd better unload."

Belinda felt around inside the canoe till she found a pack. She slung it across her back, then found a rifle and picked it up.

"I have a pack and a rifle," Claud said. "But I'm not sure they're mine."

"We'll worry about that later," Godfreya said. "Does everyone have everything?"

"I can't find my shoes," Shortpaw said. "But I didn't like them, anyway. I'd better lead. I think I know where we are."

They crossed the beach, then went up a wooded hill and down the other side into a valley. The air was damp and full of the smell of vegetation. There were sounds in the underbrush, soft rustling noises. Belinda kept hitting branches and tree trunks. She felt frightened. It was too dark, far too dark. Who knew what horrible creatures might be near?

When they reached the valley floor, Shortpaw said, "Just as I hoped. There's a trail here. I think it's the Fifty-seventh Street Trail. It will lead us straight to the spaceport."

They went along the trail, first Shortpaw, then

Belinda, then Claud and Godfreya. It was less dark here. Moonlight and starlight shone through the trees, and Belinda could make out the shapes of her companions. Her fear decreased. The trail wound back and forth between barely visible hills. From time to time, she heard a few chirps. Apparently, some of the birds were still awake. Once, she heard the sound of a brook—a soft gurgle someplace near. When she looked up, she saw stars in between the tree branches. But the moon was out of sight.

They kept on for a long time, moving slowly through the darkness. At last, Belinda saw light ahead. It was pale and steady, obviously not firelight. "The spaceport," Shortpaw said.

They hurried forward and came to a high concrete wall, topped with spotlights. They stopped. Belinda blinked, half blinded by the glare. In front of her was the moat, full of floating plants and bright green from side to side.

"Humans," a loudspeaker said. "I recognize two of you, but what about the others? And what happened to the robot?"

Godfreya stepped forward. "It's a long story. Will you let us in?"

"Certainly. Go west till you see a gate. I'll let down the drawbridge."

Godfreya nodded. They went along the moat. A little further on, there were flowers floating in it—big blossoms, some white and some yellow. Belinda saw a mechanical alligator swimming slowly through the flowers. Its back was wet and glistened.

Shortpaw stopped. "My mother told me that

those things feed on bad little rats who don't obey their parents."

"They kill whatever rats come near," the loudspeaker said.

Shortpaw shuddered, then went on. Beyond the flowers was a gate with a drawbridge drawn up in front of it. They stopped. The bridge came down, and the door beyond it opened. They went across the moat, then through the door. Inside was the landing field. They were at the southern end. Belinda could just barely see the east and west walls. The north wall was entirely out of sight. In front of her, there was concrete: a wide flat expanse, lit by hundreds of spotlights—some on the walls, others on tall poles and still others set in the ground. They were so bright that Belinda had trouble seeing. She squinted and looked around. Way off to the west of them, she saw a metal sphere resting on many metal legs. It was the lifeboat.

"Come on," Godfreya said.

They started across the field.

Behind them a loudspeaker said, "What about my story? Why are there four of you?"

Godfreya stopped and turned. The rest of them went on a few paces, then stopped too. "There are humans in Brooklyn."

"What? Are you sure?"

Godfreya nodded.

"Then all is not lost. We may still be able to win the war."

"The war is over. These humans don't want to fight."

"That's impossible. Humans always want to fight."

Godfreya shrugged, then turned and went on. The rest of them followed.

"Stop! How can I reach them? Do they have radios?"

"No."

"Then I'll have to send out a helicopter. I have one that still works. What part of Brooklyn are they in?"

Godfreya kept walking.

"Stop! Stop!" the spaceport cried, but none of them did. "Traitors! Don't you care who wins the war?"

"This is terrible," Shortpaw said. "What if this machine can get some of the humans interested in fighting?"

"Those degenerates?" Godfreya laughed.

Shortpaw frowned. "I suppose it isn't likely. But I'm still worried."

They continued across the concrete, walking very quickly now. Behind them the spaceport cried, "Fifth columnists!"

By this time, they were close to the boat. As they approached, the airlock opened. A crane swung out and lowered a platform. They reached the platform a moment after it hit the ground and stepped onto it. It started up, swaying all the time. They grabbed onto the cables.

Shortpaw's face grew pale. "I don't like heights."

"This will be over in a minute or two," Godfreya said.

Whining all the while, the crane pulled them up. They reached the airlock and stepped into it.

"Well, you're back I see," the lifeboat said. "And in a hurry, as usual. What happened to the robot?"

"We'll talk about that later," Godfreya said. "Get ready for take off."

"Is Earth unsafe too?"

"Yes. That spaceport is crazy. I want to get out of here."

"All right."

The crane swung in. The airlock closed. Godfreya spun the wheel that locked it, then led the way into the lifeboat. Once again, they hurried through metal halls. Doors opened in front of them, then shut behind them. Shortpaw kept looking around at the lightrods, the gray walls, the shut side doors. "I never thought I'd be in a spaceship. This is wonderful. But I'm frightened."

"Don't worry," Belinda said. "The boat is safe."

They reached the door into the bridge. Godfreya recited:

> *"Geyr Garmr mjok fyr Gnipahelli.*
> *Festr mun slitna, en freki renna."*

"How did you know that?" the lifeboat asked.

"I am the robot."

"Don't be ridiculous. I have eyes to see, and my memory still works. You are not a robot. You are clearly human."

"Will you please open up?"

Slowly, very slowly, the door opened, making whining and grating noises. Beyond it, Belinda saw the acceleration couches and the instrument poles beside them. On the bridge's walls, lights shone green. The ceiling panels showed pale gray concrete and rows of blue-white spotlights. They went in and looked up. "No trouble so far,"

Godfreya said. She looked around. "Well, where do we go next?"

"New Hope," Claud said.

Godfreya frowned. "Belinda?"

"I want to go home too."

"What about you, Shortpaw?"

"I'll go where Belinda wants to go."

"God damn it." Godfreya clenched one hand into a fist and hit her thigh. "Have you no sense of adventure? No desire to achieve?"

Claud shook his head.

"The idea of new planets, new societies, new ways of life has no appeal?"

Claud frowned and tugged at an earlobe. "Well, by the time we get home, New Hope may well be a new planet—to us, anyway. One hundred and eighty years is a long time. Also, I think Belinda's pattern was starting to spread there. It hasn't done that here on Earth. Shortpaw is the only Earth person who's been changed by meeting us. But think of all the people on New Hope— Geoffrey Hernshaw became a monk. Captain Laframboise became a maniac. Nigel Bloodsworth changed from a savage to a professor. Marianne Duval became a faculty wife."

"Stop that!" Godfreya shouted. "I won't listen to your crazy theories."

Claud shrugged. "In any case, I want to go home and see what's become of the pattern. And of my home village. And of New Harvard. Maybe by now natives are able to become professors."

Godfreya sighed. "Very well. We'll go to New Hope. I can go on from there alone—if the lifeboat has any fuel left."

"I got fuel from the spaceport," the lifeboat said.

"I told you I was going to. I can take off and land half a dozen times. Once I am in deep space, of course, I gather my own fuel."

"I know that," said Godfreya. "I used to be a starship captain."

"Did you?" the lifeboat said. "In any case, I'm not sure I ought to take you back to New Hope. It wasn't a place of safety the last time."

"That was long ago," Claud said. "I've just been saying that I think it's going to be a very different place by the time we get back."

"You may be right. There is something happening outside."

They all looked up. One of the concrete slabs that made up the landing field was sinking.

"Strap yourselves in!" Godfreya cried.

Belinda glanced at Shortpaw. He looked confused. She grabbed his arm and pulled him over an acceleration couch. "Lie down!"

He lay down. She strapped him in, then hurried to another couch and climbed onto it. As she fastened her straps, she looked around. Claud and Godfreya both looked ready for take off. Godfreya was moving the rods that stuck out of her instrument pole. Belinda glanced up at the ceiling panels. The slab was completely out of sight. In its place was a rectangular hole. There was something in the hole, something that moved and glinted. A machine rose out of the hole. It was made of metal and shaped like an egg. There was a huge propeller on top of the egg and another smaller propeller at the egg's narrow end. A helicopter, Belinda thought. She had seen pictures of helicopters in the Port Discovery Museum.

There was something wrong with it. It kept tilting from one side to the other. Was the gyroscope defective? Belinda wondered. Up the helicopter went, till it was well above the hole. It was still tilting and rolling. Its silver body glinted in the spotlights' glare.

"Get a missile ready for firing," Godfreya said.

"What?" the lifeboat said. "Why?"

"I'm going to destroy the helicopter."

Belinda raised her head and looked at the woman on the captain's couch. Godfreya was frowning and staring at the lights on the instrument pole. Her hair was still tangled. Her clothes were wrinkled. She looked pretty wild.

"Why do you want to destroy it?" the lifeboat asked.

"It represents a threat to Earth's inhabitants. The spaceport wants to start a war. Get that missile ready!"

There was a short silence. Belinda watched the helicopter move unsteadily across the ceiling. It didn't look dangerous. Still, if it managed to get to Brooklyn and make contact with the humans there— She thought of Conrad. He was crazy enough to go to war. It would be a new experience for him, something as exciting as the sin in Dante's *Inferno*. She shivered. In spite of their odd religious beliefs, she rather liked the rats. They were soft and furry, and they seemed to be sensible about most things. She didn't want them hurt by people such as Conrad.

"The missile is ready," the lifeboat said.

Godfreya pulled down a rod. There was a muffled roar somewhere below them. Up on the ceiling, the helicopter exploded. Fire filled two panels. Black bits of metal flew across half the ceiling. Belinda winced and cringed.

"Get us out of here!" Godfreya shouted.

"This is Lifeboat Number Eleven. I am about to take you to a place of safety. Check to make sure your safety belts are fastened. Here we go."

The rockets fired. The lifeboat shuddered. Smoke and fire spread across the whole ceiling. Over the loudspeaker, a voice said, "Criminals! Mandel-stamers!"

That must be the spaceport. As it spoke, she felt the pressure of acceleration. They were starting up.

"Lover of rats!" the loudspeaker screamed.

Up they went. The smoke on the ceiling cleared. She could see the whole landing field—a rectangle of white light, surrounded by darkness. The rectangle grew smaller and smaller. Here and there around it, she saw points of light. They were reddish in color. Those must be fires burning in rat towns. A moment later, she saw two faint gleams— the rivers on either side of Manhattan, shining in the moonlight.

The boat kept going up. Now she could make out nothing except the spaceport, a tiny patch of brilliant light. She felt the lifeboat tilt. At the edge of the ceiling, stars slid into sight. After them came the crescent moon. It still seemed enormous and unnaturally pale. She stared at it and thought, Claud was right. One hundred and eighty years was a long time. Would she know New Hope? Would it still be her home? The roar of the rockets continued. The pressure was starting to make her uncomfortable. She squirmed and felt something hard under one thigh. What was it? Then she remembered the shells she'd gathered on Brooklyn's shore. They were in that pocket. She was lying on them, being pressed against them. She hoped they wouldn't break. They were all she had to show for her long trip. Except for Shortpaw, of course, and whatever she might have learned.

BIO OF A SPACE TYRANT
Piers Anthony

"Brilliant...a thoroughly original thinker and storyteller with a unique ability to posit really *alien* alien life, humanize it, and make it come out alive on the page." *The Los Angeles Times*

A COLOSSAL NEW FIVE VOLUME SPACE THRILLER—
BIO OF A SPACE TYRANT
The Epic Adventures and Galactic Conquests of Hope Hubris

VOLUME I: REFUGEE   84194-0/$3.50 US/$4.50 Can
Hubris and his family embark upon an ill-fated voyage through space, searching for sanctuary, after pirates blast them from their home on Callisto.

VOLUME II: MERCENARY   87221-8/$3.50 US/$4.50 Can
Hubris joins the Navy of Jupiter and commands a squadron loyal to the death and sworn to war against the pirate warlords of the Jupiter Ecliptic.

VOLUME III: POLITICIAN   89685-0/$3.50 US/$4.50 Can
Fueled by his own fury, Hubris rose to triumph obliterating his enemies and blazing a path of glory across the face of Jupiter. Military legend...people's champion...promising political candidate...he now awoke to find himself the prisoner of a nightmare that knew no past.

THE BEST-SELLING EPIC CONTINUES—
VOLUME IV: EXECUTIVE
89834-9/$3.50 US/$4.50 Can
Destined to become the most hated and feared man of an era, Hope would assume an alternate identify to fulfill his dreams ...and plunge headlong into madness.

AND COMING SOON FROM AVON BOOKS
VOLUME V: STATESMAN
the climactic conclusion of Hubris' epic adventures:

AVON Paperbacks